EX LIBRIS

VINTAGE CLASSICS

T0314647

RETURN I DARE NOT

Margaret Kennedy was born in 1896. Her first novel, *The Ladies of Lyndon*, was published in 1923. Her second novel, *The Constant Nymph*, became an international bestseller. She then met and married a barrister, David Davies, with whom she had three children. She went on to write a further fifteen novels, to much critical acclaim. She was also a playwright, adapting two of her novels – *Escape Me Never* and *The Constant Nymph* – into successful productions. Three different film versions of *The Constant Nymph* were made, and featured stars of the time such as Ivor Novello and Joan Fontaine; Kennedy subsequently worked in the film industry for a number of years. She also wrote a biography of Jane Austen and a work of literary criticism, *The Outlaws of Parnassus*. Margaret Kennedy died in Woodstock, Oxfordshire, in 1967.

OTHER NOVELS BY MARGARET KENNEDY

MARGARET KENNEDY

Return I Dare Not

VINTAGE BOOKS
London

Published by Vintage 2014

2 4 6 8 10 9 7 5 3 1

First published in Great Britain by William Heinemann in 1931

Vintage
Random House, 20 Vauxhall Bridge Road,
London SW1V 2SA

www.vintage-classics.info

Addresses for companies within The Random House Group Limited
can be found at: www.randomhouse.co.uk/offices.htm

The Random House Group Limited Reg. No. 954009

A CIP catalogue record for this book
is available from the British Library

ISBN 9780099595472

The Random House Group Limited supports The Forest Stewardship
Council® (FSC®), the leading international forest-certification organisation.
Our books carrying the FSC label are printed on FSC®-certified paper.
FSC is the only forest-certification scheme supported by the leading
environmental organisations, including Greenpeace. Our
paper procurement policy can be found at
www.randomhouse.co.uk/environment

Printed and bound in Great Britain by Clays Ltd, St Ives plc

TO L. P. HARTLEY

RETURN
I DARE NOT

1. *A Farewell Performance.*

During the last three months of his public life Hugo
Pott was obliged to lunch every day at the Acorn Restaurant in Shaftesbury Avenue. He sat always at the same
table, in the same draught, and was known to eat little
save a mushroom omelette with half a bottle of *Johannis-
berger* 21. A change of any kind would have given rise to
comment in the Press and might have upset the Manage-
ment of the Acorn who liked their clients to act consistently in character. The room upstairs, though quieter,
had less prestige. So he stayed where he was and continued to eat food which he had long since come to dislike
very heartily.

Most of his companions in the downstairs room were
suffering from the same agreeable compulsion. For it is
obvious that very well-known people must be somewhat
restricted in their choice of eating places. Their patrons
like to watch them being fed, and public opinion demands
that they shall be herded together at meal times into three,
or at most four, recognised places, where any provincial
who studies his Gossip Column may know where to look
for them. So that Hugo, who was at the summit of his
career, who had three plays running simultaneously in
London, whose very shoe laces had a news value, could

scarcely expect to escape from the bondage of a Favourite Table and a Special Dish. And if anyone had told him, on that last, hot Saturday, of his approaching escape and how soon he would be lunching where and as he pleased, he would probably have felt more dismay than relief.

For he was still trying to think of the Acorn as a choice, not an imposition, and he still half believed in his own freedom. There were, after all, three other places where one could lunch. But the Acorn was the most convenient. It stood within a stone's throw of so many theatres. It was handy during rehearsals and if he wanted to pass the time of day with a fellow lion he had merely to cross the room at lunch time. Indeed, the only drawback to the place, so far as he could see, was the difficulty of getting away. He could stroll in as casually as he liked, but to stroll out was a business which required both patience and resource. For the building was fan-shaped and the only door stood at the narrow end. Hugo's favourite table happened to be at the farthest possible point from this door so that, while making his exit, he was obliged to stop and converse with every one of the lunchers at sixteen tables in between. To smile at them and hurry past would never have done. That might have looked as if all this success was going to his head. He had his reputation for Modesty to keep up.

This reputation had been acquired by Hugo along with the Table and the Dish. It carried all the hall marks of mass production. He was known to be quite consistently unspoilt and simple. In private life he was a Thoroughly Nice Young Man. He never forgot an old friendship. He never rejected a new one. He was sincerely generous to his rivals and affable without condescension to failures. He managed to be extremely amusing without saying un-

kind things. Children and animals did not dislike him.
Nor had he any vanity; he made no secret of his shortcomings and fell off horses in public with an almost royal
regularity. He would have loaded his mother with dia-
monds if he had had a mother. But he possessed no
family beyond a legendary step-aunt, who had brought
him up, and for whom he bought yachts, furs and luxury
radio sets.

His public would have been greatly put out if at any
time he had failed to do and to be all this, nor did he find
the task difficult since he really was, on the whole, a most
amiable creature, full of geniality and goodwill. A few
enemies he had, but these could offer no possible justification for disliking him save in so far as he was fortunate
and they were envious. Honesty and simplicity were
natural to him until they became so much the expected
thing as to be no longer entirely spontaneous. And if,
under the pressure of a world publicity, he gradually
ceased to be himself, the reproduction which he was at
last obliged to supply resembled the genuine article so
closely that even his step-aunt would not have been able
to tell the difference.

The Acorn at lunch time was half full of people who
had come up from the country for the day to watch Hugo
and the other half behaving in character. As soon as he
began to make his preparations for getting away they left
off eating and waited to see the performance. Hugo, conscious of his duty, obliged them. As he made his way
down the room he was conspicuously popular and modest
and unassuming. He laughed at every joke that was made
to him, caught and patted every available elbow, raised his
eyebrows, sympathised, congratulated, was very much
astonished, asked advice, gave it, and promised to ring up

in the morning. As an exhibition of hard work it was impressive, it took him twenty minutes, but he did not grudge the time or undervalue its importance. Nothing in his life, now, was more important, and he tackled the exertion superbly. The pallor of a deadly fatigue, a subtle hint of despair in his blithe grimaces, set off all this vivacity with just the necessary touch of chill like ice on champagne. Unconsciously his audience felt the flattery of it, the appeal of the mummer who hides a broken heart beneath the motley. He was theirs, body and soul, and they watched him with the affectionate indulgence of possession.

With one eye on the clock he worked his way towards the door, knowing that a traffic block might now make him miss his train. He was cutting it very fine. But for all that he gave a full two minutes to the crowning grace of his exit. Pausing at the last table of all he murmured a few confidential words to a solitary luncher there, an obscure woman of genius who played elderly bawds in Restoration revivals, and who would never get as far as a Table and Dish of her own. The longest run in her life had been in one of Hugo's early comedies and he now stopped to give her news of the next one.

"You'll come, won't you?" he exclaimed anxiously. "You *will* come, won't you? I do so want you to see it. And you will tell me what you really think, won't you?"

The poor old thing left off gobbling her *Coupe Jacques* and smiled at him. Into her shrewd eyes there stole a warmth of pleasure. She was gratified although she knew perfectly well that he did not care one brass farthing whether she came to the first night of his play or not. Her opinion could be nothing to him and the gallery would not even recognise her. But it was nice of him to say these flattering things, and nice to have him standing there talking as though she was the one person in the Acorn that he wanted to see, while all heads craned round to stare at them. Civility of that sort did not come her way very often. And though a hard life had taught her to be cynical, though she knew that his words meant nothing, that he was playing to an appreciative audience, yet she smiled a response which no synthetic kindness in him could have evoked. She knew it for real kindness inevitably exploited, and this rude strumpeting of natural virtue had long since ceased to shock her. Seeing that he was trying to stifle a convulsive yawn she sympathised, for she knew, possibly better than he did, how few constitutions are built to survive the strain of universal popularity.

"Run along," she said drily, "or you'll miss your train. You're going into the country, I expect."

"A quiet Sunday," explained Hugo in inverted commas.

But he did not tell her where because he did not expect that she would be much the wiser. Possibly she had never heard of Syranwood. He had not heard of it himself five years ago, for it had never been extensively written up. Very few of his dear friends in the Acorn would know what an adventure lay before him. For all this triumph, this table and dish summit, was not, as he had so lately thought, the topmost rung of the ladder. There were other, and steeper, heights to be scaled. Some day he might be able to dispense with his publicity agent and take all his meals in private. For a traveller like himself this trip into an undiscovered country must be made with discretion nor could he expect his companions to believe all the stories which he might bring back.

"A quiet Sunday?"

He began to fidget with one of Miss Quartermaine's gloves which lay on the table. It smelt of benzine and he was reminded of his childhood when all white gloves had smelt of benzine. Sundays had been quiet enough then, in all conscience; a day of clean collars which frayed the neck and long, bored hours of being told to behave. He could remember the stupefied hush which fell upon his aunt's house about three o'clock in the afternoon when the mid-day joint had been eaten. "Now, Hugo, for goodness' sake sit still. Why don't you get a nice book and read quietly?" "Can't I go out and play with Barbara?" "No, you can't. It's Sunday." And then the cracked bell of the chapel at the end of the road would resume its hurried summons and Hugo's aunt would go to sleep and Hugo would be sent out into the back garden to an afternoon of dreamy idleness among the chickens there. The peculiar noises of Sunday would float one by one into the quietness; a muffin man would tinkle down a distant street, strains from a Salvation Army Band would throw him into a mood of delicious melancholy, and always about tea time the dog next door would begin to bark.

"Well . . . not so quiet . . ." he conceded.

"I should say not," said Miss Quartermaine, returning to her lunch. "What's the matter with your collar? Is it too tight?"

For Hugo had been so rapt back into the past that he had begun unconsciously to rub his frayed neck. The smell of benzine had, for a few moments, abolished the work of twenty years and restored him to his lost innocence. Nor could he return to the present without a sensation of considerable giddiness, such as may beset any climber who is rash enough to look back. With an effort he forced his mind upwards again, to his goal, to Syranwood, and to the business of pleasing Miss Quartermaine. But where was she going to spend her week-end? Not, he hoped, in London.

"You've said it. I don't get asked to any stately homes somehow. Oh yes, don't look so surprised. You didn't mention where it was, so I guessed it must be something pretty ancestral. But bless you, I wouldn't have thought you were showing off."

"I know. You're much too nice . . ."

"And besides, I don't read Country Life except at the dentist's. These Family Seats are all one to me."

"It's not Chatsworth," said Hugo hastily.

"What's that?"

He was glad that he had not yielded to the temptation of saying that Aggie was coming too. She might have asked what Aggie was, which would have been very awkward. He could not have explained without seeming to show off.

"I must go!" he said tragically.

"Yes, do go. And get a good sleep. You look as if you needed it."

She smiled at him once more, and remained smiling expectantly after the glass doors had swung behind him, as if waiting to see him return. Everybody in the Acorn had glanced at those swinging doors and he ought to have pushed his pale face in again for a moment to take their applause. But he never came back.

2. *The Pleasures of Solitude*.

The street smelt of sweat, petrol and melted tar. A heat
wave had set in and Hugo blinked a little as the glare from
the pavement struck up at him. He was dangerously
exhausted and on the point of collapse. During the past
week he had enjoyed, at the most, about eleven hours of
repose, and he had not slept since Wednesday. To his
friends it seemed as though he must never sleep at all, for
he never went home before seven in the morning and had
always written something marvellous by lunch time.
But he dozed off occasionally while driving from one
place to another and sometimes even in his bed if nobody
happened to be about.

On the opposite pavement, outside the Duchess of
York's Theatre, he could see boards which said 'House
Full.' The matinée of his play there had begun. When
he went in to lunch he had gone past a long string of
patient women sitting on campstools in the sun and many
of them had recognised him. Now they were all inside.
On a Saturday afternoon, in the middle of a heat wave,
after a run of five months, he could fill a theatre. That
was why he had been asked to Syranwood. That was why
he could talk intimately of Aggie. All these things—
Aggie, Syranwood, the campstools and the 'House Full'
boards, were symbols. They were concrete expression of
his enormous success.

For between Aggie and those quiet Sundays beside the
chicken run there lay a gulf which only success could
span; and down in that gulf he might so easily have spent
a life time along with poor old Miss Quartermaine and
all the other gifted people who are just not quite successful

enough. The very thought of it made him solemn and nervous, for he was too modest to suppose that anything but the most staggering luck could account for it and he could never entirely escape from a fear that there might be, as his aunt would have said, a catch in it somewhere. The Unseen Gods might notice him one day, as he scurried along the street, and change their minds.

His car waited just a little way past the theatre, and he screwed up his eyes against the sun as he looked about for it. Bought a month ago, it did not immediately strike the eye as all the others had, but was upholstered in dark blue and slid about through the traffic like a commanding shadow. A second glance at it was indeed impressive. If only he could reach it unmolested he might look forward to the enjoyment of a good yawn in peace and solitude. Before Waterloo he might get a lot of yawning done and in the train he might even snatch a little sleep. It was in this hope that he had decided to go down by train, for if he had gone by road he would have been obliged to offer a lift to Corny Cooke, who was also going to Syranwood. Before breakfast that morning Corny had cadged for one by telephone, asserting that he would be ready to start at any hour and was about to come round to Hugo's flat. Hugo replied that he would be at the theatre all the morning and would probably go down by train. Corny asked which train. Hugo told him the wrong one. So that the threat of company on the journey had been averted. His geniality tap must be turned off for a little while, since he knew that extravagant demands would be made upon it at Syranwood. He must sleep first, yawn, sigh, not see anybody.

The door to safety was open before him, and in thirty seconds he would be almost alone. But on the brink he was snatched back. A timid voice hailed him. Turning, he found himself confronted by a very dingy fragment of the past, a dear friend of seven years ago, now left behind in the gulf. For an uncomfortable instant he feared that he was not going to be able to recall her nickname. But before he had finished giving a start of surprise he remembered and brought it out.

"Joey!" He caught at her elbow eagerly. "My Angel! How are you? How's Squirrel?"

"Oh!" said Joey, looking extremely happy. "Oh!"

She could say nothing but that, for she had run twenty yards, and had been for seven years quite desperately in love with Hugo.

"I sat up all night with your book," he hastened to assure her. "I couldn't put it . . ."

"Oh! Oh!"

"I thought it was *so* good."

"Oh!"

"And what are you doing now?"

"Oh! I tried to get into your play but . . ."

"My dear, I know. I can't get in myself. It's absurd."

"Oh Hugo! It's wonderful to see you again."

"Yes, isn't it? You haven't changed a . . ."

"Oh Hugo, it must be wonderful to be so . . ."

"Pure luck, my dear. But great fun while it lasts. How's Tiger? And . . . and B. V.? And Maeve?"

"I suppose you're in a most awful hurry, Hugo?"

Up went his eyebrows in most expressive consternation as he admitted that he was, as a matter of fact, in an absurd hurry. It was exasperating, just when he had met Joey after all these years. But he had to catch a train at Waterloo. Could he possibly give her a lift anywhere? Fate sniggered at him. He could. Since she could not get

into his play she thought that perhaps she might try the
Old Vic. Ungraceful but beaming she climbed into the
dark blue car and Hugo followed resignedly.

This time there was no audience to note the fact that he
never forgot an old friend. He had no conceivable
reason for being nice to Joey barring the fact that she
had been nice to him seven years ago. But he offered her
the same eager cordiality which he had dispensed so
lavishly in the Acorn. She was pathetic and breathless,
and she had run after him for twenty yards down Shaftesbury Avenue, and, poor thing, she looked unprosperous.
Imagination reeled before the memory of their early
intimacy. For there had been a time when she had been
the patron and he the pursuer. Obscure though she
might be, she had once disentangled him from an even
dimmer world, from his aunt's back garden, the wire
netting, and the hot, henny smell of the chicken run.
They had met at a party in Hampstead to which Hugo
had been taken by a school friend. He had gone in high
hopes because he had been told that he would meet
people who "wrote" and the drawer of his washhand
stand was, at that time, full of unpublished poems. But
the people who wrote were a disappointment. They
talked of royalties, editors and each other so intimately,
with such a profusion of initials and so many recondite
allusions that he despaired of being able to join in. Nor
had he ever heard of any of them. His hostess gave them
to understand that somebody very much heard of might
drop in later, but this never happened. The room was
hot, noisy and smoky and he ate a sandwich which made
him feel sick. At last he found himself sitting beside
Joey on a dusty divan in a corner and she was kind to
him. She listened to his shy witticisms and asked if he

had ever thought of writing a play. They agreed upon the parlous condition of the theatre, condemned commercial successes, and settled all that they would themselves have done if only they had had a little money. The stage, said Hugo, was so terribly stagey. It was, said Joey, and the Box Office seemed to be the only thing that mattered. A play with ideas had no chance.

That summer she had carried him off to Dorsetshire where she and a group of friends were leading the good life in a colony of bungalows by the sea. They too had nicknames, and they talked about royalties and editors, but Hugo could by then follow them and join in. Some of them did folk dancing, and some wore hand-dyed homespuns, and their typewriters tapped behind the curtains in their cottage windows, and they made great friends with the fishermen. It was the fashion that summer to talk Dorset dialect and to bathe, a little self-consciously, with nothing on. Hugo had been a great success. He organised moonlight picnics and wrote plays which they acted in barns and got up a pierrot troupe. He managed to instil into the whole group an energy and brilliance which it had never had before, so that it was a golden summer for everybody concerned. The memory of it had become a legend, and several of them had since earned a welcome guinea or two by writing it up.

Joey did not wear amber beads or handwoven linen but she looked sticky, and Hugo lived nowadays among women who managed never to do that, even in a heat wave. So that he was obliged to think for a moment regretfully of Caroline Chappell to whom he was reputedly attached, an astonishing and flawless creature like a magnolia tree in flower. He thought of her regretfully because she was at that moment five thousand miles away at the sick bed of one of her parents. He could never remember which, because she had so many, all divorcing each other and marrying somebody else even richer, and all continuing to worship their little Caro. She had been a trifle put out because he would not come with her, but oncoming rehearsals had kept him in London so she had taken her current husband instead. And though he deplored the separation he could not but enjoy this interval of liberty. She was perfect but, like all his other pieces of good fortune, she was exacting.

"What would Caro think of Joey?" he wondered. "And what would Joey think of Caro? Oh these women! These women!"

If there were no women in the world he would still be writing poetry among the wire netting. He could hardly go so far as to sigh for that. But in future he must really try not to collect any more of them. For at Syranwood there would be, not only Aggie, but Laura and Philomena all highly collectable, and he must be very cautious. Caro was quite enough for anybody.

Joey was telling him all about Squirrel's new novel, repeating solemnly:

"She's the best of us. Her historical stuff is so marvellous. Don't you think she's the best of us?"

Hugo agreed warmly and thought that she well might be. Looking back at it he could hardly believe that he had once joined them in those earnest discussions about their Work. Had he been laughing at them? Had he known, even then, that they were merely a stepping stone? He hoped not. After all a certain development and growth was natural to any one, and he had been very, very young. But the fact remained that there was not a single

one of them that he really wanted to see again unless it
might be that queer fellow who lived up at the coastguard's cottage and quarrelled with everybody. But then
he did not belong to the group. He just happened to be
there.

"Ever see Paul Wrench nowadays?" he asked Joey.
"He's written some marvellous stuff. Lives abroad,
doesn't he?"

Joey blinked, bewildered at being jerked out of the
small world in which she lived. Then she remembered.

"Hadn't you heard?"

"No. What?"

"He's dead. It was in the papers this morning."

"Dead? Not really. No, I didn't see. What made him
die? He was quite young. At least, not old."

"I don't know what he died of. Tiger's living with
Bunny. Did you know?"

They were crossing the river and the tide was going
out. A gull swooped low and flashed whitely past the
window of the car. Hugo thought:

"Dead? There's something wrong about that. I'd
always expected . . ."

What was it that he had always expected? He did not
much enjoy Wrench's poems though he believed that he
admired them. They were too bleak and rough. But it
was not fair that anyone so disagreeable should be forced
to die. Only pleasant people should be cut off in their
prime with half their work undone. Waste of this sort
had no ornamental grace to soften it.

"Don't you think so?" Joey was asking plaintively.

He had no idea what she had been saying so he caught
her arm and interrupted.

"My dear, I've got such a marvellous idea for a play.

Do listen. I must tell you."

He had not time to tell her much for they were turning into Waterloo Station. But it was a kind thought and Joey was radiant. Now she could go home and tell them all that Hugo was just the same, not a bit spoilt, and that he had told her all about his new play just as he used to do. Her faithful brown eyes filled with tears of pleasure. If only it had not been over so soon!

"Do you mind frightfully if I nip out here?" he entreated. "I've cut it rather fine. Benson will take you on to the Old Vic or anywhere you want to go. Good-bye, Joey darling. It's been delicious. And I must see more of you. Do let me come sometime? Will you? Will you? I should adore to. If I may I'll ring you up in the . . . good-bye . . ."

He ran very fast into the station, saw with a shock that he really had cut it fine, sprinted down the platform and plunged into the safety of an empty compartment just as the train began to move. His suitcases and golf clubs were flung in after him. The door slammed. He was alone. Flinging himself full length upon the cushions he shut his eyes.

Five minutes later the indefatigable Corny Cooke, making a tour of the train to see who was in it, peeped through the corridor window and went bustling off to spread the news that Hugo Pott had gone to sleep in the last compartment. Aggie heard it first because she was the train's most precious ornament. She had suddenly declared that she could not endure the dust of the Portsmouth road on such an afternoon and there had been great excitement at Waterloo.

She was not very much interested in Corny's news, because she had picked up a new friend on the platform, a young person looking like the Discobolos of Myron who was, in fact, a Dominion bowler. She was busy telling him how she had been obliged to take a bismuth meal and what it had looked like when it was photographed, indicating all the places on her stomach that it got to on the way. They were getting on at a great rate and the stranger was much less embarrassed than he would have been had he known who she was. A pardonable liveliness tempered his admiration, for he supposed her to be an ageing courtesan got up to look like that Lady Agneta Melotte whose picture he had seen in the papers.

"Hugo's here," chirruped Corny, putting his head into their compartment. "He's asleep."

Aggie blinked her beautiful, shallow eyes and asked who Hugo might be.

"Hugo Pott," explained Corny reproachfully.

Because Aggie knew quite well that Hugo had been asked to Syranwood especially in order to amuse her, because it had been decided that he was really too nice and too successful to be given up to that dreadful Brazilian with all the husbands. It was a rescue party, this week-end was.

"Hugo Pott," he said.

And he stared at Discobolos enquiringly.

"Which reminds me," said Aggie, growing more genial, "I'd like some tea. Or coffee. Some iced coffee would be nice, don't you think?"

"But Aggie, there isn't any. I told you when you sent me before. There's no tea car on this train."

"Why not?"

"It's too early."

"Not if I want it. I daresay the guard has some. He told me to let him know if I wanted anything. Tea will do if he hasn't got coffee. Ask him, will you, Corny?"

Discobolos, who looked upon Corny as an interfering rival, got up and shut the door into the corridor. It was a magnificent, caveman gesture and Aggie began to giggle. Corny observed them through the window for a few minutes with melancholy attention and then went on down the train. He could find nobody else for Syranwood in the other first-class carriages, but he saw several friends and exchanged news of various other week-end parties. By the time that he had worked through them all he knew who was going to stay where at half the houses on the South-Western line, and had learned that his wife had done very well at Newmarket the day before. He was glad of that for he had seen an Aubusson carpet which would look nice in his flat in Whitehall Court and he thought that he had better hurry up and buy it before anything happened.

At the end of the first-class coach he paused and considered, for the corridor was hot and the train swayed abominably. But curiosity buoyed him up and he began a survey of the third-class passengers. Here he found three more guests for Syranwood, all literary, and for a moment he looked a little blank. It was not fair of Geraldine to ask him to that sort of week-end. But then he remembered Hugo and Aggie in the coach behind and cheered up. Besides which, Gibson Grey, though a publisher, was very popular and Philomena, his wife, knew everybody. She was Geraldine's cousin. As for Sir Adrian Upward, he had quite a place of his own. Duchesses would send the proofs of their first novels to him, commanding that he should edit the punctuation. For years he had been 'that clever Mr. Upward' to any hostess who liked good talk at her dinner table, and when

Aggie's baby was born he was sent for to read Donne to her while they gave the chloroform.

"Hugo's here," vouchsafed Corny. "He's asleep."

"Who else?" asked Upward, slowly lowering his weekly review.

"Only Aggie."

Gibson Grey said:

"How useful, Corny, to have you as a liaison officer between us and the first class. Now do you happen to know . . . ?"

Corny knew everything. It was to be quite a small party. Only Laura Le Fanu, Geraldine's daughter, and Laura's husband and two of Laura's men, Walter Bechstrader and a new boy friend.

"Somebody she ran across in *Mit-Europa* last year. Name of Usher. Ford Usher. Nothing known about him except that he has discovered a cure for malaria."

Sir Adrian knew, it appeared, more than that. He had read a series of articles on Ford Usher's discovery. The cure, he said, consisted of the administration of an anti-malaria parasite carried by a mosquito called *culex pseudopictus*.

"Laura'll be busy," commented Gibson Grey. "I suppose Pott has been provided for her too."

"Oh, no," Corny corrected him. "For Aggie."

3. *Journey to Basingstoke.*

Philomena Grey looked out of the window and said nothing. But she smiled to herself because all this talk of Aggie and Laura was amusing. She could make

Aggie look like a marsh-mallow.

After fifteen years of being a good wife to Gibbie, and having babies, and rubbing in cleansing cream at night, she had forgotten what it was like to be in love. She had forgotten how the heart can stop at the casual mention of a name. All the beginning of the journey had been so exasperating and hot, and it had become delectable just because Corny came in and said: *Hugo's here.* She had thought that the power to feel so intensely must have been ground out of her long ago, that not only time but marriage would have destroyed it. Latterly she had come to identify it with her lost virginity, a thing to be remembered indulgently but not regretted. Those transports, ardours and despairs of her girlhood had never come to anything and she used to tell her more romantic friends that she had no wish to go through it all again.

But now those fifteen years of common sense had suddenly become as tiresome and trivial as an interval spent at a railway station. She had scarcely been alive at all except in moments of aching melancholy, apprehensions of waste, of power unused and youth misspent, which had sometimes assailed her on fine mornings in the spring. All the time she had been waiting, half asleep, for some kind of deliverance. And she had called it happiness. Perhaps it was, but in that case how much better to be miserable! How much better to be going through it all again.

For five minutes she stared fixedly out of the window half afraid that her face might hold some radiance which would betray her. But she need not have troubled for Gibbie was reading and Adrain Upward was saying:

" . . . The greatest loss to literature in this century . . ."

They were talking of Paul Wrench. It was one of the things people would be saying this week-end. And, poor man, he was so much more comfortable to think of, now that he was dead. For there had always been the disquieting possibility that he might one day go altogether too far. But now he could go no further. As might have been expected his last letter had been written to Corny. All last letters of poets were written to Corny.

Corny was taking a proprietary tone. So was Adrian. Paul Wrench had no defence against them now. He could no longer flout their kind endeavours. Adrian, it appeared, had tried to get him a grant from the Royal Literary Fund. Corny could have told him that it was no use. Incredible though it might be, he had contributed a poem to Corny's famous album. Corny, in a churchy voice a little raised above the din of the train, recited it, adding that Wrench had died of cancer of the throat. Corny always knew that sort of thing.

So much easier, thought Philomena, to talk about people when they were finished. Now Wrench was in the past. But he had managed to make even death appear less banal and more irrelevant than usual. For in his case there was nothing of the harmonious rounding off, the full close which sentiment requires. It was a jagged, uncouth interruption, and it added no real significance to life. He had not crossed the bar or demanded more light, but had been dragged away, protesting irritably, from the things which he wished to do. Now he would never do them, and that was all.

The senselessness of this hiatus came home to her as she looked out of the window and saw Brookwood Cemetery, which was swinging past them. Acre upon acre of the indifferent earth was strewn with haphazard pieces of stone. Crosses and slabs of marble stood up starkly among the cypresses carving the view into a thousand awkward, unrelated angles. The wreaths heaped upon the newer graves, the black figures pacing slowly down the avenues, the very blades of grass were all sunk into the same stony torpor. They had no meaning at all, for they symbolised a void space in human imagination.

"Depressing . . ." thought Philomena, as she turned her head away. "Perhaps cremation . . . but even then . . . those horrid little urns . . . one has to do something with them . . . have I ever seen a grave . . . Keats . . . I wasn't as moved as I expected to be, but perhaps that was because I was annoyed with Gibbie. He'd been tiresome . . . what was it? Oh yes, it was the day he dropped his Baedeker into the Tiber . . . fifteen years . . . and now . . . now . . . *Hugo's here* . . . don't let this be spoilt . . ."

But it was, already, a trifle spoilt. She came back to it in a different mood. Her excursion among cemeteries had stressed the precious brevity of this life which she had been wasting and she felt angry with herself. The rapture of the moment was not enough. She must begin to think ahead. The exquisite pause, the sense of standing on the threshold of new delight, had passed away from her.

Hugo was coming down to Syranwood. But what was going to happen? Did she want anything to happen? Did she intend it? And, if she was going to let things happen, at what point ought she to convey the truth to Gibbie? As an honest woman she ought, perhaps, to say something and as yet she had said nothing. There was so little to say. Some states of mind are too rare, too delicate, to be translated into common speech and she had got no further than a state of mind. To speak at all would have been to say more than the truth.

"Oh Gibbie, you know that night, that night of Stella's dance? I want to tell you that Hugo drove me home and we thought it would be fun to go down to Kew, and we got there just at sunrise and climbed in from the towing-path just opposite Zion House. Yes, I know, I've told you that part of it. But ever since that morning I've thought of nothing but Hugo. He is a little in love with me. Oh yes, I know all about Caro Chappell but I'm not worrying about her. And I don't think he was. I had on my white chiffon, and I felt I was *en beauté*: I don't believe anybody could have helped being in love with me. Of course it was partly that the gardens were quite empty and the may was out and it all looked very romantic. No, he didn't make love to me, more than he always does to everybody. But he was so delightful that I can't help thinking about him all the time. I've never enjoyed myself so much in the whole of my life. It makes me happy now to think of it. And I don't propose to stop thinking of it. But nothing happened. And I daresay nothing ever will. But if anything ever should . . . I felt I ought to tell you."

It was impossible. And yet perfect frankness had been Philomena's creed for years. It was the bedrock of a happy marriage, and her marriage with Gibbie had been happy in spite of the days when he dropped his Baedeker into the Tiber. Nothing must happen that would involve her in disloyalty to Gibbie. Their married harmony must be preserved, but there ought to be room inside it for this lovely thing, this renewal of youth. There must be room in it. Other people managed to eat their cake and have it. If one had courage, if one was

frank, there need be no disloyalty. She could think of half
a dozen instances among her romantic friends.

Now they had got past Brookwood Cemetery and were
back among the gardens of a suburb where laundry
fluttered in the sun among the aerial posts, and stout men
in their shirt sleeves mowed small lawns. She remembered
that she must change her own laundry. Gibbie's shirts
were a perfect disgrace and there was iron-mould on the
sheets every other week. She would write for the price-
list of that Hounslow place as soon as she got home on
Monday. There was a whole lot of things to remember on
Monday. A dentist's appointment must be made for
Chloe's teeth. It ought surely to be possible to straighten
them without subjecting the poor child to those hideous
wires. And Susan had begun to tread over her shoes very
badly: probably she had weak ankles and these must be
remedied. It was all the result of not having very much
money. Not that Gibbie was really poor, but he was not
as rich as most of the people they knew. Rich people
never have anything to attend to but their better feelings.
Their children's teeth are straight and they have their pick
of parlour-maids. Philomena was still looking for a
parlour-maid, because Ada's month would be up on
Tuesday week. She must go to Mrs. Duckett's Registry
again on Monday. She must make a list of all the things
to be done on Monday . . . laundry . . . teeth . . .
shoes . . . Ada . . . it was damnably unfair! For
nearly half her life she had been smothered under teeth
and laundries, when really she was not that sort of person
at all. She had married too young. She had never lived
her life. They (some hidden influences, not specified)
ought not to have allowed her to marry so young.

"Not that I blame Gibbie. I love him. Poor, darling

Gibbie! He couldn't get on without me and I'll never
. . . and the children . . . oh no, I haven't forgotten
them . . . of course he comes first, and the children.
That's solid. That's lasting. Because I shall be old
some day and then . . . those awful old women with no
ties . . . I could never . . . but I have got an immortal
soul after all, and it's smothered . . . yes smothered
under laundry baskets."

Gibbie must be made to understand. Surely, when he
loved her so much, he would give her room to live. All
that wonderful power was still in her body—the power to
charm, to soothe, to ravish, to console. She had far more
to give than Gibbie or the children would ever need. It
was not fair. She had married too soon. Somebody was
to blame. Not Gibbie; not her parents (though Mother
might have told me); not the children (they can't help
having teeth and feet, poor angels); not even Ada. But all
of them together.

She realised that she had been making furious grimaces
and that Adrian Upward, who sat opposite, was looking
at her over the top of his paper in surprise.

"I was rehearsing things to say to the laundry," she
explained hastily.

Sir Adrian tried to look as though he did not know
what a laundry did or why one should say things to it.
He had mixed so much with dukes that he had caught a
little of the ducal vagueness about the baser details of life.
He could not telephone from a public call-box without
making a muddle, and he frequently lost his way on the
Underground, which was a triumph of mind over matter
as anyone who knew his home life could testify. Philomena, remembering the smell of cabbage in the Upward
hall, asked after his sister Betsy, who had kept house for

him since the death of his wife. Adrian replied briefly that Betsy was well. And the children? They were well too, so far as he knew all six of them were, as usual, in the enjoyment of rude health.

Only by dissociating himself from Betsy and the children could Sir Adrian Upward hope to hold his own at Syranwood. For he was quite horribly and squalidly poor, and as a family man he would have been impossible. But very poor bachelors, if they can sing for their supper, have a certain appeal for the benevolent rich. So that Adrian was obliged to ignore the callow brood which he had so rashly begotten, and to suppress their obliging aunt.

Very few people had even seen Miss Betsy Upward. She was said to have a mop of short grey hair, red hands and pince-nez. But Philomena was obliged to see her occasionally because Gibbie, who was Adrian's publisher, insisted upon asking her to dinner. In many ways Gibbie was tiresomely kind-hearted. Three times a year did Betsy, in a ready-made lace tunic from the Kensington High Street, come ambling shyly in behind Adrian. She always short-circuited conversation at her end of the table and it was difficult to know who to put next to her. Nor was there any necessity for it at all. She wasn't even the man's wife, merely a poor relation who happened to keep house for him. But Gibbie thought that she was badly treated and now the mere mention of her name set the wheels of his benevolence spinning. He began asking Adrian to drop in with her one evening, though it was barely six weeks since the last time. Philomena did not support him as she should and knew that her languid warmth was obvious. But later on, if he should reproach her, she would make a stand.

C

He was always wishing these dreary women on to her. Women with whom she had nothing in common. All his friends seemed to have made a point of marrying dull wives. But where wives were concerned she had nobly done her duty. She had sat with them in polite boredom for long hours by the drawing-room fire so that he could get his cronies to himself over the port. In no way had she ever cut him off from anyone whose companionship he valued. But as regards Betsy . . .

The train came to an extraordinary jerking stop in the middle of a green field.

An idea that something was wrong occurred to all of them simultaneously. It was so much more sudden than the usual slow-down and pause. Corny disappeared into the corridor. In a surprised silence they could hear the voices of the people in the next compartment. Adrian poked his head out of the window and saw a trainful of heads, all poked out, as a whisper of the dramatic spread.

"It's a special for the Prince of Wales," he reported.

A contrary rumour travelled from the other end of the train a moment later. The engine driver had fallen down dead of heart disease.

"I wonder if we'll be long," speculated Philomena. "Wouldn't it be nice to get out for a bit and pick those wild roses?"

Gibbie at once protested. She had meant him to. Supposing the train went on? Well, of course, she had not really wanted to get out. He might have known that. But she wanted someone with whom to share the impulse. She wanted him to say:

"Adorable creature! Yes, let's!"

There were people who might have liked being left behind with her in a green field. There were women who

missed trains as they chose, who were above rules and
time-tables and Gibbie was quite capable of finding them
most attractive. But because she was his wife she might
have no whims or caprices. She was just there to see that
his children's teeth grew straight.

"I didn't really want to," she said coldly.

"And how could I know that?"

Adrian, at the window, reported that there was a bomb
on the line.

"No, but what is it really?" demanded Gibbie.

"When Corny comes back he'll tell us. I expect he's
gone to find out."

Corny had gone to find out, guided by that instinct
which had caused him to be in at a record number of
deaths. He went straight down the train to Aggie's
compartment. For it was clear to him that somebody had
pulled the alarm cord and nobody else on the train was so
likely to have done it. He arrived almost as soon as the
guard, in time to hear Discobolos exclaim:

"I tell you I never touched it. She pulled it herself.
And I suppose she'll tell you that I assaulted her. But if
ever a woman asked for it . . ."

Aggie sat, infinitely withdrawn and nunlike, in her
corner. She lifted her eyes slowly and looked at the
guard who was asking if she really had pulled the cord.

"No," she said.

"Well," began Discobolos . . .

"Now then!" said the guard sternly, "You be quiet
until you're spoken to. Did he offer to insult your
ladyship?"

"No. Oh no," said Aggie.

Discobolos, who thought the guard was being funny,
began to recover countenance. He suggested that

perhaps the little lady hadn't known what she was doing, but as one man to another . . . and he produced a case of Treasury notes.

Aggie spoke again, even more faintly. She thought the man might be drunk and perhaps they would put him into another carriage.

"Now then! Now then!" expostulated the guard. "You can't use language like that, sir. Not here. You come along with me and I'll trouble you for your name and address."

"You take a tart's word against mine? It's blackmail. That's what it is. She pulled it herself. It's a put-up thing. That's what it is. I'll get you sacked for this . . ."

"Now then. You come along out of here."

The victim was dragged into the corridor where they heard the guard saying:

"You know who that lady is? Well, she's Lady Aggie Melotte. That's who she is. And I'll trouble you to stop using insulting language. All right, Bill. Let her go."

The train started with another sudden jerk, and Corny, having witnessed the final, speechless collapse of Discobolos, went in to comfort Aggie. He wanted badly to know who had really pulled the cord.

"I'm sure I don't know," said Aggie. "He was a howwid man. Have you got me any tea, Corny?"

"No, Aggie. I told you. There isn't any."

"Oh, very well, then, have you got a pencil? I'll give you a gibbet."

She gave him *Great unaffected vampires and the moon*, but he lost because his mind was wandering. In imagination he was telling this latest Aggie story to an appreciative audience. Not that he would have much opportunity for

doing so, which was a pity. For Aggie stories had come
to be a mark of bad taste, since so many of them were told
by people who did not know her.

"L" he said vaguely.

"You've been gibbeted once for an L," scolded Aggie.
"You aren't trying. Go and fetch Hugo. Perhaps he can
be more amusing."

"Hugo's asleep."

"Well then wake him up."

Corny obediently edged his way down the swaying
train to take another peep into Hugo's compartment. It
was impossible to know whether its occupant was asleep
or not. He still lay at full length on the seat of the
carriage and his eyes were shut, but there was a taut,
forbidding look about his mouth and Corny would
rather have put his head into a wasps' nest than disturb
him. So, after waiting for a few minutes, he edged away.
Unable to face Aggie without Hugo he took refuge in a
smoking carriage with a stranger, a very large, red, raw
man with blue P & O labels on his battered portmanteaux.
This person did not look up when Corny joined him, but
after a little while a Will like a steam roller commanded
the intruder to take himself off and stop polluting an All-
White-Sahib's carriage. Corny had never been so much
aware of an ousting influence before, though mental
behests of the sort were frequently directed at him, did he
but know it. Worse still, it was an unconscious will. The
stranger was absorbed in a copy of (not the *Daily Mail*,
for Corny peeped to see) the *Lancet*. He was not merely
glancing through it, he was mopping up information
from the page in front of him with the concentrated fury
of a Hoover scouring a carpet. But the nearness of
Corny was displeasing and mechanically he flicked the

annoyance away. His soul said:

"Go."

Corny, with a faint squeak of protest, went. He took another cautious peep at Hugo and this time he met with open, hostile eyes. They stared at him without encouragement, and were tightly shut again. Even to Corny that hint was unmistakable. He went to wash his hands.

4. *The Other Life.*

Hugo hoped that he would go down the drain. All possibility of sleep had been banished by that fellow's spying. Just when he was tipping deliciously on the edge of it something would nag at him and pull him back. His relaxing nerves wound themselves up again like an automatic spring. He lay quite still on the cushions with his eyes shut and thought:

"Here is the amazingly successful Hugo Pott lying quite still with his eyes shut."

The thing was like an orchestra in a restaurant. He did not always listen to it, but it was always there. It accompanied every course in the Trimalchian banquet of his career, and in moments of solitude, like this, when he could stop to listen, the noise it made was deafening. He could hear nothing else very clearly, and his thoughts came to him in a muffled confusion.

Very soon he would get to Basingstoke and then even this much seclusion would be impossible. Once more he began to make those old, futile plans for escape, a yacht, a trip to the desert. And forthwith the train wheels began to drum out snappy little paragraphs:

. . . Lunching at the Savoy Grill yesterday I ran across Hugo Pott who told me that his next play will be completed in the Arabian Desert . . .

Hugo Pott waves a cheery good-bye. Dramatist makes home in the Sahara . . .

. . . at a farewell dinner to Mr. Hugo Pott, reading from right to left: Mrs. Chappell, Mr. Pott, Mr. 'Corny' Cooke . . .

, . . Hugo Pott takes Pott-Luck in the Gobi desert. Reading from left to right: Mr. 'Corny' Cooke, Mr. Pott, Mrs. Chappell . . .

. . . Hugo Pott, the dramatist, has fallen off his camel in the desert of Sinai (Reuter).

There was no escape; no spot from darkest Africa to Baffin's Bay where his private orchestra would not accompany him.

The train was already slowing down. It was time to get out. He struggled to his feet and looked in the glass over his head to see if there was really a smut on his nose. His face, so much photographed, so smudged with a world publicity as to be scarcely his own any more, glowered back at him. Like all his other possessions it was an asset rather than a face. A wonderful asset. For the millionth time he wished that he had not been born so Nordic, so virile, clean and candid. Fair hair and blue eyes were an impossible handicap for anyone in his situation. He scowled and the features in the glass melted into a romantic gloom. He made a grimace of disgust and saw reflected something so charmingly wry and whimsical that he groaned aloud:

"Oh help!"

The train had stopped and a porter mistook this shout

for a summons. He opened the door and began to throw suitcases about. A parting glimpse in the glass showed Hugo that the geniality tap had turned on of its own accord and he stepped down onto the platform with the expression of a successful but unspoilt young man arriving for a week-end at a country house. Gracefully preoccupied with his porter, he did not see his co-arrivals until he was near enough to give a start of genuine surprise and pleasure.

"Aggie! How delicious! You're *not* going to Syranwood? (I suppose it's all right, not a *gaffe*, calling her Aggie in public? I always did that time at Cap Ferrat.) Hullo Corny! What did Paul Wrench die of, do you know? (Perhaps I said it just a shade too loud, as if I wanted everybody in Basingstoke to hear. Well, but damn it all, so I do.) Look who's here! Gibbie and Philomena!"

But Philomena did not immediately hear these cries. She was very busy talking to Adrian Upward, and she walked out through the barrier without seeming to realise that the others were still on the platform. For she had no notion of waiting patiently at Hugo's elbow until he had finished fondling Aggie. Knowing that her rival was on the train she had been prepared for this moment. Aggie was bound to be the most important person on the platform at Basingstoke and it was a good gesture to leave her in possession of such a field. Philomena was not obliged to depend upon birth or notoriety; her setting was a garden at dawn and her appeal was lyrical. If she had any power to hold him it must keep its own terms against Aggie. Hugo could take it or leave it. He must know, as well as any one, that Aggie had the sort of face which, in a commoner, betokens adenoids, that she must be getting on for fifty, and that a lifetime of being spoilt had turned her into a vain, egotistical bore.

"Hi! Philomena! Hi!"

But she was out of the station and had got very quickly into the nearest of the Syranwood cars, so that there should be no petty manœuvring. If Hugo wanted to ride with Aggie he certainly could. Adrian Upward was a very interesting man.

"Get in," she urged him. "Get in quickly. I want to have a long bathe before dinner."

She was thinking of the artificial lake at Syranwood, among its green lawns and shady trees. Her new bathing dress, a tunic of green silk covered over with little flowers, looked like a poem. Everything that was lyrical and fresh in her, the perfect symmetry and firmness of her body, would find its background against that cool water. That was her only answer to Aggie. Let Aggie come swimming if she dared.

"Do get in, Adrian. What are you waiting for?"

"Are there two cars?" asked Adrian dubiously. "Will there be room for everyone? I can take a cab quite easily."

He knew that there were two cars, but Aggie was sure to go in the other one, and he wanted to go with her. So did Corny. So did Hugo. His eye strayed towards the barrier. Philomena saw it and flashed angrily. For snobbery was a thing which she had always detested and despised. She was as little of a snob herself as it is possible for a person of taste and discrimination to be. But then she had always known that Adrian was a snob. She had never really liked him. He was not really a good critic. His friends' books reminded him far too often of Voltaire. And his treatment of poor Betsy was quite abominable.

Brightly she urged him to engage a taxi at once, before more people got out of the station. At least she would pay him out by forcing him to explain himself. But he merely said:

"I'll see if Corny will share it."

At this point their attention was called by the chauffeur to the second car. There was plenty of room for everybody.

"Oh then," cried Adrian adroitly, "I'll stop Corny from getting a taxi."

Aggie herself came through the barrier and the question was settled without further debate.

"Two cars," said Aggie. "I see. I want Hugo to come with me. You and Adrian get into the other one, Corny."

Corny, grinning valiantly, did as he was told. Adrian followed him with a less good grace. Indeed, Gibbie was the only satisfied occupant of the middle-class car, for he knew that he would have more room for his legs where Aggie was not.

Philomena, waiting for them, managed to look as aloof as a butterfly perched on a rose. She seemed a little surprised when they all got in, as if she had not been quite sure whether other people were coming or not. And Hugo, ravished as he was at being picked out by Aggie, could not help sighing when he looked at Philomena, so gentle and serene, like a flowery glade in the middle of Basingstoke. He wished that he might have changed places with Adrian or Corny or Gibbie. The dying poet in his heart groaned thirstily. For Aggie was a business rather than a pleasure, a career rather than a diversion. Even the memory of Caro, his Magnolia tree, looked a little concocted beside the nymph-like freshness

of Philomena. He caught her eye and came close to her
car while Aggie was haranguing the station master.

"Well?" he murmured. "Have you been to Stonehenge?"

He referred to a small joke that they had shared in Kew
Gardens. For he had an excellent memory and always
greeted an attractive woman with an allusion to some jest
or confidence which had united them at their last meeting,
thereby securing an immediate recognition of intimacy.
So that he could keep a dozen irons in the fire at once, as
long as he never mixed up these private passwords.

Philomena gave him a leisurely smile. That was all
right then. He remembered, even if he did not, as yet,
take her seriously. He was bored with the idea of Aggie
already. She drove off contentedly with her sulky and
depressed companions. A taxi with Aggie's maid and the
luggage came after them, rattling through the streets of
Basingstoke. But the second car, with Hugo and Aggie in
it, dallied unaccountably in the station yard.

"Why don't we start?" demanded Aggie, two seconds
after Hugo had taken his place beside her.

Their chauffeur explained rather nervously. Yet
another gentleman was expected by this train.

"What?" exclaimed Hugo and Aggie in dismay.
"Somebody else?"

Corny would have been better than this. For the
interloper must be a complete stranger. The chauffeur
believed that his name was Usher.

"Usher?" said Aggie, as though the word had been a
little obscene. "Let him take a taxi. We can't wait. We
shall get sunstroke. We've been sitting here for an hour
at least. I don't suppose for a minute that he's come by
this train."

The man exchanged glances with his colleague. It was one of those crises which only ambassadors and domestic servants are expected to survive. How did Mr. Usher count as against Aggie? Was he too important to be left behind? The colleague nodded slightly. Nobody counted against Aggie.

"Very good, my lady."

"Perhaps he's gone already in a taxi," said Hugo, by way of salving his own conscience. "I say! What's this?"

A gladstone bag with a striped P & O label had been suddenly thrust into the car on Aggie's feet, and a large red man was climbing in after it.

"Like the wooden horse being pushed into Troy," thought Hugo, fascinated.

Nobody who knew Laura could have believed that this was her new boy friend. Even the chauffeur had his doubts and interfered to demand if it was Mr. Usher.

"It is," said the stranger. "And if you'll just move a little, Madam, I'll put my bag where it won't get in the way of your legs."

Aggie, dazed, did as she was told. The wooden horse folded himself up on the seat opposite to Hugo and the car started.

Aggie was rather sorry, now, that she had brought Hugo with her. This newcomer stirred her to a languid curiosity. She tried to remember what it was that she had heard about him. He had discovered something and he was Laura's belonging. Other people's affairs were always rather dim to Aggie, but this one struck her as amusing because it was unexpected. Much cry and little wool had hitherto been the outstanding feature in Laura's affairs. Incontinent only in conversation she was known

to dismiss her admirers at the first unmistakable mani-
festation of carnal appetite. But this one looked as
though he might be sent away five minutes after arrival
and Aggie asked herself how much talk Laura was
expecting to get out of it. For her own part she had never
been more ready to commend Laura's choice and as she
looked him over with a wanton, but not unfriendly eye,
she wished that she had known he was coming before.

Ford Usher looked back at Aggie and told himself that
she was a Society Woman. That disposed of her as
neatly as if she had been a mosquito pinned down into
one of his little specimen boxes. For though he had spent
most of his life in malarial swamps, he knew a Society
Woman when he met one, because he had seen pictures of
them in those illustrated weeklies which abound in
deserts and on frontiers. Also his mother, who had
brought up seven children by writing a very humble kind
of Gossip Column, had told him a good deal about these
creatures. She said that they were all alike, but he was not
so foolish as to believe her. Every species, as he well
knew, has its subdivisions. For instance, he was certain
that Laura Le Fanu must be quite different from all other
Society Women. He would not be coming to Syranwood
unless she were, or leaving his assistant at the Guthrie
Institute to carry out an important dissection alone. So
that he was not particularly interested in Aggie and would
have preferred the Institute smell of pitch pine and pure
alcohol to the gale of carnation which she was wafting
about the car.

"Have you ever been to Syranwood before?" began
Hugo, who felt that the wooden horse must be helped a
little.

Ford looked at him for the tenth of a second and said:

"No."

"Very hot day," pursued Hugo. "This sort of heat is so much more trying than the tropics, don't you think? Or don't you?"

"No."

Aggie giggled and Hugo gave it up. Ignoring the presence of the wooden horse he devoted himself to the business of entertaining her. With nervous rapidity he said several things which were much too good to be wasted at this point of the visit. Aggie, absorbed by the intriguing stranger, made no effort to appreciate them. He realised that he ought to study the art of saving himself up. These brilliances should have been reserved for an important moment, preferably the full publicity of the dinner table. Now he had tossed them away before a mixed audience in a station car, getting no real credit for them, nor could they be repeated later with any comfort in the presence of Aggie or Ford. Good things were not so easily come by that he could waste them like that. But he still had a lot to learn. Many of his best jokes were made under circumstances when any unscrupulous friend could steal them. He was drawing recklessly upon that precious, irreplaceable little capital of personality which had got him out of the gulf. And every so often he had a premonitory shiver of fright when he realised that the balance was continually getting smaller and that nothing was coming in. Someday it would be all gone and then he would be a bore, living precariously on the remnants of a reputation, and at last They would find him out.

But such fears, as he hastily reminded himself, were absurd. A great deal must really be coming in. This bogy of sterility was a mere consequence of temporary over-strain. His success had opened out vast new opportunities for experience. He was able to travel, to spend, to know a great variety of people, to sample fresh aspects of life. And it was sheer morbidity to look back upon the epoch of Joey and Squirrel as a period of comparative wealth. He could not really then have been getting more than he gave. And before that? Why did he keep reverting to those first days when he and everyone else had been so boringly and eternally occupied with the banal details of life, how to catch buses, how not to catch colds, and the price of parsnips? That was not life: it was merely existence. When daily bread had been secured only a fraction of soul and energy was left over for the finer sentiments. While at Syranwood, for instance, he would consort with people who had studied living itself as an art. And these must have more to give by way of exchange. Of course they would expect him to sing for his supper, but it was absurd to suppose that their fare was less nourishing than that afforded by the bus catchers. But they were more exhausting; perhaps because they demanded more.

Unawares he yawned and was at once conscious that Ford Usher, sitting opposite, was observing him with a speculative and medical eye. Probably the fellow was hoping for a case of sleepy sickness. Perhaps it was a tsetse fly that he had discovered. Hugo remembered in a vague way certain headlines, little sketch maps of some outlandish place, and a row at a British Medical Conference. He never read that part of the newspaper very carefully, but it was impossible not to have gathered something of it. He searched his mind for details.

"I think," he said to Ford at last, "that I've been bitten by a *culex pseudopictus*."

Ford showed signs of interest and asked where. Hugo,

with a glance at Aggie, said he thought it had been on his elbow. Ford explained that he meant where on the map.

"Oh, in Venice."

"There aren't any in Venice," said Ford crossly.

He decided that Hugo was not as ill as he looked; merely dissipated.

They were among the downs, going up one of those long, straight roads between chalky banks that lift away to the top of a ridge. Hugo remembered that Syranwood lay on the other side of these green walls, in a little cup filled with beech woods and sleepy hay fields. He had never stayed there, but once, some years ago, when he was merely a promising young man, he had been taken to lunch there by some friends. It was his first stately home and he had been very shy, also disappointed because it was not Tudor or filled with oak beams and minstrels' galleries, but white and classic—a square box with flanking wings, a pillared portico and a flat, balustraded roof. He had not dared to ask for the salt and his hostess seemed to think that he was some kind of colonial. But he had improved since then.

Up on the skyline of Chawton Beacon a string of young horses from some training stables spread out like a frieze. He had time to think that they were beautiful before calling Aggie's attention to them. But the thought of beauty was exasperating, like an itching spot between his shoulder blades that he could not scratch. It could give him no happiness, only torment. All the time, while he was driving and talking, hints of beauty came to oppress him. He saw, he could not help seeing, the shadow of cloud on the hillsides. His eye caught a couple of haystacks huddled together just where the grassy down and the ploughland met. All round him there was space, design and rhythm, but he was shut away from the meaning of it, and he had come to know that the promise of these things was derision. He would stop and think:

"Horses . . . grass . . . what was it I wanted to . . . what did those horses make me think I was going to . . . ? Nothing. Nice to look at. But nothing more than just what they are. Horses. They don't mean anything else. They aren't there to remind me of anything. There is no *other life*."

He could not remember a time when he had not been maddened by this sense of getting messages from some other life which he seemed to be living simultaneously with the one he knew. A delusion of immense importance hung about these hints. But he had been cheated so often that he had learnt to be wary, and, having made Aggie look at the horses, he praised the extreme competence of a certain racing play then running in London.

"Are you going to read me your new play?" asked Aggie, whose mind had been diverted to the drama. "I suppose it's terribly clever."

Hugo assured her that it was. He would adore to read it to her if it would not bore her too terribly. Her opinion would be invaluable. And his orchestra executed a flourish because now he would be able to go back to London and say, quite casually, that Aggie did not like the curtain of the second act. The ability to say such things would be a valuable stimulant and might help him to throw off this idea that his new play was filth, tripe, tossed off in a transport of boredom and fatigue, like one gigantic yawn. Even Ford Usher was looking impressed.

D

At the mention of Hugo's play he had pricked up his ears, and after a pause for recollection he announced:

"You're Pott."

Hugo sketched that deprecating little gesture which he employed on these occasions, as though he might almost be apologising for being Pott, and laughing at himself for his ridiculous fame. He quite realised that on the Outposts of the Empire it is not always easy to know what celebrities look like.

"I didn't recognise you," said Ford amiably.

Hugo thought that he was talking about photographs. He did not realise that they had met before, in the house of Ford's mother who held literary salons on Sunday evenings. For it was very long ago and Mrs. Usher was not the sort of Gossip Writer with whom he now for-gathered. Nor had he been to her house more than once. The first occasion, when, incidentally, he had met Joey, was the last. It smelt too much. The cakes were too stale and the women too shrill even for the genial Hugo. For once in his career some instinct had warned him not to become entangled and he never went again. He had no idea that he was still one of her protégés, that she had picked him up, encouraged, and pulled strings for him, and that callow young writers were still inveigled to her house on Sunday evenings by the suggestion that Hugo Pott might drop in. He only remembered that incredible old woman and her parties as a successful joke in the Joey circle. He used to dress up in a satin frock and a black wig and do Mrs. Usher at a party.

"I said to Henry James, now my dear man, I said, be sensible . . . just take the hairpins out of the coffee, please Mamselle, before you pour it out . . . poor Ed-mund Gosse came round to me in a great state about it

. . . my daughter, Mrs. Hughes Price . . . my son the medical . . ."

Ford was, in fact, 'my son, the medical.' But in those days he had been a gangling, half-grown youth and he had changed a good deal. He said nothing further to remind Hugo, and they sped on, over the empty spaces of sky and grass to where the road dipped down again.

The tower of Ullmer church stuck up among the beech trees and Syranwood showed for a moment a white shimmer of walls and a flash of windows. As they curved downwards they had a glimpse of the long, stately front of it, and the smooth lawns, and a queer jumble of stables and farm roofs crowding up behind it. Over on the far side of the valley, above the young plantations which clothed the hills, a chalky track led up to the downs again, and as Ford caught sight of it his face grew very wooden indeed, for he had been on that path before and the memory devoured him with violent emotion. He wished that he had not come on this wild-goose chase. It was no good.

And to Hugo it seemed that, instead of returning to Syranwood, he was leaving it for ever. All its beauty hung distinctly in the desolation and regret of his mind, like a reflection in deep water. He reached down to it, groped for it. The image shivered and vanished. Once more he was cheated.

Aggie said:

"I like Syranwood. It's so terribly unnatural, don't you think?"

Which was quite true. Hugo realised that his first, untutored impulse of disapproval had been right. The place was beautiful but exotic. It belonged as little to the English countryside as did its late proprietor, Otho Rivaz,

whose money came from some mysterious source in
Liberia and who might himself have walked out of
Baghdad. It was said that the Rivaz family had been
respectable solicitors in Leicestershire and that Otho had
been educated at Rugby and Cambridge, but nobody
knew for certain whether this was true or how he came to
be so rich at a comparatively early age. He spent most of
his life in undiscovered continents shooting lions and
tigers, and when in England he hunted the fox. But he
bought pictures, knew Manet from Monet at a time when
few Englishmen had heard of either, and dined everywhere. Not that he looked un-British: he had the bluff
heartiness of an eighteenth-century squire, but he
managed to combine it with the mysterious dignity of
some Eastern potentate.

Sometime in the 'eighties he bought Syranwood,
stamped it with something of his own mystery and
installed in it a wife as enigmatic as himself. Lady
Geraldine was the daughter of a bankrupt Irish peer and
had been brought up amid the splendour and squalor of a
ruined castle in County Donegal. Rumour said that she
had never learnt to read until after she was married, but
this was not true, for she annoyed Otho on the honeymoon by reading in bed. London had never seen her till
she appeared as a bride and her beauty startled the
civilised world. Nor did it ever see very much of her
again, for Otho soon removed her to Syranwood where
she remained for the rest of her life, bearing children and
entertaining house parties. His frequent absences did not
distress her and, if half the stories told were true, she
consoled herself repeatedly. But nobody, again, knew for
certain. None of the county dowagers could quite
compute the dates of Otho's departures or balance them

against the arrival of babies, nor was anybody actually named as having been her lover. She had no intimate friends, she was discreet, and she worked hard. She did all that a woman in such a position ought to have done. Her alibi, as Corny once remarked, had always been a Church bazaar.

5. *A Budding Grove.*

"I think you're so right," said Hugo to Aggie. "Don't you, Usher?"

"Don't I what?" asked Ford, starting out of his wooden trance.

"Don't you think Syranwood's terribly unnatural?"

Ford shook his head and asked what they meant.

Hugo and Aggie did not know. Indeed Aggie had merely, in the first place, repeated a remark of Adrian's. So Ford was obliged to help them along. He said:

"I suppose you mean it's been got up to look like a picture."

"Did Otho Rivaz build it?" asked Hugo.

"Oh no. He only bought it when he married Geraldine. But he did something to it. He had terribly good taste."

Hugo instantly said that people with terribly good taste always gave him a superiority complex. He was feeling happier again. He chattered gaily as the car turned out of the road into a short beech avenue. But just as they rounded the corner of the house he realised that he was going to yawn again. Laura and Lady Geraldine were coming across the lawn; whatever he did he must not start by gaping in their faces. With an immense effort he controlled the muscles of his throat and jerked his features back into a grin. Aggie got out. Ford got out. Between the ladies there was a ritual of embraces and murmured endearments:

"Aggie darling . . . how delicious this is . . ."

He might just get time to yawn and have done with it. Somebody had told him that stretching the neck upwards is a very good thing, like a chicken drinking. Taking a few steps away along the drive he stretched it and his eyes, thus lifted, encountered two other pairs of eyes just above his head. Two young girls were watching his arrival from an upper window. They hovered over the queer antics of their elders like a couple of severe young angels leaning over the bar of heaven, interested but unsympathetic. For a moment he thought that they had been waiting for him to smile at them and he did so, very charmingly, waving his hand and hoping that the poor children would not wave back so violently as to fall out of the window. But their smooth faces did not melt into any extreme ravishment of gratitude. A faint, polite spasm passed over each, as though some ghostly governess had bidden them smile at Mr. Pott. Towards waving there was no gesture.

Yet they ought to have been pleased. He recognised one of them. It was Marianne, a granddaughter of the house. He even remembered her name and called it out, pronouncing it in the correct English way "Mary Ann." For they had made friends four years ago, when he had been so shy and ill at ease, and she had taken him for a swim in the lake. A taciturn but strenuous child she had been, and she nearly drowned him, but he had liked her and her solid, old-fashioned name. Surely a creature so young and negligible (for she could not be more than nineteen even now) must like to have its name remembered and called out by Hugo Pott!

Slightly crestfallen he turned his smile upon a more deserving object and as he strolled away with Lady Geraldine across the lawn he asked, with a laugh, whether Marianne could still stand on her head at the bottom of the lake longer than anyone else.

"He's saying something about us," said Solange, the other chit. "I wonder what it is."

Marianne said sourly:

"I expect he's saying that we look like twin cherries on a pillow."

"Like what?"

"Our faces are too pink, Solange. But he thinks we're fine girls and a credit to our parents."

"Well, my parent will need all the credit he can get."

Whereat they both laughed, because the parent in question was Sir Adrian Upward. Solange was the eldest of his callow brood, but he did not yet know that she was installed at Syranwood and they hoped to give him quite a little surprise. It was time that something of the sort should be done, for Solange was getting desperate.

"But you know," said Marianne thoughtfully, "even if he does climb down, I don't see that it will do you much good. You don't want to go about with him, do you? You wouldn't like it. You'd be bored. You can't think how boring they all are. Of course I don't mean your father: I know he's very clever, and all that. But the rest of the people here this week-end, the Greys and Aggie, and Corny . . ."

"And Hugo Pott!"

"And Hugo Pott. You don't want to live in their pockets, do you?"

Solange shook her head. She did not want to go about with her father or to make her way in the world on the strength of being anybody's daughter.

"But I want him to know I'm there," she explained. "If he doesn't want me to turn up at houses where he's staying, he's got to buy me off. It's no use talking to him at home because he's never there long enough. If we ask him for anything he just looks absent-minded and says he'll be out for dinner. Aunt Betsy's tried. We've all tried, but we can't get him to grasp the idea that I must be sent to Germany. I've got to get at him from the outside. After this week-end, if I manage well, I should think he'll be more than ready to send me to Germany."

"But supposing he really hasn't got the money?"

"He can sell some of his first editions, and original manuscripts. I'll pay him back when I'm earning."

So they had planned this visit to Syranwood and Marianne promised to help in the matter of clothes, for Solange had no evening dress at all save a piece of black net partially ornamented with sequins which Betsy had bought at a sale before the war.

"You can come by an early train and choose some of my clothes," she said. "I'm so much larger than you that it will be quite easy. Packer will cut out pieces till they fit you."

"But then they won't fit you any more."

"All the better. Grandmamma will say how I've grown and get me new ones."

Early in the day they made their selection and the morning was spent in hasty dressmaking with help from Marianne's maid. But they were neither of them vastly interested in clothes, and as soon as they could they took themselves off to a room still known at Syranwood as Miss Wilson's room, after some prehistoric governess whom everybody had forgotten. Miss Wilson's room had a piano in it and Solange had brought with her some new music, a Stabat Mater of Orlando di Lasso. They had what they called a good go at it until the sound of cars in the drive told them that the house party was arriving. Solange was anxious to see what her father looked like when away from his family, so they peeped out of the window, keeping well behind the curtains.

"He's cross about something," she commented in surprise. "He can't know already . . ."

Marianne looked out and said:

"They generally arrive looking cross. I expect he wanted to go in the other car. Who is in the other car I wonder."

As soon as Adrian had been carried out of sight they leant right out of the window and scanned the drive for the next car. Solange was greatly excited at hearing that she was about to see Ford Usher, for she knew all about *culex pseudopictus*, though toxicology and not entomology was her especial passion. She knew that Ford had made his discovery on an Island in the Caspian Sea called Yeshenku. And as they hung out of their window, waiting for him to come, she told Marianne all about it. Their two heads drew close together in girlish excitement as Solange prattled of sporonts, schizonts, merocytes, merozoits, gametes, zygotes, and a-sexual cycles. But Ford, when he turned up, was a disappointment. He allowed himself to be led off by Laura just as though he had been quite an ordinary man.

"I'll never make a hero of anyone again," said Solange

bitterly. "Let's have another go at Quando Corpus, before we go down to bathe."

She went and balanced herself on the rickety piano stool and picked out the first notes of a lead which she always took wrong, humming:

Quando corpus morietur
Fac ut animae donetur . . .

But Marianne remained at the window to watch Hugo being taken across the lawn to the tea table under the cedar tree. To her mind it was a disagreeable sight, but she forced herself to watch it because she wanted to catalogue, to impress upon herself, every single thing that could be said against him. She found many, and she finished by a murmured comment which was audible to Solange.

"Anyhow it would be awful to marry a person called Pott."

She was thinking aloud, and did not expect a reply. But Solange whirled round on the piano stool.

"A man called what?"

"Pott," said Marianne in a faint voice.

"But who wants to marry a man called Pott?"

"Nobody, I should think."

"It would be just as awful to marry him if his name was Macquorquordale, wouldn't it?"

"Yes," said Marianne. "I expect so. You still don't get that lead right."

"And what did you mean by saying 'anyhow'? You do think he's dreadful, don't you? You do think he's a King Toad? What? Speak up! Don't mumble."

Marianne spoke up and said:

"Not really."

"Not really? How do you mean?"

"Most people like him frightfully."

"Nobody under fifty, I'm sure. And you don't. You can't."

Marianne shook her head sadly.

"No," she agreed. "I don't like him, very much, now. But . . ."

Solange could not help it. She began to hum:

> "*I do not like this fellow much,*
> *But I love him quite a lot.*"

Not that she meant anything in particular, except to tease Marianne for using so suggestive a phrase. So that when she saw her young friend's face she stopped, embarrassed.

"What?" she said incredulously.

Marianne nodded, whereat she threw up her hands and fell off the music stool. Finding the floor quite a comfortable place she continued to lie there and stare up reprovingly at her blushing friend.

"How very indelicate," she began after a pause.

It was. For they had often agreed that it was a breach of taste to mention such things. If one was in love one should not talk about it. To Aggie and Laura and matrons of their kidney such confidences were permissible, since they had nothing else to discuss. But by people who knew a merocyte from a merozoit it was not done.

"You began it," pointed out Marianne.

"I didn't mean to. But my dear, since we've begun being so vulgar, do tell me just a little more. I can't understand it. How . . . how long has this been going on?"

"Four years. He came here to lunch once. Somebody

brought him. He was so nice. And so . . ."

"So good-looking. I quite understand. Nobody denies that."

Marianne hesitated. Since she had begun to tell the truth she might as well go on.

"Not so very," she confessed. "He wasn't nearly so good-looking then as he is now. He used to have . . . spots . . . rather. He never has them now. I suppose he's outgrown them or something."

"I wish I could," said Solange with a sigh. "I'm just starting one on the bridge of my nose and I shall look a sight by Monday."

"Have you tried dry boracic powder?"

"Of course I have. Go on. He came here four years ago and he was spotty but nice . . . How was he nice?"

"Well, you see, he is nice."

"Never! Not now, anyhow."

"I don't know. I think he was born a nice person. And people stay what they're born, don't they? Of course he wasn't so famous then, and he had a good look to see what forks everybody else was using, and fell about a good deal on the hall floor where it's polished. And Grandmamma would keep talking to him about South Africa because she thought he was a Rhodes Scholar. But after lunch we went swimming, and I asked if he was any good standing on his head at the bottom of the water. And he challenged me. And we dived down and stood on our heads. And we stood and stood till I thought I was going to burst. I had to come up or I'd have drowned. And when I looked round for him he wasn't there. He was *still under*. Oh dear, I was frightened."

"You don't mean to say that he can stay under longer than you?"

"Umhum."

"Well, that is amazing."

Solange was impressed in spite of herself. But all this was four years ago. It did not alter the fact that Hugo was nice no longer. She got up and went to the window for another survey.

"Just look at him now! Just come here and look. He's being ever so boyish and charming over the strawberries."

"I know."

"He lets himself be photographed in bed."

"I know."

"He's a King Toad in fact."

"Well . . . perhaps . . ."

"So that you can't . . ."

"That's just it, Solange. I do."

Marianne turned away from the window with a face of deep distress, adding:

"I do. And I'm sure I wish I didn't. Because it's all true . . . all that you say. And when I heard he was coming here I thought I shouldn't mind. I thought he would just be so different that I shouldn't mind, any more than if he'd died and somebody else with the same name came to stay. But I do mind. When he looked up and waved at us just now, I realised that I mind most frightfully. He's still too like . . . too like what he was. I couldn't feel that there was any difference, though of course I know that there is. I mean I can see him as you see him, and it's dreadful, because at the same time I feel that's quite wrong. And I shall have to change into quite another person myself before I shall leave off minding."

Solange was silent and uncomfortable. She had not bargained for a confession like this and she wished that she had not forced it out of Marianne. Their pleasant,

light-hearted alliance was not built to survive such a
plunge into seriousness. There was no real intimacy between them, though they had many tastes in common,
and they could only remain friends so long as they continued to skim delightfully and flippantly over the surface
of things. She did not wish to be unsympathetic, but she
could think of nothing to say, and, relapsing from the
mature idiom which she had lately striven to adopt,
she could only murmur:

"Golly!"

Marianne laughed, for she did not easily take offence,
and it was funny to see Solange taking refuge, mentally,
behind the hockey stick and the games tunic.

"Let's try Quando Corpus again," she said.

They went back to the piano and as Solange climbed
on to the stool again she began to mumble an apology.

"That's all right," said Marianne hurriedly. "I oughtn't
to have said anything about it. It was a mistake."

6. *The Yew Parlour.*

Their clear, unimpassioned voices rose once more and
floated out into the hot silence of the summer afternoon.
Under the cedar tree the tea drinkers paused to listen.

"The girls," explained Lady Geraldine. "They're
practising again, poor things."

"Which girls?" asked Philomena. "I thought you only
had Marianne here."

"Yes, but she has a friend." Lady Geraldine paused
and then smiled benevolently at Corny. "Your daughter,"
she said.

She was pleased with herself for managing to remember the relationship. Absence of mind, always her worst failing, had grown upon her terribly since Otho's death, and she was put to many shifts by her failing memory. For instance, she was obliged to call the under-gardener Jex, in order to distinguish him from the head gardener who was called Blake, but his name was really Simmonds. Laura used to get very angry with her.

But, though absent-minded, she was not devoid of social sensibility, and the silence which followed her announcement told her that something was amiss with it. Corny had choked over his strawberries and the rest looked like people who have gone down in a lift rather suddenly. She glanced from one to another and realised that she had made a mistake. Of course Corny had no children: he had not been married more than eighteen months. But surely they had told her that this nice little girl, Marianne's friend, was somebody's daughter. Solange! Solange . . .

Helplessly she looked round for her daughter to set her right. But Laura had gone off with that man of hers—what was his name? Mr. Poe, who discovered Mosquitoes. Not that she had got the name quite right, but she knew that it reminded her, for some reason, of Edgar Allan Poe, and that she must manage to keep from muddling him up with the other young man who wrote plays. And it was very stupid of her not to be sure of the name because this Poe person had been on the carpet before, and she could never be quite certain how far things had gone between him and Laura that time when the silly girl ran off to earn her living as a Lady Help in Hampstead. Not that very much could have happened in so short a time, for Mr. Poe's mother had behaved very badly and turned poor Laura out of her house after three weeks. But for several months Laura had looked pallid and intense, as though she might be pining for somebody and she had eventually accepted Alec with the air of a nun taking the veil. Still she had left off wanting to support herself and seemed to grow more reasonable as the years went on, so that it was a thousand pities that she should have met the young man again and be stravaguing off with him when she ought to have been helping at the tea table and supplying a proper surname for Solange.

"Quite wrong," she told them all. "I was quite wrong. Not Corny's daughter. Of course not. Somebody else's daughter. Laura will remember."

Corny was the first to recover countenance and help the others out. He said that nowadays he found young girls very frightening and difficult to get on with.

"They're shy," explained Philomena. "Much shyer, I think, than we used to be."

Hugo felt pleased to hear this, he did not know why. She was shy. Perhaps that was why she had not waved to him. The little darling!

"Has shyness come in then?" he asked. "I didn't know."

"Oh yes," said Lady Geraldine. "And they're much quieter than any girls I can ever remember. And they take everything very seriously. They are always working very hard at something or other: architecture or Chinese or something like that. And they practise their music. They do nothing but practise. They never perform, as far as I can see. They don't have accomplishments, as they did when I was a girl. One can't ask them to play. They just practise because they like practising."

"When I was their age," whined Aggie pensively, "I

was always falling tewwibly in love with somebody or
other. Don't they?"

Lady Geraldine shook her head.

"Not Marianne," she said, "as far as I know. I can't
tell you about the other one . . . little Solange. We
might ask them."

Adrian Upward put down his cup in a hurry and spilt
some of his tea. Solange?

"Tell me some more," demanded Hugo.

At the back of his mind he was making rapid notes.
Because, as a modern playwright, it would never do for
him to be late for the fair. If the young girl was no longer
a minx or a dipsomaniac, if she was serious, shy, cold, and
devoted to the study of Chinese, he ought to be the very
first to know all about it. He would put a girl like that
into his next play. But he must find out what sort of
things she would do and say besides being shy and knowing Chinese. He must sit next to Marianne (or Solange) at
dinner and discover what was going on inside their funny
little heads. The opportunity would have to be made
somehow, in the intervals of amusing Aggie . . . for
though it was important that he should know all about the
modern girl he must not forget that he had other and
plumper fish to fry. Aggie would keep him busy. She
was saying now that they must all come indoors and read
'Tis Pity She's a Whore. Because she was going to play
Anabella at a Charity Matinée and during the week-end
she must study the part. To-night they would read it
again, and they could rehearse all to-morrow.

"But, Aggie, it's enormously long."

"We needn't read it all. Only my scenes. And we
don't want many women. Mrs. Grey can be the bawd . . .
Putana . . ."

E

Philomena, however, felt that the moment had come for crossing swords with Aggie. She got up and said that she was going to bathe. It was much too hot to go indoors and read plays.

"Are you coming, Hugo?"

Hugo said, in all sincerity, that he would adore to, but . . .

"Hugo's got to be Giovanni," said Aggie.

Philomena turned towards the house.

"I'm sure poor Mr. . . . that everyone wants to bathe," objected Lady Geraldine. "Can't you read it after dinner?"

Aggie explained that they would read it both before dinner and after until she was sure of her words. And she wanted all the men. There were a great many men in the play. Messengers must be sent to collect the missing men. Ford Usher must be recalled from his stroll with Laura, and Gibbie, who had gone with Laura's husband into the house for a drink, must be commandeered. Everybody must help. Because, except for the words, she was too marvellous in the part. Everybody said so. Even David Dormer, London's most formidable producer, had said so. And she looked for corroboration to Adrian, who had seen her at a rehearsal and had afterwards talked dreamily of the Duse.

But Adrian did not, on this occasion, take his cue. He was looking fixedly at two figures which had just slipped round the side of the house and were scampering across the lawn. They were wrapped in long cloaks and had bathing caps on their heads, but in spite of this disguise there was a familiarity about the shorter young woman which sent a pang through his liver. He turned to stare after them as they disappeared among the bushes by the swimming pool.

"Was that Solange?" he asked abruptly.

"Little Solange?" Lady Geraldine turned to look. "My dear Adrian! Of course! It's your daughter."

"You remember, Adrian? You saw me rehearsing at Queenie's . . ."

He made no answer. Never in his life had he been so vastly put out. Loosing every trace of urbanity he turned away with an angry grunt, a noise that Betsy knew, and walked rapidly off across the lawn.

"My own daughter," he kept saying to himself. "My own daughter! It's monstrous!"

He felt as if he should never be safe from his awful family again, as if he might find Betsy next, hiding behind a syringa bush. He was betrayed by his own daughter. Hardly knowing where he went, anxious only to escape observation, he hurried through the house into the flower garden at the back, and hid himself in the pleached alley which flanked it. He must have time to recover his composure, and somewhere at the end of the alley he knew there was a yew parlour, a snug retreat hedged thickly on three sides, with a comfortable teak bench and a view westwards over the downs. He would sit there, smoke a pipe, and decide what was to be done.

"I won't stand it," he vowed, as he tramped up the alley. "I'll teach her a lesson. I'll cut off her allowance. I'll . . ."

But he knew quite well that Solange had no allowance to be cut off. He could not afford to give her one, and Betsy had always managed to get her clothes out of the housekeeping money. He must think of some other pressure that he could bring to bear.

He approached the hedge of the yew parlour and stopped short, startled by a loud exclamation, a cry of protest it sounded, from somebody already in the arbour.

"No, Ford! No! Are you mad?"

"But, my God, Laura! Why did you send for me if . . ."

"I love you. I've said so. Isn't that enough?"

"No, it isn't."

"Hush!"

"What?"

"Somebody . . ."

There were quick, striding footsteps and Ford Usher appeared round the yew hedge, just as Adrian was making off again.

"Well?" he said, in a very unpleasant voice.

Poor Adrian had never been in such a stupid situation before. To listen at keyholes was the last thing in the world that he was likely to do. The implied accusation, and Ford's bullying underlip, coming on top of the atrocious behaviour of Solange, were too much for his temper. He returned, angrily:

"Don't say 'well' to me, sir!"

"Oh! My dear men, don't."

Laura had come round the hedge. At first she had thought it was Corny and in that case she would have stayed where she was. But she did not want her old friend Adrian to misunderstand anything, so she came round to pacify them, standing up, tall and white, against the dark background of cut yew. And they forgot that they were angry with each other because they had to look at her and wonder. She was so glowing, so alight with the emotion of her contest with Ford.

"Dear Adrian," she said gently. "I'm so very sorry. If you'll let me, I'd like to explain a little sometime . . ."

"My dear Laura . . ."

Adrian felt as though he had never looked at her before. That lovely, sulky face must have been waiting all its life for just this illumination. She took his arm and turned to Ford.

"Adrian is one of my oldest friends," she declared. "He will understand . . . everything."

"If he does, it's more than I do," said Ford stubbornly.

Laura smiled a little, but she kept her hand on Adrian's arm. And presently Ford was walking meekly away down the pleached alley, his blond head almost touching the arch of leaves above it. He had been dismissed.

"Come into the yew parlour," she said to Adrian.

"My dear child . . . I can assure you . . ."

"I want to tell you," she insisted softly. "I want your advice. You're the only person I can talk to, Adrian. You're so marvellously . . . impartial. And I want to clear my own mind about it. I want to get the whole thing put quite clearly. I feel I can talk to you as if you were God."

Adrian was almost consoled for the behaviour of Solange. Nine-tenths of him felt the charm and flattery of being compared to God. He liked the rôle of confidant and he was as anxious as everybody else at Syranwood to know exactly how affairs stood between Laura and her exotic fancy. But the eternally rebel tenth of him wondered why she should want to talk to God and suggested that if Corny or Hugo or Blake or Simmonds had arrived upon the scene they would have heard it all instead. For nothing would ever stop Laura talking about herself.

He followed her into the yew parlour and sat down on the teak bench. The sun's rays were slanting now and growing yellow instead of white so that the view of hills between the black walls of yew looked hazy and distant. Warmth and peace filled the little bower. Bumble bees, blundering in from the hay fields, and scarcely troubled to fly out again but crawled about the sun-baked stones. And it was very quiet; no noise came from the fields save the creaking of a wagon now and then as it jolted over the cut grass.

Laura leaned back and seemed to forget Adrian. She gazed out across to the molten hills as if she was staring back into some remembered land. Her long, lovely body relaxed, her breath came more slowly, and the glow of excitement left her. Gradually her cheeks recovered their usual creamy pallor, but her expression remained a little exalted and aloof. For the moment it was free of that subtle fretfulness which so often tainted its beauty, the unconscious but eternal grievance of a passionate woman frustrated. She was, perhaps, thinking, and the effort made her stern; so that her profile, standing out against the dark background of the hedge, reminded Adrian of a head which he had seen in a museum somewhere. The full lips, the nose and forehead which made one straight line, the heavy eyelids and the mane of tawny hair—they all took him back, back, to an afternoon in Rome and the Thermae Galleries and . . . and . . . yes it was . . . the head of a Sleeping Fury, and the moment of discomfort which he had had when looking at it. But he had not identified that marble composure with the restless Laura.

The silence went on far too long. He had, as he sat down, assumed the countenance of an uncle confessor, a rôle to which he was accustomed. But after five minutes this expression began to wear a little thin. At last he ventured to offer his penitent a cigarette, whereat she started, came to herself, shook her head and sighed deeply. And he became aware that, among other things, he must be prepared to be very sorry for her. This did not surprise him.

For thirty years he had enjoyed the hospitality of the rich, and he could give nothing in return save sympathy. They wanted all that he could offer, always. He patted Laura's hand and said:

"You're very unhappy."

She admitted that she was. She was wretched. No woman had ever been so misunderstood, or so falsely accused. Ford (Adrian must have heard what he said) had no right, not the shadow of a right, to accuse her of leading him on. She had invited him, as he knew, as everybody knew, as she had told everybody, to meet Walter Bechstrader, who was coming to Syranwood that week-end. Walter wanted to patronise scientific research. Ford wanted money for a second expedition to Yeshenku. Laura wanted to bring them together. Was it not a natural and benevolent wish? And had Ford any excuse for mistaking her motives?

"Well . . ." said Adrian temperately.

He was thinking of other young men who had been financed by Bechstrader, a gross but rather pathetic millionaire who had leanings after culture and looked to Laura for guidance in the matter. In the last two or three years she had helped him to get rid of a great deal of money. He had backed plays, launched musicians and published books of poetry. For Laura felt a concern for the welfare of all her admirers. If she broke their hearts, at least she filled their pockets, and though she never gave them what they desired yet they were never, from the more material point of view, sent away empty.

Now she was explaining the immense importance of a second expedition to Yeshenku. It seemed that the prophylactic parasite had mysteriously disappeared, and the attempts to cultivate it at the Guthrie Institute, from infected mosquitoes, had ended in failure. She was very technical and, as always with such women, he was astonished at her grasp of the subject. She might have spent a lifetime among mosquitoes.

"I never knew that you were so much interested in these things," he said. "You've kept it very dark, you know, Laura."

She gave him a quick look of enquiry and then laughed, with a characteristic and disarming *volte-face* towards candour.

"You mean it's all window dressing? Perhaps it is a little. But not altogether. I am interested because of Ford, you see."

"But you're more interested in Ford really?"

"Naturally. Since he's the only man I've ever . . . who's ever really meant anything to me."

"Oh," said Adrian.

He could not keep a note of enquiry out of his voice and Laura turned on him instantly.

"You're thinking of all the other people who've . . . oh, they were nothing. They were just straws I clutched at because I was drowning. I've been so unhappy. All these years. So lonely. I couldn't help clutching at happiness and pretending that my life wasn't quite empty. But I never loved them. And when I met Ford again I knew what I'd lost. I belong to him, Adrian, and I always have. He was the first and he'll be the only one, always. I've been starving. And starving people do queer things sometimes, you know. They don't just die. You can't expect them to. If they can't get bread, they'll eat stones. And that's what I've been doing: eating stones and calling it bread, all these years. Pretending I wanted this and that when it was really only Ford I wanted."

"Then you've known him a long time?"

"That's what I want to explain to you. I must make you understand the whole thing; I can't bear to know you're thinking that he's just another one. But I'll have to go back to the beginning, and I warn you it's a very sad story. Do you mind?"

"Not at all, but may I smoke a pipe?"

"Dear Adrian! Of course! A dozen pipes. What a comfort you are."

7. *A Very Sad Story.*

"You see, Adrian, when I was eighteen I wanted (would you believe it?), I wanted quite terribly to earn my own living. Can you understand why, I wonder? It was just to have the feeling that I was self-supporting. Not that I had a vocation or anything like that. I couldn't do a thing, and I'd had a wretched education. But I hated the idea of being kept. Perhaps it was because I resented seeing my mother so entirely dependent on my father. She had no money of her own ever, you know. And once I heard him scolding her because she'd over-tipped a porter. He was odd in those ways, and very lavish in others. And it seemed dreadful to me at that time. Quite suffocating! I couldn't bear to think that always, all my life, some man would have the right to question what tips I gave to porters. There were times when I even envied my own maid; at least she'd earned her money and could spend it as she liked.

"And then I used to get unreasonable terrors about the future. I thought that my father might lose all his money perhaps, and we should be quite poor. I never quite knew where it came from and I never felt safe. I used to imagine myself an incompetent, impoverished old maid, like those aunts people have. Or I used to picture myself marrying a poor man who would die and leave me with six children. It seems absurd, but I had the whole question terribly on my mind. I worried myself ill about it. I felt so unsafe; as if I'd no control over my own life when I was so absolutely dependent on other people. I thought I was useless. Of course I was very young."

And she smiled, with compassionate indulgence for the foolish girl that she had once been. Sir Alec never asked what tips she gave to porters and she had learnt to set a value on herself. But at eighteen she might have been excused for not knowing how easy it is to get money for nothing.

"Of course," she added inconsequently, "I married too young."

Adrian made a sound of agreement. He had heard this said before. Nearly all his penitents had married too young. But in Laura's case he really thought that there might be some truth in it. Alec was too old for her, and she ought to have married for love. She might have been a wonderful giver, but she was a bad taker, never knowing where to stop. And she had taken so much from Alec that her scruples about giving anything to his rivals were quite comprehensible. Also he understood, and was touched by, that young desire to work for her living. It did her credit and it should have been respected by her parents. Perhaps her whole life might have been different if, at eighteen, she had been allowed to enter a profession. For his part he was all in favour of giving girls their heads. He always advised it. Only the other day a girl had told him that she wanted to study toxicology. What girl? Solange. And now she was blackmailing him. It was monstrous. He stamped savagely on a crawling bumble bee, while Laura's deep, husky voice cooed on about the mistake of early marriages. But the name of Mrs. Usher roused him to a closer attention.

"She advertised in *The Times*," Laura was saying, "for a Lady Help. Of course I hadn't an idea what a Lady Help really is. I didn't know anything about the kind of people who advertise for Lady Helps, or know that they only do it because proper servants won't stay. She described herself as a woman writer with an interesting literary circle, to which the Lady Help was to be introduced. I thought that sounded fun! It's difficult to think oneself back into such a condition of blank innocence . . . I thought I was so bored at home that any new people would be amusing. I was a lady and I supposed that I could be a Help if I tried. She offered thirty pounds a year and my laundry and a char was kept. So I answered the advertisement."

"But my dear Laura . . . did you say Mrs. Usher? A journalist? Not surely the Mrs. Usher that I know?"

"No, I don't expect so. Nobody ever knew her except me."

"I'm thinking of a lady who is always writing to me on behalf of people I'd sooner not offend to ask me to lecture, or write articles, or stand on my head, in the interests of their pet charities. It always annoys me that they don't write themselves. Because if I accept she gets the credit, and if I refuse I get the odium. She's a sort of snob procuress, and as difficult to get rid of as the moth, once you've given her an inch. But how she ever gets into touch with the people who employ her . . ."

"Is she a widow?"

"Oh yes. Very much so. That's her strong suit. With an enormous family to support. She came to see me once and told me all about it. She was left with twenty pounds and a mortgaged house . . ."

"It is. That's the same woman. But you really don't know her, Adrian? It's not true!"

"I used to know her, though I've managed to keep out of her way for some . . ." And then the whole relevancy of this episode dawned on him. "Usher! But you don't mean to tell me that Ford . . . !"

"Of course. How slow you are! But we haven't got to him yet. You must know that I went and saw Mrs. Usher at her club and thought her quite wonderful. I'd never met anybody in the least like her before. Of course I was aware, in a way, of her vulgarity, but I didn't mind it. I'd had enough of being kept in cotton wool and I wanted to see the world. And she showed up very well at that first interview: I got the impression that she was a gallant old rattle, a bit coarse but rather impressive. And she had all the virtues that I most admired just then. She worked for her living and educated all her children and was thankful to say she'd never borrowed a penny. I thought she must have a wonderful character. She talked a great deal about money and I admired that too, never having been encouraged to mention it. I was taken in, but in the circumstances, it was inevitable, don't you think?"

"Perhaps. But my poor child, you didn't . . ."

"I did. I took the situation, and let the family think I

was going to Ireland to stay with Ellen at Lough Ashe. Ellen was in the secret and promised to forward my letters. After a month I meant to surprise them all with the news that I was earning my own living. I thought that they would accept it as an accomplished fact. But unfortunately it didn't last a month."

"I should imagine not."

His imagination was already overtasked. It was so strange that he should never have heard one word of all this before. He half believed that she must be making it up.

"I had no idea . . ." he began.

"I daresay not. Nobody has. I've never cared to talk about it."

"And you went . . . you really went to the House of Usher?"

"I went. And you couldn't ever begin to have an idea what it was like."

He made a gesture of defeat, as if willing to believe anything she told him. As a matter of fact he had a very good idea of what the House of Usher was like. Probably it was like his own.

"It smelt," said Laura.

"Ah yes. I suppose it did. Cooking in the hall."

"Oh, that was nothing. The dining-room smelt of pickles and whisky. The drawing-room, which was called the studio because it had no furniture, smelt rather like a public call-box. Have you ever telephoned from one of those places, Adrian? Gold Flake and . . . and people. Mrs. Usher's room smelt of alcohol and moth ball. Gertie's room (she was the daughter at home) smelt of benzine and . . . and various cosmetics. Not counting a general smell of dust, you understand. My room smelt of the Mamselle who was Lady Help before me and used scent instead of soap. But the basement! The larder! The scullery! Have you ever poked out a stopped-up sink?"

"No, Laura. Please!"

He put up a horrified hand to stop her, as though begging her to spare him, and reflected that this story must have some foundation of truth. She could never have evolved these details from her inner consciousness. She had really been in the House of Usher.

But Laura ignored this gesture of a fastidious man revolted.

"But it didn't discourage me, at first, as much as you might expect. On the contrary, it exalted me. I'd never been poor myself and it took me some time to realise how poor people despise each other. I was inclined to idealise anybody who worked, and I was profoundly shocked to see a noble person like Mrs. Usher living in such a smelly house. I was sorry for her. And I expect I showed it. For very soon, even on the day I got there, she began to say little things that were intended to take me down. I began to realise that I was incompetent, unable to hold my own at any respectable profession, and therefore at her mercy. But it was some time before I quite understood how low a Lady Help is rated. I didn't feel my own insecurity or re-act to it. I didn't get hurt feelings. I wasn't suspicious of being put upon. I wasn't grateful. I didn't flatter or apologise or say 'Yes, Mrs. Usher, I will do.' In short, I didn't know my place. And when I learnt it, the effect was bewildering. I want you to get hold of that bewildered element in it. I was stunned."

"But Ford . . ."

"I'm coming to him. I want you first to understand, if you can, my state of mind at the time. Because I really did set out on this adventure with a certain amount of idealism. I was an idealist in those days . . . I had a real belief . . ."

She paused for a moment, confused. Because nobody had suggested that she was not an idealist still. But she felt a great desire to make Adrian believe in the genuineness of her young impulses, whatever doubts he might entertain of her sincerity now.

"I was incredibly innocent," she assured him. "And of course I overdid it. That's my fault. I always overdo everything. Not content with the fact that I was earning my own living, I persisted in thinking of myself as a girl who was obliged to do so, who had no home to fall back on. I have a very strong imagination, too strong, and it ran away with me. The idea of a friendless girl in that house so preyed on my mind, that I began to identify myself with her. I think Corny's right in saying that I ought to have gone on the stage, you know. I do get right into the skin of the person I think I am. After a fortnight of it I *was* a friendless girl."

"But, Laura, did they know who . . ."

"No. They didn't. They thought my name was Rivers, and that I came from Ireland. I'd more sense than to let them know, or less sense, whichever way you like to put it. On the first night at supper they put me through a sort of Third Degree about my home and family and I thought I'd be found out, for I've never been asked so many impertinent questions in my life. But luckily they didn't believe a word I said. I prevaricated as much as I could, of course, and that made it sound all the more unlikely. When they asked what school my brothers had been at I got into a terrible panic because I couldn't lie exactly, so I told the truth and said they'd got scholarships, which was also true. But I saw them exchanging glances and Gertie got the giggles. And afterwards they used to ask me about my family for a joke, just to see what I would say, so I took to telling the truth, as I knew they wouldn't believe it. Behind my back, more or less, I was called the Duchess.

"And yet, through it all, I was . . . how shall I say? . . . excited. In spite of the bewilderment, and disgust, there was that excitement all the time, and a queer sense of freedom. I hated it, but I still felt that it was an adventure. I was waiting, quite confidently, for something to happen."

"And Ford happened?"

"Not at once. When I first saw him I thought him quite the most unprepossessing oaf I'd ever encountered. Such a hobbledehoy, and such loutish manners. Not that I saw much of him. He was a medical student and he only slept at home. And when we did meet he never spoke. He used to sit staring, while I staggered in and out with heavy trays. It seems that he loved me violently from the moment he set eyes on me, but I had no inkling of it."

"Oh, Laura! Hadn't you?"

"No, indeed I hadn't. This is quite, quite true. How could I possibly have known? I'd had no experience. At least very little. And it never occurred to me that a lover can expect his flame to black his boots and empty his slops. I didn't dislike him, but I just thought he was a lout. And I went on thinking that until . . . it happened.

"You must know that on Sunday evenings Mrs. Usher used to be at home for the literary and artistic circle. I used to shake up the studio cushions and put a few fresh flowers in a conspicuous place, and hide the less dead ones in a dark corner and throw the most dead away. And then, after supper, the circle arrived. Such people! I couldn't ever tell you . . . they all knew an extraordinary amount about Aggie, by the way. Much more than we do. Why is that, do you suppose? And at ten o'clock Mrs. Usher used to make a face at me and I used to go and bring in coffee and lemonade. For two Sundays I brought up all the trays from the basement and handed them round, but on the third I suddenly grew reckless, and as I went out I suggested that Ford, who was sitting in a corner looking very glum, might come and help me. I thought he might really learn manners.

"To do him justice, he came at once. We went down to the kitchen where all the cakes and sandwiches were spread out and, without any warning, Ford flew into a towering passion. I was electrified. I'd known that he didn't like being made to come to these parties, but I thought it was just bearishness, I'd never given him credit for any real taste or power to criticise. But then and there we had the whole of it: the dirt, the meanness, the pretentiousness, and his longing for something better. He seemed hardly to know what he was saying. He kept repeating that he hated it, and that he would never be able to get away from it because he was dependent on his mother, and how hopeless his ambitions were, and how lonely he was, and how he wanted to specialise on tropical diseases and would never have the money. And all this mixed up, dear Adrian, with the most touching appeals to me, and how desperately he loved me, and how my coming had made him feel that he couldn't bear this existence any more. Of course he thought I had no money either, and he could see no way out of it. I was terribly moved, and at once I felt as if

F

I must have known it always. As if I'd brought him
down there because it was time. 'I oughtn't to say all
this' he kept saying. 'You're so lovely. You're so
beautiful. I oughtn't to.' Meaning that it was vulgar
to make love to the maid. And he begged me to go
away. He said that to live as he was living was more than
any man could bear, that he couldn't sleep and couldn't
work, and when he went up to his room at night it drove
him mad to know that I had been there while he was
away, making his bed and dusting. And all mixed up
with this, the wildest diatribe about the cakes.

"She used to buy her cakes . . . now I'm slipping back
into being a Lady Help! Did you notice how I said 'she'?
I found myself talking about 'her' just like that, to the
charwoman. She used to buy her cakes in a bargain basement on Saturday, stale ones that hadn't been sold during
the week. They wouldn't have been half so bad if she
hadn't always chosen cream ones. And there was a particular heart-shaped horror, quite rancid, of bright pink
marzipan, which had gone on for three weeks because
nobody could bring themselves to touch it. When Ford
saw that it was put out to go up again he went Berserk.
He snatched it up and hurled it into the scrap pail. So we
went upstairs without it. And Mrs. Usher, who was
already very much put out with me for taking Ford downstairs at all and keeping him so long, asked me where it
was. Ford said baldly: 'It's gone bad.' And somebody
gave an audible snigger. I suspect that Mrs. Usher's pro-
visions were a standing joke with the circle. She looked
for a moment as if she was going to suffocate and then she
told me to go and bring it up in such a way . . . there
was something in her tone . . . a sort of snarling insult.
I've heard maids and people say they've been spoken to as

if they were dirt, but I never knew what it meant before. I don't know how I got out of the room.

"I ran into the hall and up to my room, Ford rushed out after me and called, but I took no notice. I flew up the stairs and he came after me, so white and furious that I was frightened. We were both shaking. We couldn't speak. We looked at each other and there didn't seem anything to do but fall into one another's arms, so we did. We clung to each other as if we'd been drowning.

"We couldn't stay there, up in my room, so we went out on to the Heath.

"Have you ever been on Hampstead Heath on a summer night, Adrian? A hot summer night? No, I don't expect you have. Well, it's like a . . . a Dionysian festival. In the moonlight, under the bushes, wherever you go, you seem to be climbing over prone couples, most of them apparently in flagrant delight, as Corny says. We seemed to be walking in a place where restraint didn't exist. We were exalted enough already, and the atmosphere didn't calm us down. In fact, it was catching. We found a fairly solitary place and sat down under a bush, but there were still faint rustlings and whisperings all round us. Perhaps it made no difference though. Perhaps the same thing would have happened wherever we had been. I think it was bound to happen from the moment that he touched me.

"I was out of myself. I'd lost all count of anything I'd ever known before. It didn't seem to matter in the least that he was an oaf, and his family quite terrible, or that he was only interested in people with elephantiasis, or that I'd only been in love with him for twenty minutes. He was so immensely powerful, compared with anyone I'd ever met before. He was carried away, and he took me along with him. The things which I'd thought important, didn't seem to matter in the least. And after all, people's minds aren't really the most . . ."

Laura broke off suddenly and the heresy upon the tip of her tongue was never uttered. For she had discoursed so often, and so earnestly, upon the opposite theme. She had been discoursing on it to Ford before Adrian interrupted them. A marriage of true minds, she had said, was all that ought to matter. And she had tried to dismiss with contempt that other point upon which Ford was so blindly importunate. Where was she?

Adrian again offered her a cigarette. He was extremely anxious to make her go on, and to say nothing that should disturb this mood of candour, though he could hardly believe that it would sustain her quite to the end of the story. And even as he held the match for her she seemed to grow more cautious. When she went on her progress was not so headlong.

"After all," she pointed out, "we had a certain amount in common. Music, for instance."

"A great link," agreed Adrian.

"Ford really knows a great deal about music. He reads scores. He likes reading scores better than going to concerts. Isn't that odd? He says that he can hear them in his own head so much better than anyone can play them. He says that's the only way to hear them perfectly. His attic was full of scores and he used to read them in bed. When I made his bed in the morning I always used to find symphonies or quartettes tucked away under the pillow. I'd once tried to talk to him about music, but he was abrupt and surly."

A bleak way to enjoy music, thought Adrian, and not much akin to Laura's enjoyment of the Opera. But she evidently thought that it was. The indiscretion upon Hampstead Heath, towards which she was so cautiously wending her way, might be explained and excused on the grounds of a musical understanding. And he could not help figuring to himself how Aggie would have told the same story. There would have been a good deal more rough stuff and nothing about scores under pillows.

"I was sorry for him," continued Laura. "But it wasn't that. And I was frightened and miserable. But it wasn't that. It was . . . I don't want to dwell on this rather shy-making part of it . . ."

Now they were really getting to the point and Adrian was on tenterhooks. But she seemed to draw back and reconnoitre again, like a person approaching a barbed-wire fence.

"I'm afraid I was curiously childish in some ways. I'd no experience of that sort . . . of course there had been one or two rather transcendental affairs with Julian's friends . . . and I'd been rather taken with Gibbie . . . and I'd thought endlessly about the subject. What girl doesn't? But I'd never really understood . . . Oh! Is that somebody in the pleached alley? Listen!"

"You ought to have a little grill put in the back of this hedge," said Adrian irritably.

They listened and heard footsteps coming nearer.

"I'll have to finish telling you another time," murmured Laura with not unmixed regret. "Why, Hugo! How frightened you look!"

"I am," said Hugo. "I thought this was a safe place to hide in. But I'm interrupting you. I'll go."

"Oh no."

"Oh yes. You're telling Sir Adrian all about it. Don't say anything you might regret afterwards."

Laura lifted her eyebrows and Hugo felt at once that this facetiousness would have gone down better with Joey. Adrian said rather crustily:

"I thought you were reading a play."

"We haven't begun yet. Aggie is still dressing and the rest of us are waiting about. She has to rehearse in costume because that helps her to remember the words. If she sends anyone to find me, say I'm waiting in the kitchen garden."

He disappeared again and Laura called after him to try the white currants because they were marvellous.

"Well?" demanded Adrian.

"Well . . . where had I got to?"

"Hampstead Heath."

"Oh yes. Well, when we got back to the house . . ."

"You hadn't begun to go back yet," Adrian reminded her.

"Hadn't I? Well, we did. We went back. And I thought we were engaged. So did Ford. But it hadn't been explicitly discussed. It was quite late when we got back, so late that the party was over and everyone in bed. Only Mrs. Usher's typewriter was tapping in her room. We crept past it and said good-night. And that was the last I ever saw of him. I lay awake all night, not able to think of anything, just spent and . . . and devastated. I felt as if I had to see him again before my life would begin to go on. But when I got up in the morning I found that my door had been locked from the outside. I'd been shut in. That frightened me. I couldn't bring myself to rattle and call. I waited. I heard them all go down to breakfast. And I waited for Ford to come. I was sure he would. But of course he wasn't given the chance. And presently I heard the front door bang. I knew he had gone to catch his train. And then, after a while she came up and let me out. The charwoman was on the landing and heard all she said. She told me to pack up and go or she'd send for the police and have me put out. She said that she'd had trouble of the sort with another of her sons, before, and she ought to have known better than to have a girl of my type in the house, and that young men weren't saints and she didn't expect them to be.

"I know now that she had nothing to go on. She only knew that we'd been out late and the rest was all guess-work. But at the time I thought he must have told her. . . . I don't suppose I had many wits about me that morning. She talked about her duty as a mother to get him out of this scrape; I know she meant me to think he'd told her, even if she didn't say so. I can't remember. I can't remember exactly what she said. Only the night-mare horror of it. And I wasn't sure of anything, even that he would stick to me. I knew he regarded me as a servant. And I wanted to run away. So I packed my box and marched out of the house and took a taxi to Waterloo.

"It wasn't till I got to the station that I realised I had no money at all. Only threepence-halfpenny. I'd never had any wages paid and it hadn't occurred to me to ask for them. The taxi man wanted his fare. I was at my wits' end. He was horrible and made a great fuss and shouted till quite a crowd collected. He kept shouting to the other taxi men: 'Hi, Nobby! Look at 'er ! She ain't got no money. Took my taxi from Hampstead and now she ain't got no money. *And* I carried down 'er boxes.' You've no idea what it's like to have no money at all. And it was August, you see. I couldn't think of anyone in Town that I could borrow from. And at last a man in the crowd paid my fare and took me into the station. I was so bewildered

and so anxious to get away from all those staring people
that at first I was grateful. But not for long. He suggested
that we should go and have a drink somewhere quiet.
And then I realised that I'd been picked up. He was
worse to get away from than the taxi man. I don't know
what I should have done if I hadn't suddenly caught sight
of Alec. I didn't know him well, but he had stayed here
once and I felt: any port in a storm. I flew after him and
asked him to lend me a pound. And the last clear memory
I have is of Alec, looking quite at sea but very courteous,
fishing out a notecase.

"After that it's all blurred. He was very kind. He saw
at once that I was in trouble, and took charge of me. I
suppose he got rid of my corner boy. I don't know. He
took me home himself: at least he must have managed to
disappear before I actually got home, for I don't remember
arriving with him then. But he came down a week or two
later and asked me to marry him. He knew most of the
story. Not about Ford, I mean, but about the Ushers. I
told him on the way home, I think. I remember the shame
and humiliation I felt when he looked after me so beautifully. Things that woman had said, horrible things, kept
coming back to me and I felt they were true. She said I'd
never starve because there would always be some man
quite ready to look after me.

"When I got home I told most of it to my mother, not
everything, and she helped me to keep it from my father.
But she didn't understand, and when Alec appeared she
urged me to marry him at once. She said I would be much
happier married. So I did. I hadn't really the spirits or
the energy to fight about it, and Alec was very kind. I was
so wretched, and felt that anything would be better than
waiting and waiting to hear some word from Ford. Be-

ıse he knew how to find me. I'd told him where I lived,
ıt night, and what my real name was. But he never
ote and he never came, and I began to believe that his
ıther was right and that he was glad to be out of a
ape. I was ill and miserable, and marrying Alec seemed
be the only way to put an end to it, and he was so good
me, and my mother was so insistent, that I gave in.
"But Adrian, do you know, Ford did come, and I never
ew. I never knew till last summer when we happened
meet in Austria. When he got home that night and
ınd me gone he was in despair. And next day he rushed
wn to Basingstoke and eventually found his way over
: downs here. He actually got as far as that little white
th you can see on Ullmer Ridge, when he saw me down
low, riding with some man or other who was staying
re. He knew at once that it was I because of my hair.
ıd he asked an old shepherd up there who I was, and the
ın told him, and pointed out Syranwood. I suppose he
ıde out that we were great people in these parts. Any-
w, it frightened Ford. He didn't know what to make
it. He thought I'd been playing with him. And he
:ned round in a rage and walked back to Basingstoke.
ıt if he hadn't, if he'd come down and claimed me, I
ınk I'd have gone with him, anywhere. We were born
: each other, and it's been fate, nothing but fate, that has
ıarated us. He has never looked at a woman since, and
. . I have never known a moment's happiness."
This was quite true and Adrian admitted it. Unhappi-
ıs hung about her perpetually. All the people who
ʒed her were terribly sorry for her. And she was ready
share this unhappiness with Ford, a consciousness of
ʒiding fate, a rubicon never quite crossed.
"I've told him that he has all of me that matters

already," she said. "But I can't do what he wants. I can't
go off with him and leave Alec. Even for his own sake I
can't. It would be madness . . . at this stage in his
career . . . his work *ought* to come first. If I love him I
must insist on that!"

"Poor Ford," murmured Adrian.

Laura turned her sad, wild eyes on him, full of a mute
reproof. He should have said:

"Poor Laura."

He hastened to say it. Perhaps it was Poor Laura, after
all. Because Ford, at least, had *culex pseudopictus*. If her
story was true, and he believed a good deal of it, she was
in the right when she called it a sad one. Ten years had
taken more from her than they had from Ford. She might
talk of her vows to Alec, and of Ford's career, but she was
thinking of the change in herself.

"You don't love him now as you did then, Laura,
whatever you may say."

"I can't. But does anyone? Doesn't the best of us . . .
get lost, somehow, very soon?"

Adrian agreed hastily, taking refuge in a melancholy
generalisation. In his rôle of chorus as well as confidant
he felt that some reference to the common lot was needed
to round off this very sad story, and he quoted,
sombrely:

"There's not a joy the world can give, like that it takes
away."

"How true!" thought Laura.

And how good was Adrian! How unfailing in his
sympathy, and how apt to clothe the harsh contour of the
passions with a soothing mantle of sentiment. He could
quote beautifully.

"O could I feel as I have felt, or be what I have been,
Or weep as I could once have wept o'er many a
vanished scene——
As springs in deserts found seem sweet, all brackish
though they be,
So midst the withered waste of life, those tears would
flow to me."

"Dear, dear Adrian."

8.   *The Lake.*

Nothing like Poetry, thought Adrian, and then remembered unexpectedly that Paul Wrench was lying in a German mortuary, with his bleak, thin nose sticking up in the air.

"Did you know Paul Wrench is dead?" he asked.

Laura sat up in dismay.

"It's not true!"

She felt the loss to literature almost as keenly as he did. And they began to disinter episodes in that queer, unornamental life with a comfortable sense that it was over. But this was no subject to keep them sitting long in the yew parlour and soon they were pacing slowly back towards the house. Laura suggested that there was time for a bathe before dinner. But Adrian shook his head. He cut a lean figure in a bathing suit and he wanted to avoid, as long as possible, an encounter with Solange. So he set off towards the library, intending to write an article, a few first impressions of Paul Wrench while the subject was still fresh in his mind. But, on opening the library door, he heard a racket within which, for a moment, kept him standing on the threshold. The greater part of the room was hidden by a large leather screen and behind it he heard Corny say:

"Were every drop of blood that runs in thy adultrous veins a life, this sword (dost see?) should in one blow confound them all. Harlot! Rare, notable harlot, that with thy brazen face . . ."

It had crossed Adrian's mind that he might be intruding upon another *tête-à-tête*, but the reference to the sword reassured him. Peeping round the screen he saw Aggie, in cloth of gold, standing with joined hands. Hugo, pale green with fatigue, sat on a table and clutched a prompt copy. Adrian had never seen that drained green shade on any face but once, when he had been taken on a yacht to the tropics and one of the cooks, crazy with the heat, had jumped overboard.

"Why do you wear a halo?" he asked Aggie. "Surely that's not necessary for Anabella."

Aggie explained. The proper head-dress had not come yet and she was obliged to wear this pearl cap which had done duty in the last tableau where she had posed as an angel. Her maid, not able to understand that Aggie ever acted anything more terrestrial, had stupidly failed to remove the halo. However, it was very becoming. She turned to Hugo for her cue.

"The man, the more than man . . ." prompted Hugo.

"The man, the more than man that got this spwightly boy . . . you ought to wush at me with a dagger, Corny."

Adrian, after another glance at Hugo, did a kind thing. He broke up the rehearsal, insisting that Aggie ought really at this point to go up and practise all her labials in front of a glass. He told her straight out that she mooed rather over them.

"Say 'the man, the more the man' ten times over," he urged, "and then you'll see what I mean."

Aggie looked a little peevish, but Adrian was known to be a good critic and she was known to take her work seriously, so off she went. And Hugo was at last free to go for a swim and cool his aching head.

Solange and Marianne had been bathing ever since tea and Ford very soon joined them. But they took little notice of one another. For a time the lake had been given up to sheer athletics. Ford, powerful and plebeian, had done trick diving by himself at one end of the pool. The girls rode on a rubber horse, played with some diving discs and did good work collecting the rose leaves which showered down upon the water and grew sodden. There was no shouting, splashing, or noisy laughter. Then, as the shadows lengthened, Philomena made her appearance and the gathering became more social. Seeing no sign of Hugo she decided not to go in at once. Her green silk tunic would stand the water, but it did not look its best when it was wet and the freshness of the colouring was lost. So she sat on the grass under the rose bushes and enjoyed the cooling air. Hugo would come sooner or later and Aggie was doing herself no good by being so autocratic. He had given Philomena a look, when he was dragged away, which was entirely reassuring. And now, all the time that he was reading 'Tis Pity indoors (rehearsals were no treat to him) he would be longing for the lake and more congenial company.

She had devised a most original bathing cap, so transparent as to make her hair into a gold frame, and confined by a little wreath of flowers. But she took it off as she lay on the grass, enjoying the feel of the soft breeze on her skin and blowing through her hair. She was not in a hurry. She was not impatient. She was consciously happy. The smell of mown grass was pleasant, and the rose petals drifted down on to her hair.

One end of the pool was in shadow now, but beams of dappled light fell on the diving scaffold. Over and over again did those two indefatigable girls climb up and stand there, poised solemnly for a moment with their arms above their heads. Then they would skim downward, straight into the water with hardly a splash, like a couple of fishes. Their thick shrimp-coloured caps hid their hair completely and their faces were like nuns' faces, pink and null. In their bodies, as they lifted their arms, there were youth and vigour but little grace. Philomena envied them nothing. She was glad not to be a girl any more. Could anything, she asked herself as she watched them, be more unknowing than the way they moved? Marianne was going to be a magnificent creature, a second Laura, but at present she just seemed to be too large for herself. And Solange was as straight and spare as a boy. No. There were no points about being a girl. One had it all to go through. One married the wrong man too young, and one lost virginity, not, as poets believe, in the twinkling of an eye, but gradually like something pounded up in a mill. Nor was it enjoyable, though one tried to think so at the time. One had a lot to go through before enjoyment became a possibility.

And she looked with grave satisfaction at the slim soundness of her own legs. They were perfect, from waist to ankle, long, smooth and white, almost more beautiful than her arms. She had avoided that sharp bisecting line at the mid-thigh which is the blemish of so many bathing dresses. Her tunic hung loose in rounded petals to the knee, over a brief *maillot*, so that when she moved or swam, there was always the gleam of white flesh through silk. The sense of her own beauty possessed and exalted her so that she was lifted clear out of yesterday's indecision. She was sure of Hugo and she was sure of herself. No anxieties or scruples beset her, for she knew that she could get anything she wanted so long as she preserved this sense of rightness and balance. She could do as she pleased, nor was there any need to wonder what was going to happen. Nothing would happen unless she willed it.

"But it shall," she thought, with a faint, reckless tremor of anticipation. "I'm going to go on with it."

Lady Geraldine came down to the lake. It was always rather a shock to see her there, for at sixty-eight she looked her age. She came padding over the grass in a queer wrap made out of some oriental shawl, bright red but a little moth-eaten and smelling of camphor. Her gnarled old feet were thrust into leather sabots, and on her head she wore a battered rush hat.

"Such a noise in the library," she complained as she sat down on the grass beside Philomena. "I heard it as I came past the window. Poor Aggie is saying a piece all about strumpets . . ."

Nobody else in the world ever called Aggie poor. But Geraldine had always done so, and, like most of her vagaries, it might possibly have been a piece of malice. To her it was as if no years had passed since poor Aggie was a lumpish girl of fourteen whose nose always bled in church.

Philomena peered into the ravaged beauty of that face and wondered, not for the first time, what was really at

the back of Geraldine's mind. She was as mysterious as
the Queen of Sheba. There was no plumbing the depths
of her inward emancipation. For complete submission to
Otho in every detail of existence had taught her how to
hide herself, and behind a wall of disconcerting vagueness
she led a lawless and independent life. Nobody had ever
penetrated into that uncomplicated country, and her
lovers knew even less of her than Otho did. If there had
ever been any lovers. Philomena would have liked to be
sure. But nobody was sure. That tranquil simplicity had
blinded everyone.

Now she gave a shock to Ford by taking off her wrapper
and standing up on the bank in a salmon-pink chemise
made of very cheap artificial silk and trimmed with cotton
lace. Philomena remembered once more that if you are
rich enough you can do and wear anything you like. And
Ford, who saw that even this garment was shortly to be
removed, dived quickly under water. But his panic was
premature, for beneath her chemise she wore a faded
black bathing dress with an anchor embroidered on the
front of it. Taking off her rings she hung them on a twig
of a rose bush, pulled an oilskin cap over her tousled
white hair, and jumped into the pool. She was still a fine
swimmer though she had given up diving.

Up to the far end, by the diving board, she went, and
then back again, the oilskin cap travelling swiftly and
silently over the water. And behind her, swimming in a
row, came the pink heads of Solange and Marianne and
Ford with his hair plastered down over his eyes, for they
had all been seized with an impulse to do a couple of
lengths before coming out.

Philomena was beginning to feel chilly. The sun was
nearly off the pool and to be looking blue would spoil

everything. But she was relieved to see Gibbie come bounding from the house. Evidently the rehearsal was over and Hugo would soon be on his way. Gibbie burst into the pool with a jocular splash and began to be funny with the rubber horse. The quiet was over.

"Are you going out or coming in?" he called to Philomena on the bank.

"We're all going out," replied Lady Geraldine, as she climbed on to the bank. "It's nearly dinner time. Beata!"

Marianne, who was used to being called after any of her aunts, came swimming to the bank edge.

"Have I arranged the table?"

"No, grandmamma. I think Laura's doing it."

"Aren't we a man short?"

"No, we're even numbers unless Mr. Bechstrader comes. I think I remember how Laura's done it: you, Mr. Pott, Aggie, Mr. Cooke, Solange, Uncle Alec, Mrs. Grey, Sir Adrian, me, Mr. Grey, Laura and Mr. Usher."

"Humph."

Geraldine looked at Ford's head as it sped away down the lake again.

"Have I got to have them both? Is there anybody besides Laura who knows anything about mosquitoes?"

"Solange does. She knows a lot about them."

"Ho, does she? Well, why not . . . oh, I suppose we'd better leave it to Laura."

Philomena bit her lip angrily. Adrian and Alec! Why should she have to sit between Adrian and Alec? And Aggie, of course, was to get Hugo. She glanced across the lawn impatiently to see if he was coming, for she had suddenly grown tired of waiting for him. This hour, which was to be her own, was flying past; it was being

G

wasted. All her contented assurance fell away from her as she thought of Adrian and Alec, and the cruel shortness of life. At this rate the week-end would soon be over and she would go back to London having missed her chance. If anything was to happen she must make it happen immediately.

As soon as he appeared on the other side of the lawn she climbed to the highest dive, a board in a pollarded willow, where she could stand with green leaves behind her. And she stayed there just long enough before she dived, so that he could see her and wish that he had come out sooner. Her white legs flashed under the silky water and her yellow head with its flowery cap came up. Hugo was standing staring on the bank.

"Philomena?"

He leapt into the water beside her and the girls immediately retreated from the bath as though it had been contaminated. Seizing their cloaks they made for the house, followed by Ford. Lady Geraldine, sitting on the grass, had gone into one of her long Sibylline trances, so that Hugo and Philomena had the pool to themselves, undisturbed by Gibbie who plunged merrily about with his horse in one corner.

Hugo did not want to swim, or to dive, or to exert himself in any way. He craved to be simply at peace. But Philomena was so beautiful that he could not be at peace. Something stung him between the shoulder-blades as when he had seen the horses on the hill. He was reminded of something, an image, a snare, cheated man that he was. For beauty, instead of remaining a pleasure, still masqueraded as a promise, and he could not tell what it was that he desired. Perhaps it was simply Philomena.

Floating on his back he looked up at the sky and the

rooks streaming homeward across the golden zenith. The water was getting chilly. Damn Aggie! She had spoilt his bathe. She had kept him away from Philomena.

"I'm glad you're still here," he said. "And I'm glad the others have gone away. I don't like crowds."

"Is Corny coming?"

"No, he had to catch the post. He writes to his wife every day, you know."

Philomena laughed, as people always did when they remembered that Corny had a wife.

"I can't get used to it," she said.

"I know. It does bring things home, doesn't it? This world depression I mean. One can hear of the unemployed, and fluctuating currencies and trade slump without losing hope. But I did feel that things must be in a very bad way indeed when Corny had to marry. Have you ever met her, Philomena?"

"No. I never meet those racing people. But she's been pointed out to me . . . all teeth and tweeds. She must be at least fifteen years older than Corny. But so, so rich!"

"That explains it from Corny's angle, but . . ."

"Oh, she married him because he looked so like her first husband, who was a jockey. Corny told Gibbie so."

"I never thought of it, but he is exactly like a jockey. Oh, I say, don't go out yet."

"I've been here for hours and it's getting cold."

She got out of the water and stood warming herself in the last of the sun, while Gibbie disappeared into the shed to put away the rubber horse. And Hugo floated in the water at her feet, looking up at her beseechingly.

"Can you see yourself in the water?" he asked.

"No. It isn't still enough."

"That's a pity."

He climbed out too, and they waited for the rippled surface to settle so that they could look down to their own faces, drowned under the shadow of the bank. Hugo caught at her elbow. It was cold and drops of lake water fell off it like pearls.

"I suppose you know," he said gravely, "how beautiful you are. Or don't you?"

But he spoke to the face in the water, rather than to the woman beside him. If only he could plunge down there, into that green deep world which was so much more beautiful because it was an illusion. He would dive down and down and stay there for ever. *How long can you stand on your head at the bottom of the lake?* For ever!

A belated rook, flapping over their heads, jarred the air with a single derisive caw, and he roused himself.

"Philomena!"

"Yes, Hugo?"

"I'm desperate."

"Poor Hugo!"

"You know what's the matter. Or don't you?"

"Of course I know."

"Then . . . come away with me."

His plan of escape dissolved into gloom as the gangplank of a steamer flashed upon his inward eye. That was no way.

"I must talk to Gibbie," murmured Philomena.

Talks to Gibbie, scenes, packing up, customs houses, trouble with Caro, more publicity, the divorce court: that was what it meant. He had been mad.

"I don't think Gibbie would mind, Hugo. He understands me. If I came for a little while . . ."

"For a little while?" echoed Hugo blankly.

His mind had scarcely adjusted itself to this amazing idea before they were startled by the tolling of a great bell in the Syranwood stables. It swung out over the hay-fields so that shepherds on the downs might know that their betters were about to dress for dinner. In the house hot baths were being turned on and maids were laying dresses reverently on beds. There was a girding of loins in the butler's pantry, and the cook and her satellites knew nothing of the cooling day.

Smoke rose from the cottage chimneys in the valley. Ploughmen and their wives sat at supper with the day's toil behind them. Out in the fields the last wagon had creaked through the gate into the lane. But at Syranwood the curtain was about to ring up on the biggest drama of the day, and all those upon whom the success of the evening depended were settling themselves into harness. Dinner must be cooked and served and in due time ninety-six plates, seventy-two glasses, twelve coffee cups, thirty-six spoons, seventy-two forks, and sixty knives would come back to be washed, not to mention dishes, sauce boats, salad bowls and cream jugs.

And yet, in the mellowing light, the house looked as if every one in it had gone to sleep. The sun had dipped suddenly behind the trees, but the sky was still full of gold and the cedars and yews, massed against all that glory, looked quite black, while the line of hills was turning rapidly to indigo. In the hall it was dusk. Hugo paused there amid the litter of dogs and hats and garden baskets and dishevelled copies of *Proust*. He said:

"Don't risk anything you value for me, my dear. I'm not worth it."

"I'll talk to Gibbie."

9. *Talking to Gibbie.*

She had no maid with her, but one of the housemaids had put out her new black dress on the bed. She looked at it doubtfully, wondering if she should wear it after all. Perhaps it was too sophisticated. She did not want to be seen in competition with Laura or Aggie, and the cut, which commanded respect when she dined out with Gibbie in Regent's Park, would pass unnoticed here.

Gibbie's things were arranged on a smaller bed in his dressing-room, hot water steamed in brass jugs in the basins and the door of the bathroom stood open to show that the first bath was ready. And the whole place smelt like a room in the country, of mignonette from the large bowls on the dressing and writing tables, and of fresh, lavendered linen. The incense of cut hay drifted through the window. Philomena knew them all so well, these country smells, just as she knew the view from the window, the gracious curving line of hills and trees, but for the moment she felt impatient of them. They were old, and they had been going on a long time, while she was in a hurry. So she pulled the curtains, turned on the light, and slipped out of her damp bathing suit.

She was still in the bath when Gibbie came into his dressing-room. He called to her:

"Are you nearly through?

"Yes."

He opened the door and looked in, peering through the clouds of steam at the ravishing creature who belonged to him. He had been married for fifteen years. Though he still had ardent moments this was not one of them. He said:

"I didn't lock the bathing shed, because I couldn't find the key."

Philomena gave him a sombre look and he asked if anything was the matter.

"Nothing."

"Then why are you eyeing me like that? What have I done?"

"Nothing."

He knew better than that. Trouble of some sort was brewing. But he did not press the point, and merely said:

"Well then, hurry up. I want a bath too."

Philomena hurried up. She powdered her back, tugged a comb through her curls and hooked the tight-fitting bodice of her white dress under her arms. With lipstick she carefully accentuated the heart-shaped line of her mouth with its full lower lip. And then she went to talk to Gibbie while he tied his tie.

"Hullo!" he said, "you've not put on the artichoke, after all."

"My black dress? No. I haven't."

"I thought you brought it down especially. Isn't it your best dress?"

"It's not as becoming, really, as this."

"I agree. But I thought all those criss-cross lines were supposed to be very fashionable."

"Gibbie, you remember a talk we had before we were married? When we were engaged?"

Gibbie did not answer, because he was brushing his hair, and she had to repeat her question. Then he turned round, a wooden brush in either hand. There was a puzzled look on his face ('his nice walrus face,' as Geraldine said when the engagement was announced).

"Which talk, dear?"

"About being free."

"Did we talk about being free?"

"Of course we did. Surely you remember. It isn't so terribly long ago."

"Fifteen years," said Gibbie unnecessarily.

He showed no signs however of remembering their talk and presently he added:

"You know I often feel as if I'd been born married . . ."

"Do you? I don't. And I wish you would try to remember. We had a most important talk and we agreed that freedom is the one really vital thing in marriage. Surely you remember."

"I can't say that I do. Was it that day when we went on a bus and your hat blew off?"

"No. Do listen please. This is serious. Really you mustn't pretend that you don't remember. Because we settled some important things then. At least, I hope we did. We agreed that we were both to be perfectly free."

"And aren't we?"

"I don't know if we are or not, because we haven't put it to the test. I said then (oh, you must remember this), I said if ever you fell in love, temporarily, with someone else, I'd try to understand. As long as you came back. As long as our home, and our children, didn't suffer. We agreed that two people can never be quite everything to each other, and that to try was to shut each other up in prison. And that marriage ought to be as full and rich an experience as possible. And that really civilised people wouldn't deny each other new experiences . . . and . . . and other friendships . . . don't you remember now?"

"Extraordinary," commented Gibbie, as he pummelled his head with the hair brushes, "what a lot being married teaches you. I must have been half-baked."

"I don't think it's half-baked," said Philomena crossly.

"I know you don't. But I do. I talked a lot of hot air in those days I suppose. But I know now that it wouldn't work."

"I can't see why not.   If you came to me and told me that you'd fallen desperately in love with . . . with . . . well, say with that girl you admired so much at the Tyrrells the other night, that Mrs. Drew, and that you wanted to go off with her for a little while, I think I'd try to understand."

"I'm sure Drew wouldn't. His head looks as if it had been shut in a door. I shouldn't think he's ever understood anything. And he's so much bigger than I am. Try somebody with a little tiny husband."

Philomena nearly stamped. It seemed as if he was determined not to take her seriously.

"You've gone back on your word then," she exclaimed. "You didn't mean what you said about freedom. I married you on the understanding . . ."

"That I'd fall in love with other people now and then?"

"Not you necessarily."

"Oh? Both of us?"

"Why not?"

"Philomena! Are you serious?"

"Quite serious."

"You mean that it's not only my duty, but yours as well . . . my dear girl, what are you driving at?"

At last he had grasped the fact that there was something behind all this and that she was not merely chattering out of idle sociability. She was trying to tell him something.

He put down his brushes before he asked the next question.

"You haven't fallen in love with anyone, have you?"

He had come to the point a little too soon. She had meant to tie him down first, to remind him of his early promises and extract an admission that he still held by them. Even then it would not have been easy to pass from the general to the particular.

She took the offensive.

"You promised. And it's not fair to go back on it now. But you've never been fair to me, Gibbie. You never look at me yourself, and you're not prepared to let anyone else look. You take everything for granted."

She spoke of parlourmaids and teeth and having Betsy to dinner and childbirth and laundries and her immortal soul. She pelted him with reproaches, and her ammunition was so varied that he hardly knew where to turn. It seemed that he had done nothing but wrong for fifteen years, and if he tried to justify himself on one charge he was immediately tripped up with another. Undoubtedly he had been, for many years, the most inconsiderate, the most crassly complacent husband in Regent's Park. He would have laughed if the threat of something worse ahead had not sobered him.

"And what's at the bottom of all this?" he demanded at last. "What have I done to-day? Do come to the point."

"I'm perfectly prepared to be open with you. I would never do anything without telling you. And I want you to understand that I put my home first. Nothing would induce me to shirk my responsibility there. When the children were babies I gave up my whole life to them. Nobody could say that I haven't done my duty by them and by you. And I'm perfectly prepared to come back and be a good wife to you, Gibbie. It isn't that I don't love you. I do. But I'm something else, besides being your wife. I have a life apart from you, and I don't see anything wrong in that. As long as it is frankly admitted. A great deal of me is being wasted. I'm still young, and the life I have to lead is too narrow. It's stifling me. You don't really want me . . ."

"Philomena!"

"Not all of me. Why should you? After fifteen years it's a wonder if you know I'm there at all. I think it would do us both good if we took a little holiday away from each other. I think we should love and appreciate each other more. But I'm not going to do what some women do, because I think it's wrong. I'm not going to deceive you. I trust that there will never be any need for deceit or subterfuge between us. We're both civilised people. Surely we can talk things out?"

"We'll have to," said Gibbie gloomily. "Do I understand from all this that you want to take a lover? That there is somebody . . ."

"Yes. There is. But I'm not going to do anything that you won't agree to. And I have some justification in expecting you to see my point of view because of the opinions you expressed before we were married. You've never said before that you'd changed them."

Gibbie was impossible. He chose this moment to regulate his watch. And then he started going round the room, picking things up and putting them down without seeming to know what he was doing. At last, with an effort, he asked:

"Who . . . ?"

"That doesn't signify, just at present. I'll tell you, if we can agree on principle. But if we can't agree I don't think I'll tell you. Because, of course, if we can't agree I'll give him up. You come first, naturally. It'll be my happiness that I give up: my right to be myself. But I'll give it up if you wish it. I can promise you that. I'll never see him again."

"You mean to say that this fellow has asked you . . . has actually suggested . . ."

"Gibbie! Don't be so furious! It's . . . it's uncivilised . . ."

"Somebody I know? One of our friends?"

"You've said hundreds of times that jealousy is a degrading thing and that a liberally minded man ought to . . ."

Gibbie pulled himself together and spoke more quietly.

"That's quite true," he agreed. "But one isn't always able to do what one ought. I'm sorry. At least, I'm not sure if I am. It seems so monstrous . . ."

"Why monstrous? What on earth is there monstrous about it? I love you, and I love him too, in a different way. And I don't see that I'm taking away anything that belongs to you, by giving what he wants to him. If you're thinking of the mere aspect of physical intimacy, that's barbarous. I want you to consider the emotional side of it. What do you gain by repressing my feeling for him? Don't you think that emotional experience makes people richer, not poorer? And the richer I am, the more I could give you. Yes? Come in!"

A maid had tapped at the door to know what time Mrs. Grey would like to be called in the morning and if she would have breakfast in bed and whether she would take coffee or tea. When she had settled these points Philomena went back to the dressing-room. Gibbie was still

sitting on his bed, looking as though he had been
through a railway accident. His hair stood on end, his
clean shirt was crumpled, and his walrus face was mottled
with diverse emotions. Grief, fury, and bewilderment
buffeted him in turn until he could hardly have said what
he was feeling. He looked at his wife in a dazed way and
asked if she really had come in five minutes ago and told
him that she proposed to take a lover. He looked so
forlorn that she felt obliged to deal more gently with him.

"Yes I did, Gibbie darling. But please don't look so
miserable. If you mind terribly, I won't go. You will
come first, always. Do understand that."

"I can't understand anything."

"I told him that I could do nothing, promise nothing,
until I'd talked to you."

"You told him . . ." Anger for a moment got the
upper hand. "What right had you to tell him anything of
the sort? Good God! He must think me a . . ."

"No, he didn't. This sort of situation isn't as unusual
as you seem to think. After several years of marriage it's
almost inevitable. I know of more than one case . . .
and if it's dealt with frankly, it needn't mean disaster."

"But you couldn't have thought . . . Philomena, what
has happened? What has suddenly come between us?"

She was just about to say that it was not sudden when
she paused. A wave of sick doubt broke over her. She
was unsure of Hugo, of herself, of the whole business.

"How can you love him? What is he to you, that I
can't be? Do try to explain."

Against the solid reality of her relations with Gibbie
she tried to evoke the image of Hugo, the appeal which
he had made to her, the love, it must be love, which he
had awakened. But the image in her mind was as unreal

and shadowy as the face which had looked up at her from the waters of the lake. She tried to think of Hugo and she could only picture herself, her own wasted life. He was a mystery, a cult, a symbol, the embodiment of the youth that was slipping away from her. But apart from that, he had no solid existence. He was not real, as this blustering, walrus-faced husband of hers was real.

"He . . . he needs me . . ." she said faintly.

He had said he was desperate. And he looked desperate. He wanted something very badly. She had known that even before this flame was lit between them. And her thoughts went back to a night some months ago when he had taken the author's call at a successful *première*. His face, in that blaze of light, had looked so pale beside the faces of the actors in their make-up. For a moment she had not recognised him. And he had taken the leading lady's arm and patted it while he said the right, charming, modest things. But all the time she had felt as if it was a ventriloquist's doll speaking out of that stiff green face. A scene of desperation had been before her even then, in spite of the glamour, the applause, and in spite of Mrs. Chappell in the stage box. She had felt so sorry for him, without knowing why, that she had mentioned it to Gibbie when they got home. And Gibbie had said, very seriously, that he would rather row in the galleys than be a playwright any day. But Gibbie had not understood. It was not, it could not be, anything to do with Hugo's profession.

Gibbie was saying:

"You don't love me. You don't love me any more."

"Oh, but I do. Indeed I do. Can't you understand? Please, please don't be so unhappy. I won't . . . oh plague! We must go down. Just look at the time!"

10. *Dinner*.

Again the great bell in the stables was tolling out the hour. Since its last ringing the light had changed and faded. The sky had paled to a placid aquamarine. Late blackbirds whistled on the lawns, and in the borders all the flowers glowed in the waning light like little lamps. A first star trembled over Chawton beacon. It was the most beautiful hour of the day, but it was, at Syranwood, a time for being indoors and eating.

As Philomena and Gibbie came downstairs they saw all the house party streaming across the hall into the dining-room, for Geraldine never waited a minute for anybody. She led the way, swathed in several wedding veils. Three weeks before she had discovered that she had nothing to wear in the evenings, so she had unearthed these white elephants from her wardrobe, cut holes in them for her head and arms, and slung them on. A string of emeralds dangled and caught in the uppermost, and her hair was still a little damp from bathing.

After her came Aggie and, clutching at Aggie's elbow, Hugo.

Then a spare, grizzled figure walked out by itself: Sir Alexander Le Fanu. He walked with his head bent down, so that Gibbie and Philomena had a good view of the bald patch on the top of it, worn smooth and shiny by the constant friction of a lawyer's wig.

Laura swam out next, in a white dress so marvellously cut that she might have been poured into it. Airy draperies floated behind her and some of them dragged on the floor so that Ford, who followed close behind, had to do a war dance not to tread on them. The top of

his head was not, by any means, bald and, with his broad
shoulders and long arms, he looked rather like a dancing
bear; while Corny, who trotted after him, might have
been his little keeper. But he was the reason of the white
dress, as Philomena, looking down in dismay at her own
skirts, immediately realised. And yet Laura was asking
them all to believe that Ford had come to meet Bechstrader. Philomena sniffed. She had never pretended to
tolerate these goings on. An acknowledged love affair
was one thing, but these vague appropriations were quite
another. She had always said that Alec ought not to put
up with it, and Gibbie had said so too. It was the man's
business to keep his wife in order.

And then, since everyone of importance had crossed
the hall, she joined the procession, leaving Gibbie to
follow with Adrian and the two girls.

For the dramatic meeting between father and daughter
had taken place in the drawing-room, while everyone was
drinking cocktails. And it had gone off unexpectedly well,
owing to the elegance of Marianne's best frock, a stiff
yellow moiré with a big bow, like a bustle, at the back.
Adrian, who had never seen his daughter so well dressed
before, was as impressed as they had meant him to be.
She was, indeed, extremely pretty; far more striking than
the stalwart Marianne. She knew how to move, and she
made her entrance demurely. In the five minutes before
dinner she played her cards to perfection. Supported by
her friend she managed to seem at home and unself-
conscious in these somewhat formidable surroundings.
The two girls, though not exactly of the party, absorbed
in their music and other youthful pursuits yet added both
charm and grace to the group. People made much of
them, and their aloofness gave them distinction amid the

sophisticated intimacy of their elders. Adrian watched them and drew a deep sigh of relief. At least the disgrace which he had feared, when he saw her in a bathing suit, was to be spared him. She knew how to behave. She was not going to show him up, or be too savage a reminder of his home, and the week-end need not necessarily be spoilt. He was conscious of an enormous relief.

And yet he trembled a little, wondering what else she had in store for him. If she could manage to be as unexpected as this there was no knowing what weapons she might have in reserve. But they might come to an understanding. And in any case he must, for the time being, make a show of pride and pleasure, or else be made to look supremely foolish.

Presently she came across and greeted him with agreeable composure.

"I survive," Adrian told her. "You will be glad to know that I survive. What . . . what . . ."

He made the vague, cultured little gesture of a man seeking the right word. Solange waited, smiling expectantly. He never made those passes in the air at home. There he always knew exactly what to say.

"What are you up to?" he pronounced at last.

"Guess," said Solange darkly.

All the others had gone into the hall and he courteously made way for her. She swept out, the stiff skirts and the bustle bow giving her the wherewithal to sweep. Adrian felt a genuine spasm of pride and said to Philomena, as they took their seats:

"I find that I have a daughter."

To which Philomena, who had not yet forgiven him for his attempted desertion at Basingstoke, felt inclined to reply:

H

"High time too."

They were both aggrieved at the arrangement of the dinner table, and Adrian, who had not been prepared for it, felt the slight most keenly. It was natural that Hugo, who was so much in the fashion, should sit between Geraldine and Aggie. But there was no reason why Ford Usher should be sitting on Geraldine's left, for his conversation, despite the efforts of Laura, was non-existent. And it was a mystery why Corny should be so much thought of. Plenty of other people were quite as amusing, yet he never got poked away among the young girls and the husbands as Adrian now was.

At the more desirable end of the table an immediate spate of chatter broke out. Hugo was rapidly and nervously earning his right to be there. For as yet he was still on trial and he knew it; so that he must sing for his supper with an extra flourish of bravura, stimulated by the sense of being judged by new, and unusually stringent standards. The mass produced, synthetic geniality of a theatrical garden party would not pass muster here. Aggie, Laura, Geraldine and Corny were all listening to him and they were savage critics if not good ones. Unlike his colleagues in the Acorn, they did not devote nine-tenths of their energy to their profession so that they were able to take their pleasures strenuously. It was his new ambition to be a worker and yet to be able to hold his own, socially, with those who were not. He did not belong to them, and it would be foolish to pretend that he did, but the points of difference must be brought out with a subtle and engaging skill. He might not be too flippant, or too serious, nor might he tell stories, like a professional entertainer. What they liked, what they required, was that he should distil a fine essence of amusement for them out of any topic that came up.

If he had not been so tired, and so inwardly depressed, he would have been more sure that he could do it. At times he was inclined to envy Ford, whose inarticulate mutterings were only heard by Laura, and, if passed on by her to the general company, were first given point and translated into intelligible English. But he drank a good deal of champagne and hoped that he was holding his own. They were attentive enough, and he was an adept at window-dressing. He believed that he was getting through. Had they demanded even better he might have supplied it. But they were none of them worth that; no people in the world were worth it. He thought that he had gauged pretty accurately the demand that any one of them might make, and it was some time before he remembered that two of the party were still unconquered. He had meant to observe Marianne, or Solange, during dinner, and make up his mind what was going on inside their funny little heads. They had not smiled at him, as they ought, and he must find out why.

The thought of this small problem revived his flagging spirits. He leaned round Aggie to have a look at Marianne and was rewarded by catching a glance from Philomena. Automatically he gave a slight nod, as the sickening memory of his recent folly returned to him. But he must not think of that now, or it would spoil his dinner. These things sometimes settled themselves. And what was Marianne doing, chattering so volubly to Gibbie? It was not what he had expected, especially in a young woman who, even four years ago, had impressed him with her taciturnity. Straining his ears he thought he could catch the words *culex pseudopictus*. She was pouring out some long and dramatic story so that Gibbie could

scarcely get in a word edgeways. *Culex pseudopictus!*
Aggie interrupted and reclaimed his attention before he
had time to build up any theory about it.

Marianne, as a matter of fact, was talking so much
because she was sorry for Gibbie. The poor man was
plainly in trouble and his eyes besought her to take the
burden of conversation off his shoulders until he should
have collected a few of his straying faculties. So she
racked her brains for something to say and began, at
random, to retail all that she had learned from Solange
about the importance of Ford's discovery. As the soup
and the fish were served she described, in great detail, the
first expedition to Yeshenku.

Gibbie was dumbly grateful to her and took in nothing
that she said. But with the entrée he grew clear-headed
enough to ask:

"Where is this place . . . Yeshenku . . . what
country is it in?"

"I don't know what it's in. It's an island in the
Caspian Sea. And nobody gets malaria there. Because the
mosquitoes don't carry it. Because they don't catch it
from the people so the people don't catch it from them.
You see?"

"Not quite. Which starts not catching it first?"

"Why, you see, when you get bitten by an *anopheline*, a
malaria-carrying mosquito, you get a parasite from it.
And then you go giving the parasite to another mosquito.
And the mosquito gives it to another person. And that's
the way it goes on. The parasite is a cell called a sporozoit,
in the salivary gland of the first mosquito that bites you.
And in your blood it changes to a schizont. And that
turns into a merocyte, and that turns into hundreds of
merozoits, and makes you ill at the same time. That's why

the fever recurs, whenever there's a fresh batch of merozoits poisoning your blood. And they turn into sexual forms, microgametes and macrogametes. But nothing happens to them when they're inside you. Only, when another mosquito bites you, they get into its stomach and breed oöcysts, which split up into sporoblasts, and they turn into sporozoits and get into the salivary glands again. You see?"

"I see. And how big is a sporoblast?"

"That I don't know," said Marianne regretfully. "I shall have to ask Solange. I shouldn't think they can be very large if there are hundreds of them in one mosquito."

"Go on. Tell me some more."

If she would only keep on like this for a little longer he would have time to pull himself together. He could never be grateful enough to Geraldine for putting him next to Marianne in this crisis, for any of the others might have seen that he was not listening. And if he was to get through the week-end he must try to shelve the issue between himself and Philomena. She had no right to give him such a jolt when they were staying away. She ought to have waited until they got home. There could be no violent hurry, no real reason for bringing it all up at a moment when they both needed to be in good spirits. This lover of hers, this nameless villain, was hardly likely to turn up at Syranwood. She must have spoken on an impulse and on another impulse she might, just possibly, take it all back.

"And when he got there he found that the whole island was simply crawling with mosquitoes," Marianne was saying. "In fact, they'd none of them been so bitten in their lives."

"Well may they call it Yeshenku," muttered Gibbie.

"What?"

"I was merely quoting. You've heard of the old lady who said, 'Well may they call it Stonehenge, for I've never been so bitten in my life'?"

Marianne pondered for some time before she said that she did not see the point.

"There is none," Gibbie assured her. "It's a middle-aged joke, and merely silly. Go on. Who were bitten besides Ford?"

"Mr. MacDonald and Captain Rankin. But they didn't get malaria, though many of the mosquitoes were ano-phelines. But they had something else, a very slight fever, not unlike malaria, but much less serious and confined to one attack. And when they took specimens of their blood they found they'd got quite a new parasite, and it killed the malaria sporonts, because they tried. It was like a kind of inoculation really. But for months they could not make out where it came from until they noticed one of the mosquitoes that were biting them. They'd thought it was a *culex* and hadn't bothered. But it wasn't. It was a new species. *Culex pseudopictus*."

At this moment Hugo leant forward and looked at her down the table, and she left off talking abruptly. For she had seen the same thing that Adrian noticed when he broke up the rehearsal, the dumb distress, the flash of an almost insane appeal. He caught her eye and seemed to listen anxiously, as though he thought that she might be saying something important. And then, when Aggie touched his elbow, he jerked himself back.

The truth, which she had half guessed already, broke in upon her mind, and with a new, painful insight, she saw that four years had indeed not changed him. The new person that she had supposed him to become had not ousted the old, but the two were bound together in a gruesome partnership, like convicts on a chain. And the spectacle of his bondage so appalled her that she nearly ran out of the room.

"But he hates it!" she cried to herself. "He hates and loathes it!"

A grill dish was bumped gently into her elbow and she was recalled to the necessities of the moment. There was poor Gibbie to be talked to.

"The only difficulty," she resumed rapidly, "is that they've lost the new parasite. They can't cultivate it. They infect a mosquito, and it simply disappears."

Gibbie's fixed, attentive smile had grown glassy. He heard not a word. For he too had seen how Hugo looked down the table and had caught that glance exchanged with Philomena. And he too had, in a flash, divined the truth. A thousand confirming circumstances assailed him. Of course, the man was Hugo.

It was so inevitable that his anger subsided and, with a gloomy precision, he was able to review the facts. He remembered that in past years he had always been a little afraid lest something of this sort should happen. She had been in many ways a wonderful wife. If it had not been for her support he would never have left his old firm and set up for himself. It was she who had managed to make their poverty, during the next three years, more than bearable. She had never worried or complained. She had always been considerate to his friends. She ran his house beautifully and she had borne him three fine children. Often, but perhaps not quite often enough, he had been amazed at his own luck. Especially when the babies were born had he raged against the injustice of an arrangement which demanded so much more from her than from him.

He had felt that she would ask in meal or in malt, some ultimate compensation from him and from mankind. And he had inwardly vowed that she should have fair dealing.

Now the day of reckoning had arrived. She was making her demand. And at least she had been honest about it: or rather, had tried to be honest, for her method of broaching the topic had not been quite fair. It looked very like a trap, but he believed that the guile of it was unconscious. And she had offered to give up her lover. Her happiness, she called it. He must remember that. He ought not to under-rate that offer. She had appealed to him, to his generosity and to his sense of justice.

What, supposing this were not to be his but an abstract case, what would the Good Man do?

Philomena seemed to have no doubts about it. She had hinted very plainly that his outraged feelings were mere prejudice, the survival of an uncivilised tradition of ownership. Perhaps she was right. But she was asking much more than that. She was expecting him to wear his horns, not merely with submission but almost with enthusiasm, as a badge of civilisation. To give her up altogether would be an easy fate compared with this. If she had wanted her freedom, he could have understood better. But she did not ask for that. She merely asked for leave to take a lover.

Such things had, he supposed, been done before. He knew of cases: husbands and wives who lived in amity with openly unfaithful partners. But he had never imagined that they were done in cold blood. It was surely an unforeseen situation, accepted after it had come about. The good man might very well be commended for refusing to divorce a wife whom he still loved, and who was willing to live with him. And how far was his own case parallel to these? He must talk it over with Philomena again.

Catching her eye, he smiled slightly, and she saw at once that he was not angry any more. It was an immense relief to know that; for, as long as he was not angry, she could do anything with him. She knew what was passing in his mind; his expression of heavy speculation was familiar to her. By some miracle of good luck he had lost himself again in that maze of abstract reasoning which was like a foreign country to her. He was asking himself what the Good Man would do; turning his case into an academic problem to be thrashed out by a couple of earnest undergraduates. Philomena, who had never in her life asked herself what the Good Woman would do, was immensely diverted. So often she had seen him like this, lost and helpless, until she had pity on him and made up his mind by one, swift, unreasonable decision. Soon she would make it up again. She would secure everything. She would have her own way. She would enjoy the pleasures of romance with the right to call herself an excellent wife, the adventures of youth with the settled future of middle age. She would eat her cake and have it.

Genially and in soaring spirits she turned to poor Sir Alec and wrung out of his work-parched brain a few sparse drops of conversation. He could talk about dry fly-fishing and the Bar, but she could not sustain many exchanges on the first topic and the fear of being a bore kept him rather short upon the second. Twenty years before, as a youngish man, he had greatly desired to keep up interests outside his work, and certain relics of that odd ambition had become habits. He still took little books of poetry about in his pocket, in the hope that he might some day find the time and energy to read them. And he still tried not to tell legal stories. So they talked about Jane Austen and Philomena, suppressing a yawn, thought, as she always thought, what a pearl Alec would have been if he was not so overworked and if he had married somebody nicer. A good wife would have made him so happy, and she had nothing but condemnation for Laura, who would not keep accounts, who took a pride in being unpunctual and who refused to have children. So she cooed away to him, and completely turned her back on the sulky Adrian who had once more displayed his snobbishness. And she actually succeeded in making Alec laugh three times before the arrival of asparagus silenced them.

By a strange tradition this fastidious company laid down their forks and seized the limp and oily objects in their fingers, dangling them high in the air. It was not a pretty sight: but nobody thought this except a small page-boy, recently imported from an orphanage, who was assisting at this dinner as a first step on the road to footmanhood. Having never seen asparagus eaten before, this innocent was overcome with giggles and had to leave the dining-room. Whereat it was decided that he would never do in house service, so he was apprenticed to a garage. And did very well. So that this asparagus course was the turning point in his career.

Corny took advantage of the silence to be repeating some poetry. In his churchy voice he could be heard reciting those lines which he had already recollected in the train, the lines which Paul Wrench had written in his album. Everybody began at once to say things about Paul Wrench. But Adrian did not say his bit, because Philomena had already heard it and Marianne, on his other side, was too young to know how good it was. He thought of those "First Impressions of Paul Wrench" which he had begun to write in the library before dinner, and which would be printed in his Weekly next Wednesday. And he thought of all the grave lamenting which he would be called upon to do in the next ten days. And suddenly he asked himself if he really cared a bit.

Literature had lost one of the brightest buds in its coronal. He, as a 'louse in the locks of literature' (for so, in a spasm of disgust, did he term himself), ought to be greatly concerned. But did lice mind what happened to buds? And did he feel any genuine sense of bereavement? He did not. The loss of one of his own front teeth would have distressed him infinitely more. He cared so very little for literature, when it came to the point. It was all humbug. Everything in his life was humbug, just as everything in Paul Wrench's harsh, unpretending life had been as real as a gravel beach to bare feet (a good simile and one which he must use in his impressions).

"For what have I lived?" he wondered, as he dangled the asparagus over his head.

To write, twenty years ago, a life of Voltaire which had become a minor classic.

To eat asparagus in the houses of the rich.

No. That was not being fair to himself. He could have done without the asparagus. He was not a sensual man, and he valued his company above his dinner. The major portion of his honesty had not been sacrificed for a mess of pottage. He had been betrayed by a far more insidious temptation, by the attempt to ignore every element in life which did not fit in with his ideal of freedom and urbanity. Being a poor man, he had made shift to pretend that he was not, because the truth of poverty interfered with this

mirage of an exquisite existence. And this, in itself was
not ignoble, had he not been reduced to suggesting that
gilt was gold. If these stately homes, this life of the
leisured, had been all that he pretended, then any sacrifice
might have been worth while. But they were not. And
in his heart he knew that the great patron whose influence
had first moulded him to this ideal was a paltry liar, a
romancier de concierge in disguise. Such a world had never
existed outside a novelist's imagination. The surface
might be produced. At Syranwood the surface was
almost flawless. The mechanism, the apparatus, the
dinner table, the flowers, the women's fair, long-chinned
faces, the bloom of the peaches in the Wedgwood
baskets, it was all exquisite. And beneath the surface it
was all your elbow: nothing exquisite about Aggie, or
Corny, or Laura, or the parrot-house noises they were
making, no originality, no freedom, and no beauty
beyond that which money can secure. Yet for them, and
for their like, he, who had once known value when he met
it, had sacrificed his muse. He had taken Hugo's plays
seriously, because they were in the fashion, he was
jealous of Corny, he had quoted Byron to Laura and read
Donne to Aggie as though childbirth must necessarily
hurt her more than other people.

But he had remained a gentleman. Nobody could
deny that. He was perhaps the only really well-bred
critic of any standing. A gentle suavity distinguished him
amid the hysterical squeals, the pompous grunts of his
colleagues. In these days of tabloid culture he might still
call himself something of a scholar. He had a sense of
proportion, a scale of reference, and he had done a little
towards keeping up the old standards. In thus taking
stock of himself he ought not to be unfair or to miss out

what might remain to his credit. He could condemn without being personally offensive. How many of his contemporaries could do that? And he could praise without exaggeration. Or very nearly, for he still wished that he had not once been betrayed into comparing Hugo with Congreve. And he had stood out against the dangers of intellectual arrogance; his tastes were catholic and humane and he gave a fair hearing to everybody. He had never been ashamed to confess that the second-rate could often charm and entertain him. In fact he had created the *cachet* which now surrounded the word 'competence.' He read detective novels, he went to murder plays and made no bones about enjoying them.

And to struggling writers of merit he had given many a helping hand. He published them in his Weekly. He got the Prize Committees upon which he sat to give them awards. He used his influence to get them Civil List pensions. He was notoriously kind to promising young men, talking to them delightfully and without condescension, and giving them reviewing to do. His benevolence had even included an offer of friendship to Paul Wrench at a time when Wrench's friends were never very easy. Nobody would ever know how much he had tried to do for that unfortunate creature. A certain successful stock breeder from Darlington had once consulted him in a scheme for patronising the arts. On being told that Wrench was a good poet on the point of starvation this man was greatly impressed. He had offered a pension of £250 for three years, on the condition that Wrench should produce at least two volumes of poetry during that period, a reasonable stipulation and calculated to stimulate industry.

Of the subsequent scene Adrian could not, even now,

think without a flush of vexation. He had been prepared
for a certain amount of surliness, but Wrench's language
had passed all bounds. And now the foolish fellow was
dead. He had never been anyone's enemy but his own,
and he had achieved fame in spite of himself. East
Prussia was the devil of a way off. If it had been
nearer there might have been quite an impressive
gathering at the funeral. But nobody would go as far as
that.

"Except me," decided Adrian surprisingly.

He found that his mind was made up. He was going.
He wished to be there. And that was his answer to these
furies which had been scourging him. Even if he was too
late for the ceremony he could at least stand for an hour in
meditation beside the poet's grave, in a windswept
cemetery on the shores of the Baltic. Among them all he
would be the only one to whom Paul Wrench meant as
much as that. Nor would he mention the expedition to
any one else. It should be made for his own satisfaction,
to prove to the Furies how much more the loss of a poet
meant to him than a gap in his front teeth. If he, a poor
and busy man, could afford this journey, there must
surely remain some grain of idealism in his spiritual
composition. Unkind friends, jealous rivals, might call
him an old snob, a week-end essayist, but the tribunal in
his own heart must acquit him.

And afterwards it might gradually leak out.

"Did you know Adrian actually went to Wrench's
funeral?"

"Fancy his caring as much as that!"

Posterity might couple the name of Upward with that
of Wrench's grave.

Reassured, he saw the women prepare to leave the

table. He was quite himself again, which was timely, for his reputation as a talker had grown on port.

11. *Nightstocks.*

The drawing-room was rich with a bloomy dusk and Laura turned on one or two lights. All the night whispers and smells drifted in through the windows on the wings of vagrant moths. Unconsciously the women dropped their voices to a lower key, tuning themselves to the twilight as they fluttered about the dim room, powdering their noses and discussing Hugo. Their soft, murmuring laughter was like the cooing of doves.

"I've always been so fond of him . . ."

"Such a pity . . ."

"A creole, isn't she?"

"But darling, aren't creoles black?"

"Do you know I've never seen her."

"Aggie! It's not true. You couldn't have helped . . ."

"Really too well dressed, in that spit-and-polish American way. I expect she always wears afternoon dresses in the afternoon."

" . . . and invariably in the weekly papers . . ."

"Somebody ought to disentangle him. He's much too nice . . ."

"And the money he must be making . . ."

"Aggie! We think it's your mission."

"Don't you think that Aggie ought . . ."

Nobody asked what the girls thought, for Hugo, though not much their senior, was no affair of theirs. So they handed the cigarettes in silence and slipped off as

soon as they could, through the long windows on to the
terrace behind the house.

The moon was rising and there was only a little fleck of
pale sky left in the west, to show where the sun had been.
The girls ran down the garden paths, between the clipped
box bushes, and paused by the fountain pool. In the wan
light there was no difference between Marianne's pink
chiffon and the yellow she had lent to Solange. They
were two flitting wraiths and their low-pitched voices
hardly broke the quiet of the summer night. Only one
thing in the garden looked whiter than they did, and that
was the long bed of lilies by the south wall.

"Do you like lilies?" asked Solange, pausing to sniff.

"No," snapped Marianne.

"I thought you didn't. Why?"

"They're like Aggie—too good to be true. You
think: how wonderful! And then the smell makes you
sick. And you see there's a brown dead leaf hanging
down somewhere on their stalks."

Solange laughed. She had fewer reasons for disliking
Aggie.

They went down the path, past the lilies to a place
where peach trees sprawled against the brick and a great,
untidy bed of night stocks sent out an aromatic blast.
The struggling, insignificant flowers stood out like a
faded Milky Way of small stars. Even at night, in their
hour of glory, they were nothing to look at. But their
scent was more than a scent. It was a world. It filled the
soul with a transport of hope and melancholy. Solange
and Marianne stood in silence, sniffing vigorously.

"If lilies are like Aggie," said Solange, "then night
stocks are like you."

"*Euphemei.*"

"What?"

"It's Greek."

"I didn't know you knew Greek."

"I don't really. Miss Fosdyke used to teach me some, but we never got further than things like: 'Oh that I might be buzzed about by bees' and 'the hoplites escaped their own notice rushing about in the market place.' But I learnt *Euphemei* from my Uncle Julian. It's a polite way of saying 'Shut up'."

"How can anyone escape their own notice?"

"The Greeks could apparently."

Solange meditated for a moment and then said:

"It would be a lovely thing to do. I suppose you'd say that animals did. But you mustn't be cross if I say that night stocks are like you. They are. Horrid people don't know about them, and they're just as good if you stand near them or go half a mile off. Whereas a lily, especially a Madonna lily . . ."

"I'd rather be a dead nettle than a Madonna lily."

"Oh? Do you think dead nettles are bad flowers?"

"Harmless. But uninteresting. Listen! There's a nightingale. No, it can't be! It's too late."

Far away, in some elm trees across the hay fields, they could hear four long, clear whistles. But the music was so faint that a burst of laughter from the house soon smothered it. Aggie's voice, raised in glee, came through the drawing-room window.

"He bit her? Not Sally?"

"No, no! Not Sally. Netta."

"Poor Sally! How she would have enjoyed . . ."

"It's not true!"

"But Philomena! Where?"

"Oh, only on the shoulder. And his aide-de-camp . . ."

The voices dropped and Marianne said:

"They're having fun now we've gone."

Solange said:

"Funny to think of Aggie disentangling anyone!"

Marianne would have thought it funny if she had not still been so unhappy. She was listening for the sound of the men's voices coming into the drawing-room, and a few minutes later, in a sudden significant lull of the women's laughter, she heard Adrian saying something about 'Charles' Wain over the new chimney.' Breaking suddenly away from her friend she flew lightly up the path and on to the terrace outside the drawing-room window. Inside she could see Hugo, talking to her grandmother. He was still there. And she darted away again, her pale skirts brushing the glass as if she had been a bird blown past the window.

"What was it? What did you run away for?" demanded Solange, as she returned.

"To see if Aggie has begun."

"Has she?"

"Not yet."

"I wonder . . ." began Solange.

"What?"

"You'll be offended."

"I expect so. But that doesn't generally stop you."

"I wonder you don't disentangle him yourself."

"How . . . ?"

"Oh, anybody could do it. He's as vain as a peacock. Just let him see that you haven't fallen at his feet."

"I meant what for? Why should I?"

Voices echoed under the arch of night. They were all coming out on to the terrace and the garden was full of pale, fluttering skirts. The two girls sought safety in the pleached alley, where they were hidden.

"We're safe here," said Marianne. "They'll all go and look at the lilies. They're Aggie's favourite flower. She'll tell him to come and smell them with her."

"Hope he gets his nose all yellow," muttered Solange viciously.

"He'll remember not to, I expect. He never escapes his own notice."

"Oh Marianne, you can't! You really can't . . ." she could not get her tongue round the indecent word. "You can't . . ."

"I do."

"Then for heaven's sake why don't you lift a finger to get him?"

"What good would that do?"

"You'd be better than Aggie. At least you can disentangle him from that."

Now Lady Geraldine was calling to them. She wanted a note taken over to the rectory inviting the parson and his wife to dinner on Sunday. Voices echoed the summons from under the apple boughs, and between the box bushes.

"Ssh! Don't answer," whispered Marianne. "Don't you see, it isn't Aggie, or that Creole person, or anybody like that that he needs to be disentangled from. It's much worse . . ."

"Mary . . . Anne! Solange! Mary . . . Anne!"

"It's himself. You see? Himself. At least, not that, but the person he has to pretend to be. He doesn't want . . . he doesn't like. . . . Oh look! Let's run!"

One end of the pleached alley was darkened by the figure of Corny, who had been sent to look for them. They fled down the leafy tunnel only to fall into the arms of Hugo who was coming in at the other end. Solange swerved to avoid him, but Marianne was caught, picked up, carried out into the moonlight, and set on her feet as if she had been a large doll. She did not resist. But when he released her she shook out her skirts and waited haughtily for an explanation.

"Grandma wants you," said Hugo.

He was speaking, of course, in inverted commas, and she ought to have appreciated the audacious fantasy of it. Heaven help her if she supposed that he naturally talked like that, and saw no difference between Lady Geraldine and the grandmother of some brood at Gunnersbury. It was a bromide, so obvious that nobody ought to have been able to mistake it.

Marianne thanked him stiffly and walked away.

"The modern girl," mused Hugo, looking after her, "has no sense of humour. No sense of humour at all. That's another thing to remember about her. She is, as certain of the Americans say, dumb. She's a dumb-bell."

But was she?

"Tell me," he said to the first fluttering frock that he met under the apple boughs, "tell me more about the modern girl."

"Hugo?"

The flutterer was Philomena. He was not going to be let off.

Hesitation had never been one of Hugo's failings. In a crisis he did not waver. Bitterly though he might regret his moment of folly, that abortive, misguided gesture towards escape, he had no intention of retreat. That would have been too foolish. He must go on as he had begun. Philomena was obviously expecting some kind of demonstration. He made it.

"Aggie," she told him recklessly, "is waiting among the lilies."

"Like somebody in a Victorian poem?" He dismissed Aggie. "Lilies always give me hay fever. Come into the moonlight, Philomena. I want to look at you."

"I can't stay now. I've got to play bridge. I just wanted to tell you that I've spoken to Gibbie."

"Oh?"

He wanted to say:

"Gawd's teeth!"

But he restrained himself, though he did think that she might have given him time to digest his dinner. As long as she was beside him, he could not find his position entirely regrettable.

She was such a rest from Aggie.

"And what did Gibbie say?" he asked, rather faintly.

He liked Gibbie. He ought to have kept out of this, liking Gibbie as he did. Now they would have to avoid each other at their Club. It was absurd. But his boats were burned. Entwining Philomena's waist more firmly, he asked what Gibbie had said.

"I think he . . . understands."

"What?"

"We've discussed it before, you know. And we both feel the same about these things. We don't want to prevent each other from living as completely and beautifully as possible. I told him that I wouldn't go with you unless he understood. I said I'd give you up if he hated it too much. Because you see, Hugo, I do put my home first. My home, and the children, and Gibbie. I'd have to go back to them eventually, you understand?"

"You mean that Gibbie doesn't . . ."

"He did at first. But just now, when we came out into

the garden, he said to me that he would try to understand, and not come between me and my happiness."

Extraordinary fellow, thought Hugo, resentfully. For often, in unregenerate moments, he had thought how nice it would be to make love to Philomena. But he had always regarded Gibbie as an obstacle.

"Gibbie," she explained, "is civilised. He doesn't think he owns me. He's liberal minded."

Too damned liberal by half, agreed Hugo to himself. But then he remembered how liberal he had always been himself. He had written a play about a wife who made a very successful experiment of this sort. Having said and implied so much, in his time, about sexual freedom, he was bound to believe in it, and he made a great effort to think all the better of Gibbie. But certain early impressions die hard, and he found that he was thinking the worse of Gibbie. A deceived husband is by tradition an object of ridicule, but a complaisant husband ranks even lower.

He remained silent and meditative so long that Philomena began to feel uncomfortable. She grew oddly anxious to rectify any mistake that might have arisen about Gibbie's manly spirit, and she explained that Gibbie had never been a person to stand any nonsense. He had his ideas of wifely duty and he expected her to live up to them. Hugo must not think that Gibbie would put up with anything.

"If he thought I wasn't pulling my weight," she boasted, "he'd leave me. He isn't one of those men who let themselves be made fools of."

Hugo gulped attentively. The situation was beyond him, so he left it alone. If he did nothing, and said nothing, but just went on pacing round the garden, something might happen to solve it all. He might wake up and find that he had dreamt it. Or Philomena might turn out to be pulling his leg. But her next words startled him.

"We'll go at once," she said.

"But darling . . ."

"If you can get away."

"But darling . . . I can't. I can't possibly go away just now. Not right away. The rehearsals of *Beggar My Neighbour* begin next week."

"Oh Hugo!"

She had forgotten that wretched play. Of course he could not go away. The whole thing would have to be postponed. And, now that she had spoken to Gibbie, postponement would be so uncomfortable.

"What are we going to do?" she asked mournfully.

He had skilfully guided her into the yew parlour, where the moon still lurked behind the black hedges and the distant hills were only the dimmest shadow against the sky. Turning to her, in the warm darkness, Hugo began to make the only possible reply. But she drew back.

"Not now, Hugo! Not till we can go away. I wouldn't feel it was right."

"You extraordinary woman!"

"It wouldn't be fair to Gibbie. We must just be friends till then. And after we come back. Do you see?"

Hugo argued with her, and though he could not convince he came very near to overcoming her. Her feelings were stronger than her principles and Hugo was skilful at pressing his point. Indeed there is no knowing how far they might have got towards settling their difficulties had not Lady Geraldine appeared, drifted round the yew hedge, her lace veils catching on the branches. Peering without ceremony at the couple on the teak seat, she sank down beside them and asked if that was Mr. Usher?

"It's Hugo," explained Philomena, composing herself.

"Why do I want to call him . . . no, don't move. There is plenty of room for three. Though I think poor Aggie is waiting for you, Mr. Swan. She has begun to pick all the lilies, and I'm afraid, if you don't go soon, there won't be one left. I said to her: 'Aggie dear, why are you picking my lilies?' And she said: 'Well, why doesn't he come? I want to rehearse with him.' Poor Aggie is always so impatient, you know."

Hugo, half glad and half sorry at the interruption, said that he would go. He hurried gracefully away, and the two ladies waited until the sound of his departing feet had sunk into the silence of the night. And then Lady Geraldine asked:

"What is that young man's name?"

"Pott. Hugo Pott."

"And I called him Edgar!"

"No, Geraldine. You called him Swan."

"To remind myself that it isn't Edgar. That man who wrote the House . . . the House of . . ."

Geraldine's silvery voice, tuned to the moonlit dusk and the nightingales, sank pensively. But presently it rose again.

"Philomena. I don't like to find people in compromising situations. Especially in the garden."

"But Geraldine!"

"Kissing and cuddling, Philomena! I saw you. And you call yourself a respectable woman."

"We love each other," said Philomena defensively.

"I guessed as much. But that is no excuse."

Philomena bit her lip with vexation. Geraldine, of all people, had not the faintest right to talk in this censorious strain. The Rivaz collection, as her seven children were called, could never have been accumulated without a certain amount of kissing and cuddling, in the garden or elsewhere. For in the family circle Otho, the Tyrant, was only credited with two of them: Mathilde the eldest, the mother of Marianne, and Dominick the youngest, born after Geraldine had taken a protracted tour through Central Africa alone with Otho, and some negro porters. It was the only time that she had shot big game too, and it was unfortunate for Dominick, for he had inherited the paternal bull neck. Mathilde and Dominick were indubitably Otho's children. Whereas Beata, Lionel, Charles, Julian and Laura were all as handsome as they were varied in type. So that it was perfectly ridiculous for Geraldine to sit there, happed up in wedding veils and talking like a district visitor. She had done all that Philomena was too modern and civilised to do. She had deceived her husband frequently under his own roof, deceived him with the most blatant and expensive consequences, and all she cared for was a cynical parade of appearances. Probably she had had dozens of lovers, and now she was shocked and disapproving because Philomena contemplated one.

"Decorum," she observed, as though she had been following her young cousin's thoughts. "As long as you don't underrate the importance of decorum you can do whatever you please. You can recite the Black Mass in Canterbury Cathedral and nobody will think of protesting, if you do it in an evangelical manner. I remember, when I was a young girl I heard a parson asked to say grace at my father's house. I'm afraid he was not a very religious man, or else he must have been a little tipsy, for he got up and said: *To all which, Oh Lord, we most strongly object.* But, my dear, he said it in the right way, and nobody thought it odd. It was a lesson which I have never forgotten."

"I don't underrate decorum," replied Philomena, with some spirit. "But I hate deception. I don't intend to lie to my husband, even if it's decorous. Gibbie knows everything. I daresay that may seem shocking to you. But at least it's better than a life of furtive little intrigues."

"Oh, undoubtedly," agreed Lady Geraldine at once. "But tell me, Philomena dear, I've always wanted to know, how do you manage?"

"Manage?"

Philomena winced at the word. It was the idiom of an older generation, and it recalled a number of uncomfortable episodes. It implied a discreet concealment of the indecorous. One managed when one took small children on a long railway journey. Her romance was being reduced to the level of the nursery.

"I'm going away with Hugo," she explained hastily. "Of course, there can be nothing between us while I am with Gibbie. And when we come back the whole thing will be over."

"Over? Oh I see. But how wonderful to be able to know that!"

And Geraldine sighed. For she had a great admiration for women who knew when these things were over. Not to clutch, not to cling, to take lightly and to relinquish gracefully, how many tears had it not cost her to learn that!

"You'll forgive these questions, my dear. Things are so

different nowadays. And so you go away? Where?"

"I don't know where yet," said Philomena.

Something warned her that Geraldine was going to ask where she generally went, and she did not want to admit that she had never done such a thing before. So she hurried on.

"Don't you feel that jealousy between husband and wife is a mistake?"

"It shows very limited interests," agreed Geraldine. "But when are you going, then?"

"That depends. Hugo has a play coming on. I expect it will be about six weeks before he can get away."

"Oh, has he? I thought they never began new plays at that time of year."

"Most people don't. But Hugo can. He says it will have settled nicely into its run by the autumn."

"Six weeks? Dear me! That runs you very near to the summer. What are you doing about the children's holidays?"

Philomena did not answer. For Geraldine knew as well as she did that the Greys were sharing a house in Skye with Beata. Philomena was to be there through August, in charge of both sets of children, while Beata was to take duty in September.

"Of course, Beata might exchange," calculated Geraldine.

But her tone implied that everything would have to be explained to Beata before she would do it.

"I haven't really made my plans," said Philomena evasively.

Making plans, like managing, was another thing that the elderly did. Philomena hated making plans and thinking ahead. She had had so much of it, and of remembering not to ask anyone to dinner on a Thursday because it was cook's night off, fixing September for Nannie's holiday, and getting in enough food to last over Easter Monday. She would go mad unless she got away from it sometimes, and here she was, actually making plans in order to get away. She was thinking:

"I might squeeze it in between Hugo's play and Skye if I can manage to get a new parlour-maid by then."

Her holidays with Gibbie had always been snatched like that. They had been achieved in the face of obstacles, and liable to alteration if a boiler burst or a child came out in nettle rash. But to plan an unofficial honeymoon was monstrous.

"Perhaps it would be better to wait for the autumn," suggested Geraldine helpfully. "Often you get such nice weather in October."

Philomena jumped up and said that she was cold, and that Laura had said something about bridge. For if this went on five seconds longer she would lose heart.

In spite of Gibbie's goodness, his undeniable generosity she could not help feeling that things were still very unfair. It was not as if other people did not succeed in doing these things. They happened every day without any obvious orgy of planning. But some people can act upon impulse and others cannot.

The flower garden was deserted. But as she passed the laurestinus hedge which veiled the kitchen wing she heard a frantic rattling and splashing. The unseen slaves were hurling themselves into the endless task of washing up. There was a whiff of steamy air and the impression of hot people working at break-neck speed. She hurried petulantly past, hating to be reminded of effort. There was too much effort everywhere. It was impossible, unless one had a lot of money, to pretend that life is a haphazard and impulsive thing. Even here, though carefully concealed behind laurestinus bushes, the basic effort was still present. And flowering shrubs are expensive. Gibbie could afford to pay servants, to transfer the real effort of his household to shoulders other than Philomena's, but he could not afford to keep those shoulders out of sight. And the beautiful freedom upon which they had agreed was impracticable because it cost too much.

12. *Miss Wilson's Room.*

The house was lying awake and empty. She went up the steps from the garden and all along the terrace, peering through the windows into hushed, shadowy rooms where lamps burned solitary. Nothing moved except the fluttering moths, and in the library she could see the top of Adrian's head as he bent over an article on Paul Wrench. He seemed to be the only person indoors.

At the far end of the terrace something unusual struck her eye. Just down below, by the south wall, she looked at a void blank where, an hour ago, there had been whiteness. The lily bed had completely disappeared. She stood staring at where it should have been as if she expected to see those fantastic silvery spikes come back again. When Corny emerged from the bushes she could only point and gasp:

"Aggie?"

Corny said that several people had expostulated, but when Aggie was impatient she did not seem to know what

she was doing. And afterwards she had gone and stood
with the lilies in her arms for a long time, lost in thought,
under the lamp in the hall. Fletcher, the butler, coming
out of the service door, had got quite a turn. A scene not
unlike the Annunciation, said Corny: Aggie, amid a hay-
stack of lilies and the modest, virginal Fletcher, recoiling
against his green baize door. But it had all been Hugo's
fault for not coming.

"Not coming?" echoed Philomena. "He did come,
surely. A long time ago. He went especially to find her."

"He never arrived."

"Then where is he?"

Corny eyed the façade of the house. He was the only
person in it who could have said straight off where each
guest was sleeping. He always knew those things five
minutes after arriving anywhere.

"There's no light in his room," he said.

And he looked thoughtful, for he liked to know what
everybody was doing, all the time. He knew that the girls
were practising music again, that Aggie was pacing from
room to room in a fury, that Gibbie and Alec were playing
billiards, and that Laura was keeping Ford in order until
Bechstrader should arrive. The whole of Corny's evening
was spent in trotting about from one group to another
like a conscientious little sheep dog.

He took Philomena through the garden door into the
hall, which still smelt strongly of Aggie's lilies. They
passed out on to the drive in front, where there was a
noise of singing. The girls had left off practising and
were amusing themselves.

"Perhaps he's in Miss Wilson's room?"

Philomena looked doubtful. But then she remembered
that Hugo had been asking for information about the

modern girl. He seemed to be harping on the subject.

"We might look," she agreed.

He had been there for about twenty minutes, and was lying on an old sofa in the corner. It was not a very comfortable sofa, for the springs were all gone. Laura and her sisters, Marianne and her cousins, had all lain on it in turn, to rest their growing backs, while their governesses read aloud Motley's *Rise of the Dutch Republic* or Prescott's *Conquest of Mexico*. But he found himself at ease upon it. Repose began to steal over him and his muscles loosened. The girls had pleasant voices and they took no notice of him whatever when he came in. They did not mind an audience as long as they could ignore it.

Philomena and Corny looked about them for a moment and then sank on to chairs amid all the scattered music and untidy, girlish possessions. Marianne's tapestry, bright and intricate, sprawled over half the table, but had been pushed aside to make room for a microscope that Solange had brought. The floor was covered with pins, relics of their hurried dressmaking in the morning, and great trays of drying lavender stood in a corner.

"There's Hugo," whispered Corny, suddenly perceiving the sofa in the corner.

Hugo opened one eye, smiled at them, and shut it again. For the moment he was feeling very safe, like a ship that has drifted into harbour. Marianne's voice, gentle as the moonlight, wafted him on. Like a benevolent and propitious wind it filled his drooping sails.

How nice it would be, he thought, to go to sleep hearing this music, and then, after a hundred years of repose, to wake up and find it still there. He was nearly asleep already and for a timeless instant he dreamed his old dream of the High Road and the Low Road. Miss

Wilson's room had melted into Oxford Street and you were driving along it in a car, consumed by a dreadful, craving anxiety. Because somewhere just after the Marble Arch there were two roads, the High Road and the Low Road. And if you took the first it led you into Oxford Circus. But if you took the second you went down and down and down, till the houses stood on high cliffs on either side, down through a gorge to the sea. And the Low Road ran out along a shore towards mountains and lakes full of vivid, clear colours, more beautiful than anything seen in the waking world. But it was hard to find. He had been there once, but he could never find it again. He knew how the bay curved round into a long peninsula. He could have drawn it. He must have seen it, at some time, though it was difficult to believe that anything so lovely could be seen and forgotten. The High Road and the Low Road . . . the Low Road. . . . He was awake again, and Marianne's voice still sang on:

> . . . *qui fait rêver les oiseaux dans les arbres,*
> *Et sangloter d'extase les jets d'eaux.*
> *Les grands jets d'eaux sveltes. . . .*

The other life, vast, serene, enchanted, lay all about him. He sank into it while the voice rose and fell on a last cadence:

> . . . *Parmi les marbres . . .*

Into the final tinkling, tender drops of music broke Corny's sibilant whisper.

"This," he hissed, "is the way one ought to spend the evening, don't you think?"

A kind of tremor passed down the averted backs of Solange and Marianne. But they continued to take no notice of their audience. People had a way of coming in like this to listen, of an evening, but they soon went off again.

"Sing this," murmured Solange, snatching up the austerest song that she could find.

And Marianne began uncompromisingly:

> Oh Lord! How long must I
> In this dark prison lie?

Solange did not place the chords quite right, so they did it again. Three times over did Marianne ask how long she must lie in a dark prison, and Corny began to fidget. Hugo, irritable and wide awake, sat up on his sofa. He thought that he had never heard a more annoying song. It was like a cold bath. And, as it went on, it translated his agreeable dream in harsh fact.

> Where but faint gleams of Thee salute my sight
> Like doubtful moonshine, in a cloudy night. . . .

"I'm going to bed," announced Hugo.

Corny scuffled out after him. For by this time Walter Bechstrader would have arrived and there would be drama of some sort going on downstairs.

"But are you really going to bed?" he asked Hugo when they were outside the door.

"Yes," snapped Hugo. "I'm tired."

He strode off and Corny sent after him a glance of faintly puzzled disapproval. It was much too early for the life and soul of the party to be going to bed. Straws show

K

which way the wind blows and Corny was a connoisseur in straws. He shook his head slightly as he set off downstairs, and foresaw himself agreeing with his friends that it was A Pity. Not at once perhaps, but before very long.

Bechstrader had come, as a peculiar booming monologue, going forward in the drawing-room, assured Corny before he got to the bottom of the stairs. It was like the note of a benevolent and cultured gong. For Laura, discovering that he would be obliged to go back in the course of Sunday, and that the time at her disposal was short, had lost no time in introducing him to Ford. She was determined to vindicate the importance of mosquitoes.

But she had not intended, at this stage, more than a general exchange of politeness, and controversy was beginning much too soon. The real business of the evening should have been done in the library, well after midnight, when Walter had been worked up to it. It took a little beating about the bush to mellow him, but after he had laid down the law for a couple of hours he would generally become malleable and put his hand in his pocket.

Her plans were miscarrying. For nobody would have expected Walter to know so terribly much. The usual river of words flowed from him, all about nothing as it seemed at first. But presently, to her horror, a definite meaning emerged. And a very unpleasant meaning it was, as coming from a rich patron. For though he was very interested to meet Ford, and though he knew all about Yeshenku, it appeared that he did not believe in *culex pseudopictus*. Somebody had been getting at him. Some rival had put ideas into his head. For the whole trend of his monologue, and the number of authorities which he misquoted, bore witness to a recent interview with some

other expert. And there were, after all, many eminent
people who thought that Ford's conclusions were moon-
shine.

Laura grew angry and nervous. She looked at Ford
appealingly, hoping that he would wake up and defend
himself. But he said nothing. He merely puffed at the
cigar which had been given to him and looked at Walter
in contemptuous silence. Nobody helped her. Lady
Geraldine had gone into one of her trances, while Aggie,
temporarily recovered from her sulks, was amusing the
company by doing her famous imitation of a monkey
eating nuts, making sudden screeches which disturbed
Walter as much as his undeviating flow exasperated her.
Each privately thought the other ill-mannered.

Walter, growing more benevolent as he grew more
damning, told Ford with a smile that *pseudopictus* was not,
probably, a *culex* at all. It was an anopheline, of a species
already well known to entomologists. Whereat Ford got
up and walked away. Laura's failure became apparent
to everybody in the room.

"Now, Ford," she exclaimed with a laugh, "the gaunt-
let's been flung and you mustn't go away. I don't know
the answer to this, or I'd take up the challenge
myself."

"For people who know anything about the subject,"
said Ford, "there is my article in the last issue of the
British Medical Journal. In that I have answered, to the
best of my ability, the more serious criticisms which have
been levelled against my work. But I have never met
anybody before who took Mr. Bechstrader's view. It is
obvious that he has not understood the arguments against
me, so that I would find it very difficult to set him right."

"You've the great body of professional opinion against

you," said Bechstrader, rather angrily.

"I know. And it takes me all my time to hold out against that. I don't propose to bring my case before the man in the street until I've secured the attention of the people who matter."

Walter Bechstrader, who had never been called the man in the street before, gave an enormous sigh of astonishment. Like a deflated balloon he seemed to shrink and shrivel. For nobody who wanted his money had ever refused to listen to him respectfully, and in return for patronage he liked the innocent pleasure of being treated as an equal.

"Well, well," he said dazedly. "Well, well!"

Laura's smile covered a paroxysm of sick dismay. She ought to have known how it would be. The whole plan was a mistake, and she had been aware of it, the moment she saw Ford getting out of the car with Hugo and Aggie. He had looked bleak and red and anxious, and he had a air of hurried purpose. He was like somebody coming on business, a piano tuner or an undertaker, not an interesting young *protégé*. And he had worn a dreadful hat which had lain about in the hall ever since, to remind her of his shortcomings. She could not think why somebody did not take it away. Perhaps the servants really thought that it belonged to a piano tuner. Everybody must know that he had come for some definite purpose and he had shown them all that it was not for Walter's money.

As if this was not already too much, Aggie, who was in a nasty temper, declared that they were to play 'Platitudes' and that Ford and Laura were to go out first.

"Oh no!" cried Laura. "Let's send Adrian and Corny."

"They can go after," said Aggie. "I've thought of such good ones for you and Mr. Usher."

"What?" asked Ford alarmed. "I can't. Is it something highbrow?"

"Not a bit. You go out and we choose a bromide for each of you, and then you come in and hold a conversation . . ."

"I can't hold conversations . . ."

"And you have to see which can say your bromide first."

"Come on," said Laura, with a black look at Aggie. "Let's get it over."

They went out into the hall and she began at once to scold him.

"You were perfectly impossible. You were very rude to him. And you came here especially to meet him."

"Did I?"

"You want to go to Yeshenku again, don't you? And you want the money to do it? Yet you won't even be civil to the man who might give it to you. I know he was tiresome. But you can't care terribly much for your work, if you put your personal vanity in front of it. What does it matter how you get the money as long as you get it?"

"But Laura. I won't get it. Your husband's friends can hardly be expected to finance me when they know . . ."

"Ssh!"

A servant came through the baize door and they had to change the subject.

Ford looked doubtfully round the hall, so different from the halls that he was used to, where the stairs hit his nose as soon as he came in at the front door. The beauty and grace of Syranwood astonished and depressed him, for he was not insensible to these things and had a correct, well-judging eye. But he had become resigned to doing without them, and was content now to divide his life between the Guthrie Institute and his mother's house at Hampstead.

"Is it because you don't want to give up all this?" he asked suddenly.

"Hush. We can't talk here. People keep coming through."

Syranwood had frightened him before. When he saw it first, from the path over Ullmer Ridge, it had frightened him so much that he had run away. He had thought that she could not possibly be ready to give up 'all this' for him and his poverty. And for that cowardice she had since reproached him bitterly. She had said that those three weeks of hard work in his mother's house had meant more to her than anything in her life since. She had complained of her great unhappiness. If it had not been for her reproaches, for that unspoken appeal, he would never have dared to come again. And he had not come to be made a fool of but to clear the matter up.

"If you've no use for me after all," he said, "I'll make peace with your talkative friend. But you must say what it is that you really want, and you won't."

"I want to help you."

"Why?"

Corny called them back into the drawing-room before Laura could explain why. A platitude was whispered to each in turn and they advanced to their chairs. Ford exclaimed loudly:

"I can be led but not driven!"

Too late the rules of the game were properly explained to him. As Hugo remarked, when told of it next morning, one shouldn't play parlour games with a wooden horse.

So Gibbie and Adrian were sent out. They did their best manfully, but they were not funny enough to rescue the evening, and the party broke up early. Corny felt that, on the whole, he had collected no conversational fodder for the coming week. There was nothing to report save, perhaps, a certain oddness in the behaviour of Hugo. Something was amiss there. Aggie was dissatisfied, for one thing, and it was upon Aggie that the temperature of the week-end depended. Hugo had been summoned to amuse her and all his brilliance, all his success, should have been laid at her feet. But he had not quite risen to the occasion, though he had made them all laugh at dinner. Without knowing it they were reacting to the overstrain which had been, hitherto, so carefully hidden. Hugo had no business to be so tired, and if he was going to show it, he had better not have come.

So thought Corny, as he saw them all off to bed. On principle he was the last to go, for he hated the idea of missing anything. He hovered in the hall, pouring out glasses of orangeade for the women, and watching them go upstairs. Had Hugo exerted himself they would not have been doing this before two o'clock in the morning. But soon they had all vanished save Bechstrader, whose gong was now resounding in the library as he told Adrian about literature. Corny thought that he had accounted for everybody, but in order to make sure he took a last turn round the garden.

The night was still beautifully warm, and the moon had grown smaller as it sailed far above the trees to the empty top of the sky. The laurestinus hedge now screened a silent kitchen wing, for the last plate had been washed and the scullions had gone creaking up to their attics. A late night smell had begun to rise from the garden, a smell of earth and the flowers of other years, and the night stocks were a little less heady. Corny trotted round the box-

edged paths, skirted the kitchen garden, and took a peep
into the yew parlour. A fragment of white on a rose bush
caught his attention. It was a piece of Honiton lace, torn
out of one of Geraldine's veils, and he smiled as he
examined it. So that was where Geraldine had been in the
half hour that he lost sight of her: sitting in the yew
parlour, probably with Philomena.

Round to the front of the house he went, to inspect the
dim, grey expanse of lawn and the swimming pool. His
glowing cigar-end bobbed and dipped round the edge of
the water. When he stood still he could hear, although
there was no wind, a faint rustle and whisper among the
leaves, as though some life was stirring there. Everything
else was immobile, static in the moonlight. And yet the
earth was rushing on through space.

He sighed.

He hated being alone, because his unshared thoughts
were all very melancholy. But he was obliged to conceal
that, for a life sentence of buffoonery had been passed
upon him. At school he had been popular because he was
considered to be funny, and it had been so ever since. He
did not know why because he never felt very funny, but
people continued to laugh when he said things. Had he
ever indulged in a personal extravagance, had he fallen in
love or got religion, they would have taken it as a monu-
mental joke. It hurt his feelings. Once, when taking a
world cruise with Aggie and some of her friends he had
dived into a shark-infested bay to rescue a drowning man,
and even this act of heroism had been received with ill-
suppressed mirth. The idea of Corny being eaten by a
shark had convulsed the whole party behind his back. He
knew it and believed that in the worst event they would
hardly have been able to keep straight faces. And though

they listened to him civilly when he recited poetry he had
never been able to communicate the thrill which certain
lines could give him. Always, when he began, did he hope
to electrify his hearers, and invariably he was crushed by
the limitations of his own voice. His one success had led
to his marriage. Arriving at a very mixed house party in
the company of Mrs. Worthington, known as the Racing
Widow, a *tête-à-tête* in the car had been forced on him and
he had at first found it difficult to sustain a sporting conversation. But a remark which she made about hounds
reminded him of a certain famous passage in *A Mid-
summer Night's Dream*, and he quoted it. Mrs. Worthington was deeply impressed, regretted that she read so
little, and asked the name of the author several times.
Corny was passionately grateful to her, and a marriage
ensued which was received by all his acquaintances as the
crowning jest of his career.

He came to a standstill and threw a small pebble into
the lake. It fell with a plop, and the widening rings
caught the moonlight as they spread across the water. In
a perfect circle they spread and spread until they kissed
the grass at his feet. Soon they were gone and the water
was as still and dark as before. Again the thought visited
him how the dark lake, and the solid downs, and the trees,
the fields, the village and the sleeping graves in the
churchyard were all being rushed through space at a speed
so inconceivable that it seemed like immobility. His body
went with them, but his soul stood still. He was not yet
entirely, like the dead in Ullmer Churchyard, a part of
time and space. The idea fell into his mind like the pebble
into the lake, and expanding emotions spread and spread
across his being. He quoted aloud:

Rolled round in earth's diurnal course,
With rocks and stones and trees.

But the words when spoken did not match the magnitude of the idea. His voice had been cold and prim. It had no echo. He tried again to achieve that noble resonance which should have filled the night.

"R-r-r-rolled r-r-r-r-round . . . Oh my God!"

13.   *The Good Man.*

A red cigar-end, like an errant firefly, was bobbing round the far side of the lake and he made after it hopefully, only to track down Gibbie, who was scarcely worth pursuit unless it might be for information about the book trade.

"Good-night, Gibbie!"

Gibbie growled a civil reply and hurried off into the house. He told himself that Corny was more like a black beetle than it was possible for any man to be—dark, shiny, hollow and ubiquitous. Nobody was safe with Corny in the house. He was the sort of person who might almost be found hiding under the bed.

Bechstrader's gong was still booming in the library, but in the drawing-room all the lamps had been turned out. Gibbie mixed himself a drink and stood for a moment at the garden door before going up. He heard the stable clock strike one, and thought:

"It doesn't feel as late as this."

His cigar prevented him from smelling the earth and

the ghosts of last year's flowers, which haunted the sleeping thickets. His trouble stood round him like a stiff tent, holding off the influence of the night and all possibility of quietude. He shook himself and finished his drink. It was time to go up. Sooner or later he would have to do it and perhaps she might be asleep.

She was not. He heard her calling as soon as he went into his dressing-room. For she had been waiting for him, lying alone in her big bed, and she wanted to re-open the whole, wretched business. But he could not face it. He had done his best for one day. Talk about it any more he could not. Any more discussion would only make him angry again. So he pretended not to hear her gentle summons.

"Gibbie!"

He wound up his watch and took out his studs.

"Gibbie!"

He sat down on the edge of his bed and began to do his accounts for the day, writing in a little note book all that he had spent, working backwards to the paper which he had bought that morning at Baker Street Station.

Tip to Porter at Basingstoke.   1/6

    ,, ,, ,, ,,   ,,   1/–

Railway fares . . .

"Gibbie!"

She would go on like that all night. He got up heavily and opened the door into her room.

"What is it, Philomena?"

"Why didn't you come in and say good-night to me?"

"I thought you might be asleep."

"Didn't you hear me calling?"

He said nothing to that, for a moment, and then, bidding her good-night, he turned back towards his room.

"No, Gibbie. Wait. I want to talk."

"Philomena . . . I can't talk any more . . . about it . . . to-night."

"I'm terribly unhappy."

"I don't see why you should be."

"I don't believe I can go."

"Go? Where?"

" . . . go with him . . . go away with him."

"Oh? So you mean to go away with him? I was wondering what your plans were."

His voice, in spite of every effort, sounded bitter, and Philomena looked startled.

"Are you . . . angry again?"

"You must give me time to get used to the idea."

"Probably you won't have to get used to it. Probably I shan't be able to go."

"What?"

"A lot of chance I have, tied hand and foot!"

"Who is tying you?"

"Oh, not you. It's nothing to do with you."

She did not mean to insult him. She was thinking of her practical difficulties which would remain however compliant Gibbie might be. But her words sounded contemptuous and to him they were a turning point. He felt a new, cool anger which was far more formidable than the first explosive recoil.

"I'm going to bed now," he announced.

"Do you realise that Ada has given notice?"

Gibbie clutched his head and stared at her.

"What on earth has that to do . . ."

She explained and he advised her sombrely to let Ada

rip. But that just showed how far he was from understanding.

"You've never understood me."

"No."

"And you've never really loved me."

"That's a good thing perhaps, if it's true."

"I'm nothing to you really."

She burst into sobs and said something inarticulate
about Julian Rivaz, a name which he could not bear to
hear in such a dispute.

"Philomena! Don't!"

"I think he was the only person you've ever come near
loving. If you'd cared for me half as much as you cared
for him, I should have been a happier woman. In your
heart you're always thinking of him and always missing
him, and always arguing things out with him. And as he
was killed when you were twenty you've stayed twenty
ever since. If you could only get back to that time, and
before, when you were at school, I believe you wouldn't
mind if I were dead. If you could wake up one morning
and find you'd dreamt it all, and that you'd never married
me and never had the children, you wouldn't feel the
faintest pang of regret. You play at being a good husband, and a good father, and a hard-working publisher,
but your heart isn't in it and you don't ever really believe
in it . . ."

Gibbie went into his dressing-room and shut the door
on her. It was impossible to argue, for there was so much
truth in what she had said. It was just like her to hurl it at
him after pretending to admire him for fifteen years. He
sat down on his bed and finished doing his accounts. The
routine of maturity, which he had so zealously imposed
upon himself, had almost become second nature. The

Good Man does accounts, takes out Life Policies, and knows where he stands, especially when he has incurred the responsibility of a wife and family. And Gibbie, who hated money, who yearned for the contemplative life, sat balancing his day's expenditure like a practical business man, unaware that very few business men would have worried so much about the halfpennies.

His heart was not in it, and his real life had been at a standstill for many years. Ever since the death of Julian he had been marking time, feverishly active, but stationary. He had lost all sense of going on, of development, so that at times it seemed as though Julian, crumbling in a French cemetery, was still more alive than he.

Philomena had been right. He had loved her and the children, with a conscientious and whole-hearted energy, but there was no emotion behind it so strong as that which carried him backward to Julian and the past. His boyhood had been too happy. It had been an Idyll, a romantic dream, but it had led him nowhere and he had awakened to a drab and uninspired daylight. Yet, when sentimentalists declared in his hearing that schooldays are the happiest, he had always protested, rather from conscience than from conviction.

His halfpennies balanced, he crept wearily into bed and turned out the light. And the image of Julian bore down upon him from the past, still radiant, still mocking. He saw Julian's face blaze for a moment against the tingling darkness, so real and so near that he was almost comforted. For this bright ghost still kept him company. He could evoke it in a moment. His memory at least had never failed him, and he never had to ask himself how Julian really looked. He had forgotten nothing.

Julian had been a very beautiful boy. At school his

beauty had been a recognised and somewhat ambiguous joke. Many people had worshipped him and he took it all as a matter of course. Another face swam up from the dusty corridors of time, a pale and long-nosed face, the studious features of poor Pickup, who had been accused of standing on a hassock in chapel in order to get a better view of Julian reading the lessons. And behind him blinked the enigmatic Hilliard, who talked in his sleep, and was once heard to mutter:

"Don't let's talk about Blenkinsup any more. Let's talk about Rivaz."

Julian, in the face of these ardours, had been cold, caustic and quenching. He was a disappointment, as the more sentimental of his followers very soon discovered. But once, when Gibbie saved a House match, he had made a demonstration. He put an arm round Gibbie's shoulders and they walked half the length of the playing field in that posture. Gibbie still felt a little faint when he thought of that blissful climax. Oh, but Philomena had been quite right!

Yet she could know nothing, no woman could ever know, the strength of those early passions. He had spoken of them sometimes and she had laughed. Or else she had been slightly resentful. She could never understand the idealism of such a relationship or the world in which it could exist; and when he tried to convey it to her, with its turbulence, crude energy, and cheerful grossness, she had always shrugged her shoulders and said that boys were disgusting little creatures, far more sentimental than girls and so incredibly coarse.

"Even if you weren't immoral yourselves," she complained, "you seem to have done nothing but make jokes about it. Everything you say only makes me more determined to send Martin to Bedales."

Women, thought Gibbie, as he creaked and turned in his bed, can never know anything about men, since their first care is to enslave those qualities which they cannot comprehend. They fill the world with shows and shadows and their tactics are those of the trident and the net. What chance has the bright armed gladiator against this ancient, Protean enemy? Had the Good Man ever triumphed in a battle with his wife? Was there written on the pages of history any Socratic argument which might have silenced Xantippe?

"Perhaps he beat her," thought Gibbie, hopefully.

But he feared not. The Good Man rules by moral force alone, and if he has not got any moral force he complains to nobody but his Creator.

Philomena, in her own bed on the other side of the door, listened to the creak of his springs and wondered why he did not go to sleep. She wished that she had not broken out in that way about Julian. It was silly. Perhaps Ada would stay until August to oblige. But it would not be easy to arrange and Geraldine had been so discouraging. *How will you manage?* She had thought that she was managing so cleverly. At dinner she had been quite sure of success. But now that she was faced with all the obstacles it hardly seemed worth while, especially since Gibbie was so restive. It had been a great pity to mention Julian, just then, and she would not have done it if she had not lost her temper. She had thought all those things for years, but she had never actually said them. They were a grievance, she knew that: they were all part of her contention that she had married the wrong man too young. But if Gibbie were now to begin upon a long course of asking himself whether he had ever really loved her, she had only herself to blame, for she had put the idea into his head. One should never say those things. It was like opening a door without knowing where it led. Perhaps she had better abandon the whole scheme before they got themselves into worse difficulties. It was very hard on her, and poor Hugo would be broken-hearted. She only hoped that the children would realise some day what sacrifices she had made for them, or conversely that they would never know, because the world, surely, was growing saner and their lives might be different. She did not know what to do about Ada. She wished she could get to sleep. Gibbie's springs creaked again and she turned on the reading lamp by her bed as she petulantly searched for an aspirin.

Gibbie saw the narrow crack of light under her door, and realised that she too was awake and restless. He tried to picture her thoughts in that amorphous thing which she called her mind, and he felt suddenly a great longing to go to her, to lose himself, to hide from his bitter meditations. She could offer him the refuge of her woman's world. For real life, the male life which he had lived as a boy becomes with manhood too vast and bleak a thing. Humanity cannot survive without some subterfuge, some shelter from the winds that scourge it. If women were like men, he reflected, if they were not enervating and consoling, the whole race would be liable to perish from too much spiritual exposure. Only the epicene require candour between the sexes. That is why the Elizabethans, and indeed all the poets of the more virile ages of the world, were so much taken up by the idea of woman's falseness, her 'jestings and protestings, crossed words and oaths.' Really they liked false women. They needed them. They could not have endured anything else. They wanted

L

some respite from the intolerable burden of their manhood.

Yet it was her falseness which kept him from her. Their conversation before dinner came back to him and he grew certain that she had set a trap for him. She thought him a fool. *It's nothing to do with you.* She did not even trouble to hide her contempt for him. His resentment stood firm against her and in the flood of doubt and misery which was sweeping him away, he began to cling to that resentment, to brace himself against its stability. He resisted the impulse to go to her, and presently he turned on his own light, meaning to read himself to sleep. But he had not got further than three pages when a terrific bumping and thumping broke upon his ear. An extraordinary noise was going on somewhere in the house. At first he thought it was a slight earthquake, but the sound came nearer, as if someone was throwing something violently downstairs. Philomena was tapping at his door. She put her head in.

"Gibbie? Are you awake? What is that noise?"

He sat up in bed and suggested that it was the servants.

"Do you realise the time? It's nearly three o'clock. Somebody is throwing something downstairs. I believe it's a burglar."

"No burglar would make a noise like that."

"Oh Gibbie! Do go and see."

"You always think it's a burglar and it never is."

A still louder crash was too much for his curiosity. He climbed out of bed and put on his dressing gown.

"I'll just look out on the landing and see if everything is all right," he said.

Philomena came to the door of her bedroom and stood there listening while he hurried down towards the bumping.

14. *Night and Day.*

A lady, dressed for a journey even to her gloves, was kicking a very large dressing case down the shallow polished stairs. At his exclamation she turned round and glared up at him. It was Aggie.

"What am I doing?" she echoed. "What do I look as if I'm doing? I'm getting out of this house."

"But . . ."

"And I'm dragging my own box downstairs because nobody answers the bell. I've rung it twenty or thirty times. Either it's out of order or else my maid is drunk. I had to pack the thing myself."

"But Aggie . . ."

"Don't mop and mow like that, Gibbie. Carry it down for me."

"But Aggie, there's no train."

"No. I don't suppose there is. I must have a car."

"Everybody is asleep."

"Then they must wake up."

"But Aggie, what's the matter? Why do you want to hurry off in the middle of the night?"

Aggie told him furiously that Syranwood was intolerable. She could not stay there an instant longer. Her bed was like a sack of potatoes and faced north, whereas anybody who cared about her must know that she could only sleep facing east. She thought that she had got hernia trying to push it round. The bell was a mile off, by the door, so that if she had had a heart attack in the middle of the night she would have had to die in her bed. She shouldn't wonder if she was going to have another baby, and it was very bad for her to be upset. So she was going.

At this point the staircase, which had been but dimly lighted, sprang into a yellow glare, for somebody overhead had turned on the chandelier in the hall. Softly padding feet were heard and presently Lady Geraldine appeared, wrapped in the same red shawl which she had worn at the bathing pool, and wearing on her head an antique mob cap, nodding with rose-coloured ribbons. She looked infinitely older and more wizened than she had seemed by daylight.

"What is the matter with you, Aggie?" she asked severely.

Aggie explained and when she got to her probable condition, Geraldine said:

"Fiddle."

Aggie began to cry.

"You can go if you like," said Geraldine. "But I won't have my servants roused. You must carry your own bag into Basingstoke."

"It's not a bag," sobbed Aggie.

She began a tirade in which her own health, the mattresses of Syranwood and Laura's morals were the main themes. Also she said that it was very unkind of Geraldine to ask all the boors and popinjays in London to meet her.

"They seem to think they've come here for a rest cure."

Geraldine laughed.

"Take her bag up to her room for her, Gibbie."

"It's not a bag . . ."

"And come with me, Aggie. I'll give you a *cachet fièvre*."

"I've had a whole boxful of *cachets fièvres*."

"Then I'd better give you an emetic, I should think. Come along."

After a little dosing, Aggie consented to go back to her own room, though she said, before they parted:

"I shall never feel quite the same towards you again, Geraldine. You've been very cruel . . ."

"Not at all. I sympathise . . ."

"No you don't. You said fiddle. It was unforgivable. . . ."

"Well, I'm sorry. But it is fiddle, and you know it."

"You don't know how unhappy I am. You've had such a different life, Geraldine."

"Indeed, it's not my fault. I asked that Jug man down here especially because I was told you liked him. I can't help it if he's a disappointment."

"You've had your life," persisted Aggie sulkily.

She took off her hat and gloves and threw them on the floor. While Geraldine picked them up and put them away she got into a pair of lace pyjamas.

"Decorative but scratchy," commented Geraldine, looking at them. "I should get into something more comfortable if I were you. It's half past three."

Her tone suggested that half past three was a final hour and Aggie began to cry again, sobbing out an incoherent story about such a touching man and a railway communication cord.

"He's probably spending the night in the cells, poor boy. How tragic life is, Geraldine."

"Aggie!"

Geraldine's voice was so peremptory that Aggie stopped crying.

"Yes?"

"Don't put up your umbrella before it rains. It's waste of time. Look in the glass."

"I'm hideous. I've been crying."

"No you're not. Crying never makes you hideous, or you wouldn't do it. Look in the glass. There's no need for all this panic."

Aggie turned round and looked at herself in the long glass of the wardrobe, a little cautiously at first, but with renewed composure.

"The light is very dim," she said doubtfully.

"You can look at yourself in the dressing-table glass if you like."

Aggie turned her fair head this way and that, stretched her long neck and smiled. All the admiration which had been poured out before her, for nearly thirty years, had given an uncanny rarity and glamour to her loveliness. She was not merely a beautiful woman. Philomena and Laura were that. She was a unique woman. There were plenty of Philomenas and Lauras. But there was only one Aggie. When people looked at her, when she looked at herself in the glass, it was this silvery aura of legend that they saw.

"But some day, you know," she said, growing pinched again. "Some day . . ."

"Not yet."

"I've always said that."

"Poor Aggie."

"If you say Poor Aggie again . . . I'll burn your house down."

Yet Geraldine, as she pattered off to her own room again, was really very sorry for poor Aggie. These first, dreadful premonitions were the worst. Nothing afterwards was quite so hard to bear. It must still be only in the middle of the night, when the ticking clocks become audible, that panic stretched out its icy paw and touched her. To-morrow, next week, some new enthusiasm would lend her wings and she would escape from time's pursuit. But not for ever. The terror would come back, the clocks would tick louder and the pauses in the night would seem longer. She would not grow old easily: she was too vain, too spoilt, had lived too long upon the lotus food of adulation. When the last time came she would meet it without fortitude; she would clutch and struggle and become a bore.

For Geraldine it had all been easier. As the wife of Otho she had acquired great practice in endurance and the stoicism of a slave. She had known from the first that the world is a hard place and with great skill she made the best of it. Her farewells to youth had been made with serenity and grace, unmarred by any impulsive returns. But they had not been made without suffering. Even now she could never make up her mind which had given her most pain, the first love or the last: the first when she had demanded so much or the last when she had expected so little.

Her room, which took up the whole of one wing, had windows on either side of it so that she could look out on to the lawn, the garden or the stable roofs. It was a vast place, smelling faintly of camphor, and filled with sofas and chairs covered with a bird's-eye chintz. At first sight there seemed to be no bed in it at all. Long ago there used to be a large four-poster, but when Otho died she banished it and put in a corner a small box ottoman, very hard, narrow and uncomfortable but blatantly single, as though she could not enough assert her right to sleep alone for the rest of her life. Over the mantelpiece hung a large portrait group of Otho, herself, and the Rivaz collection, painted in a manner of an eighteenth-century conversation piece. It had been done about the time that she used to lie awake listening to the clocks, but there was nothing in her portrait to indicate this. Her Titian hair was flung up from her forehead into an elaborately waved confusion which ended in a coil very far down on the back of her neck. In the approved manner of the day she presented the torso. She was presenting it to Otho who, for his part, was strenuously pointing out a fine copper beech upon the north side of the lawn. Clinging to her skirts was that infant Dominick, begotten in the swamps of Africa, whose Rivaz bull neck made him so creditable an olive branch. Mathilde, also with a bull neck, leant affectionately upon her father's arm, and completed the foreground section of the group. The swarthy Charles, the Celtic Lionel and the golden Julian were kept busy with a pony in the rear, while Laura and Beata, red-haired like their mother, gambolled with a puppy.

There were a great many other pictures: pastel portraits of all the children, and water-colour sketches of Lough Ashe, Geraldine's old home, done by her twin sister, Helena. And there was a small Benozzo Gozzoli, a Martyrdom of St. Stephen, which Otho had given her after Dominick was born.

Beside the ottoman couch, on a small table, a spirit lamp was burning. She had just lighted it when poor Aggie began bumping about on the stairs. It was her habit to make tea several times during the night. Even in youth she had been but a light sleeper, and now, in old age, she scarcely shut her eyes. The long hours spent alone among her pictures and chintz sofas would have been rather tedious if it had not been for these cups of tea. She seldom lay down on the bed, but would wander round the room with a rug, perching, now in one chair, now in another, like an old bird on a bough. She would doze off for a few minutes and then drink more tea until the first grey light began to struggle with the flame of her candle and she could reasonably call it morning. Then, putting on another cap and a slightly thicker shawl, she would sit down to her writing table and begin letters to her children, to Lionel in China, to Mathilde in Rome, to Dominick in Egypt, and sometimes, absently, to 'My darling Julian' or 'My dearest Charles' before she remembered that they were in Heaven. An odd, roosting nocturnal life she led up there among her chairs and sofas.

When she had drunk her tea she went impatiently to one of the windows to see whether it was night or day, and found the world midway between the two. Darkness had vanished and the light was elfin. It came from nowhere and lay over the trees and stable roofs with a bluish pallor, destroying all colour and making everything look flat. On the roof immediately below her slept Solange and Marianne in a couple of camp beds. Their bodies were shapeless lumps under the tossed army blankets and their pillows looked dingy, but their tender faces, turned up to the sky, were like sleeping flowers. The grandmother gazed down at them for a long time, pondering. A deep sigh escaped her. For Marianne asleep made her think of a garden in the early morning, when no footstep has marked the cool sparkle of the grass. Her face was smooth and blank, with its innocent eyelids, and her young breast under the blanket rose and fell serenely. But her soul was not far away, for when a little wind, the first wind of dawn, blew down from the hills and fanned her hair, she stirred and smiled in her sleep. Turning on her back she flung out a hand as if to a friend who had kissed her.

"Soon, very soon now," sighed the old woman at the window. "Whose kisses will wake her to-morrow? The first time and the last time. What agony!"

Turning back to her room, where the candle flame still fought back the day, she settled to rest for a moment on a sofa by the writing-table. And she prayed that Marianne might not, at any rate, grow into a Laura or a Philomena, wasting the precious years. For the interval between the first time and the last is very short, and when it is gone it is gone for ever. These poor young women all talked too much. For Aggie she could find excuses, for Aggie was, as it were, making hay in the twilight. But for Philomena and Laura she had nothing but contempt. They wanted these Potts and Ushers, did they? Such names too! But why talk about it? Geraldine had never talked except perhaps a little at first when, in her inexperience, she had found it necessary to confide in Helena. She remembered going out in a boat to the summer-house on the island at Lough Ashe. It was a Sunday afternoon in September, soon after she had been married to Otho, and he had sent her on a visit home while he took a trip down the Amazon. She had enjoyed her freedom. The young cousin whom she had always wished to marry had been there and they used to row about on the lake. In those days they called it deceiving one's husband, and she had said to Helena afterwards:

"Do you think it was quite right . . . on a Sunday?"

Absurd question! But she was hardly older than Marianne. And how the church bells had chimed that Sunday evening, echoing over the water and the bracken and the birch trees of the Island! The bracken was turning and the rowan berries were red, and the bells rang: Ding-dong-right-wrong-ding-dong, and Helena said:

"As long as Otho doesn't find out."

For her own part she had always thought it wrong to

deceive anybody and she soon learnt to hold her tongue. She had given and taken a great deal of happiness when once she got past spring, that treacherous season of romantic expectation and unfulfilled promise when the sap rises in the trees and the heart is filled with melancholy and a sense of mis-spent youth. Summer is much better than spring, she thought drowsily, because it lasts longer. And Charles, pulling Julian in a little go-cart along the box-edged path of the kitchen garden, was going much faster than she could run even though they were only little boys and not yet in Heaven. She picked up her long skirts and ducked her head under the apple boughs as she ran after them, calling. And her father's steward, Michael M'Ginty, with his grey whiskers and pot hat, stepped out from a clump of hollyhocks and said solemnly:

"Her leddyship is in the big Markay."

Because there was a garden party for the Lord Lieutenant and a band was playing by the shores of Lough Ashe, and she must keep the children out of the way. And the cocks and hens were clucking and crowing, and the bells rang across the water: ding-dong-right-wrong——, so loudly that she woke and found that the grey dawn had turned to broad sunlight. Hens were clucking in the stable yard and the bells of Ullmer Church were ringing for an early Celebration to which, out of kindness for Mr. Comstock, she ought to go. But first she would drink some more tea. She blinked at the sunlight, innocently pleased to have slept so long.

15.   *The Wooden Horse.*

The two girls in the camp beds were stirring, awakened

by the church bells. Tossing off their blankets they climbed in at the staircase window and scampered up to get their bathing things. It was the moment in the whole day which they liked best, for they could generally count upon getting the pool to themselves.

"And after breakfast," said Solange, as she tied on her cap, "directly after breakfast, I must get after my poor father, or he'll slip away without giving me an opportunity. This is probably the turning point of my life. The field-marshal's baton is going to be taken out of the knapsack."

"How is your spot?" asked Marianne.

Solange looked carefully in the glass and said that perhaps it was not going to come to anything after all. And then she began to arrange her cap at a more becoming angle.

"You needn't bother to do that," Marianne told her. "There won't be anybody else in the pool."

"Oh, but there is. I saw somebody going out as we passed the staircase window."

"Oh, bother! Never mind. It's probably only Mr. Usher."

Quite so, thought Solange, as she gave a last tug to her cap. And since Mr. Usher was the most important person in the house one might as well look as decent as possible. Anyone but Marianne would have guessed as much from all this cap-tugging.

It was Ford Usher. He was swimming up and down with a sullen energy and even before breakfast he had the air of a man who is putting in time because his business is at a standstill. His furious strokes sent ripples up on to the grass and the rose petals which had fallen in the night went sailing about like little boats. But his greeting to the girls was amiable enough and he offered to blow up the rubber horse for them. It was a long time since any man staying in the house had been equal to that job.

"Won't it give you pneumonia?" asked Marianne, as she watched him puffing.

Ford shook his head, not wishing to waste breath on an answer.

"Could it give a person pneumonia?" asked Solange in surprise.

"Some doctor who was staying here once said it could," answered Marianne. "So grandmamma said that the under-gardener had better always do it."

Ford took the horse away from his lips in order that he might comment on this. But in time he caught the glint in Marianne's eye, and saw that no comment was needed. Instead, he said pleasantly:

"You're so sharp you'll cut yourself."

Solange and Marianne, who had not heard this witticism since they left the nursery, both dived to the bottom of the lake in mirthful embarrassment.

"Nice kids," thought Ford.

The head of Solange bobbed up again and she asked him abruptly if he knew Dr. Eckhardt of Freiburg.

"Why, yes," said Ford, in some surprise. "He came up to the Guthrie last time he was in London. Do you know him?"

"No. But I want to. I want to go and work under him. Because he's the best toxicologist in the world."

"He is," agreed Ford. "But what do you know about it?"

"Nothing," said Solange hastily.

She dived again, but Marianne, who was floating and listening, explained:

"She wants to be a toxicologist. But she's got no money."

Ford was even more surprised. Seeing her dressed in Marianne's clothes, and knowing her to be the daughter of Sir Adrian Upward, he had imagined that she must be rich. When she came up again he looked at her with greater interest.

"There are ways and means, you know," he said.

She had them all at her fingers' ends; the endowments, and the travelling scholarships, but they were for people with degrees. She had no certificates. For the most part she was self-taught, though she had seized on every opportunity that came her way. But without a degree in science she could not even work at the Guthrie Institute.

"I don't know about that," said Ford. "Come up one day and see my department, won't you? And we could talk it over, perhaps."

Solange grew pink with pleasure and hoped that Marianne would think it was all because she was going to get a close view of *culex pseudopictus*.

They sat for a long time on the steps of the diving scaffold. Ford was interested and amused, and as he talked he thought how nice it would be to get back to the Guthrie Institute. For so many weeks it had been spoilt for him, ever since Laura came in one day, and peered at his test tubes, he had worked with one eye on the door. Just as, long ago, he used to sit in his attic at Hampstead with his books in front of him and listen for her foot on the stairs. He would think of her, and then try not to think of her, until body and soul were locked together in a kind of desperate inertia, and his mind began to run upon violent remedies. He could not possibly go on like this. He must put an end to it. He had come to put an end to it, but whenever he tried to bring this necessity before her she would begin to talk about Bechstrader.

"We must be going," said Marianne, "because the people will be coming out of church, and they take the footpath past this pool to get to the village. It's the quickest way and everybody uses it for early Service. Grandmamma doesn't like us to be bathing too blatantly on Sunday."

Ford climbed reluctantly on to the bank and betook himself into the house. While he was shaving he watched, from his window, a long line of people climb over a stile and go streaming in single file on a path across an uncut hayfield. This communal life of the countryside was a new thing to him, for he had spent his time either in towns or in outlandish places where he encamped as a stranger. He had no roots anywhere. Presently he saw Lady Geraldine coming across the lawn and reflected that she had just been kneeling at the altar on a perfect equality with the yokels in the field. Yet they would touch their hats to her once they were out of church and both gestures were traditional rather than reasonable. And he felt that Laura's position was immensely strengthened by this mysterious background of tradition. He ought never to have come to Syranwood. He should have sought her out in London and forced the issue there, where they were upon common ground. In London he would have known what to say to her. But in this place she could always escape him by suddenly identifying herself with all those rooted conventions and assumptions of a rural community, and he would find himself, as he irritably put it, up against the whole bag of tricks.

That he had once prevailed was of little significance, for then she had been, not at Syranwood, but on Hampstead Heath. Otherwise it could never have happened, and it seemed to him sometimes as if her whole policy, in bringing him down to the country, was to make him understand this. If he were to stay much longer he would begin to doubt if it had happened at all. His memory of that final episode had always been curiously uncertain. No clear picture came back to him, only the knowledge that he had been quite mad about her and that his passion had ended in a delirium from which he had emerged unsatisfied. Perhaps they were both too young and inexperienced, and he had been in too much of a hurry, afraid that she might escape him. He remembered his desire and he supposed that he had got what he wanted, but the achievement had eluded him.

But she must know. She must remember. And with that memory in her mind she must either hate him or want him back. Unless, and this suspicion occasionally crossed his mind, she simply wanted to punish him for a humiliation which she had never forgiven. In which case he was playing into her hands, writhing and plunging like a hooked fish while she mocked him with gentle advice. A violent spasm of rage shook him. His hands trembled and he cut his chin, which bled profusely.

"I can't even shave in this damned place," he thought. "In monsoons, yes. I'm O.K. in a monsoon. Take more than a monsoon to start me hacking myself about. But here! I shall cut my throat next if I'm not careful. Now I've made a mess of the towel. Oh well, serve 'em right."

When he had staunched the cut and changed his collar he went back to his post of observation by the window. Laura was on the lawn now, talking to Mrs. Comstock, the Rector's wife. They carried Prayer Books in their hands and their faces were devoutly pensive. He could hardly believe his eyes. Though he was himself an agnostic, he had a puzzled respect for believers, especially if they were women. She had been taking the Sacrament, and only the God to whom she knelt could know what to make of it. But perhaps she was not as wicked as she seemed. Perhaps she did not mean to be so cruel. Even if she loved him as much as she said she did, there might still be some excuse for her ambiguities. For, after all, he was asking a great deal. She would have to give up 'all this' for him and his £500 a year. Her courage might well fail her, as his did when he seriously thought about it. £500 a year was probably not enough, and he would not have blamed her for saying so. But that was the one thing which she could never be induced to say.

Presently she looked up and caught sight of him at his window. And her smile, as she waved to him, was friendliness itself. He could not keep away from her. He went down meekly to join her and they strolled about the garden, stopping to look at the withered, untidy mass that had been night stocks the evening before. His pain and bewilderment made his face look a little more wooden than usual, but only his mother would have noticed it.

Laura still held her Prayer Book, but he averted his eyes from it, as if it was a talisman which she was using against him. And it was. For he could not ask her if she remembered Hampstead Heath while she brandished it in his face. So he listened in dumb rebellion while she talked about the little old chapel on the downs which was to be restored with the money collected for the Ullmer War Memorial, and of the windows to Julian and Charles which her mother was giving, and how she would like to show him the designs. She was very gentle, and very much wrapped up, for the moment, in her family. All

M

through the languors of a fully choral Celebration she had
been pondering upon their mournful case and she wanted
to make him understand that it was as hard for her as it
was for him.

"We'll go up to the chapel this afternoon," she said.
"It's a lovely walk."

Ford jerked his head despairingly and said that a lovely
walk would be of no use to him.

"Ford! You're not making it easy . . ."

"I didn't come down here to go walks. I came to talk
to you. I must know what you want to do."

"Dear Ford, I've told you. I can't do what you want."

"Why not?"

She looked down regretfully at her Prayer Book.

"Because of Alec," she murmured.

"You don't love him."

"He's my husband."

Ford picked a rose and began savagely to tear the petals
off. The gesture annoyed her and she took it away from
him, saying:

"Don't."

"What do you mean? He's your husband. If you mean
the vows you made in church, well, you've broken them
already. You promised to love him and you don't. You
did it against your will. You told me so yourself. Even
church people don't call that a marriage. Is it religion
that's worrying you?"

With a Prayer Book in her hand she could easily have
said that it was. But it was not true. The discipline of her
church had never troubled her and she always felt that
God understood if nobody else did.

"No," she said. "It's something deeper than that."

"There's always one thing that I want to say to you,"

pursued Ford, looking anywhere but at the Prayer Book, "but I don't know how to say it. You'll be angry. It's this. Doesn't it make any difference that you . . . that you belonged to me first?"

"Don't, Ford. Don't speak of that."

"But I must. It makes all the difference. You oughtn't to have married him. You ought to have married me. And now it's all cleared up between us you can set it right. You can leave him and come to me and I'll marry you as soon as you're free. He'll divorce you, I suppose? Only there is this. We'd have to live on £500 a year. Is it that that you can't face? Do you think £500 a year enough?"

She did not answer because they had reached the flagged path under the house and she could see Corny's head bobbing behind the curtain of a first-floor room. Probably there were others watching them. And she thought that Corny might have heard the last sentence about £500 a year. With a small pressure on Ford's arm she enjoined caution.

"I suppose," she said, speaking to Corny's curtain, "that £500 wouldn't be enough to go to Yeshenku again. How soon do you want to go?"

"As soon as possible," said Ford, with a scowl up at the window. "We're held up till we can get more specimens."

"Because of the zygotes you can't trace? But where ought they to be, Ford? I mean, where did you expect to find them?"

"In the midgut," said Ford.

"Of the mosquito?"

"Naturally," said Ford. "If it was our own midguts we wouldn't have to go and look for them in Yeshenku."

Corny, sure that this conversation might be openly

overheard, poked his head out of the window and wished them a good-morning. He said that Aggie had a temperature.

"In the walls of the stomach," particularised Ford.

"But you find sporonts in the salivary glands?"

"Never in a mosquito we've infected ourselves."

"Very odd. But they must pass it on somehow. Perhaps it comes out in a second generation. In their eggs or something."

"Oh, that's impossible . . ." began Ford. "At least . . . it's so unlikely that we've never considered it."

"But why shouldn't it?"

He stood still and pondered.

"Because it never happens with any form of the malaria parasite. Anophelines . . ."

"But this isn't a malaria parasite. You said that in many ways its history differs . . ."

"I know. And that's why we haven't sufficiently . . . have you got a telephone?"

It seemed as if she was never going to get him away from the house again.

"I'd like to get on to Macdonald, my assistant at the Guthrie. We dissected some specimens yesterday and he mayn't have thrown away the carcasses. It's just possible. It's worth looking. He'll be there. He lives at the Guthrie."

"Telephone after breakfast," suggested Laura.

"But I ought to get on to him at once. He may throw away those carcasses."

"And if he hasn't?"

"Then I must take the first train back . . ."

As soon as he had finished his business here, he was going to say. He looked quickly and questioningly at

Laura, and saw that she was biting her lip. His mind came back, refreshed, to the business in hand. He must settle it or he would never get back to his zygotes. And he walked her briskly away from the house to the bottom of the garden.

"It will be breakfast in five minutes," he said, "and you haven't told me what you are going to do."

"But I have told you, Ford. I can't come with you. It's impossible."

"Because I'm too poor?"

"No. Not that. I'd willingly share poverty with you. But I've married Alec. I oughtn't to have, but it's done. And I'm bound to . . . to give him value for his money."

Ford gave a short laugh.

"That's good! You give him value for his money. What do you give him, I'd like to know? He looks half starved. Value! He has to work twenty hours a day for you, and a lot of fun he must get in the other four!"

"All successful barristers overwork . . ."

"You think you give him value? You call yourself a good wife? When you go about complaining that you're not happy and you oughtn't to have married him? What kind of a wife do you call yourself? You're worse than a kept woman. You steal everything. You take everything and give nothing."

"And when I did . . . when I did . . . you threw it back in my face."

"But I can tell you this. It's not good enough for me."

"You shouldn't have let me go that first time. It was all your fault."

"Now I've got my answer and I know where I am. You just want to keep me hanging round. It's not good enough. You ask me down here . . ."

"To meet Walter Bechstrader . . ."

"And then you come at me with a Prayer Book and a lot of hysterical nonsense about loyalty and friendship being all that matters . . ."

"So they are."

"You're not loyal to him. You're not loyal to me. He keeps you on velvet, and kills himself to do it, and what do you give him? A privilege that you won't give to me because you say it's not worth anything. If it's worth so little why does he have to pay so much for it? If it's worth such a lot, you're lying when you tell me that I have the best you can give. You're cheating both of us."

"Because I've been cheated," said Laura in a low voice.

"You?"

She did not know how to explain, or tell him that he was being unfair, and that she really had more desire to do right than he supposed. She had principles but they never seemed to help her. She knew, only too clearly, what she ought to be, but she could never make up her mind what she ought to do. It had been a mistake to marry Alec. As his wife she could never be what she ought. But her conscience rose up against any attempt to right that mistake.

"It's quite true," she thought bitterly. "I'm not a good wife to him. I'll try to do better."

But how? Well, to begin with, she would dismiss Ford.

"Who's been cheating you?" he was asking.

"Nobody has. But you see, Ford, I'm not, as you say, a good wife to Alec, because I can't be. Because he doesn't call out the . . . the strength in me that I might have had. But I could have been a good wife to you."

"Could you? Then . . ."

"Once. But not now. Don't you see? That's the point. I've changed. I've gone down hill. I think we've both changed. You're harder and more selfish and more worldly than you used to be. You don't really want the risk of going off with me. And if you lost your post at the Guthrie through it, I think you'd hate me. You want me so much that you've worked yourself up into thinking you'd be equal to it, but very soon you'll be glad that you escaped. You don't really want me for a wife now. If I had consented to become your mistress again, without leaving Alec, you would have been perfectly happy. We could once have given something better to each other. When we were younger, and had more faith. But not now, after our lives have grown apart for so long. I had so much courage then, and I haven't got it now. The same thing which made me go to work for your mother might have strengthened me to make our marriage a success, in spite of our being poor, and divided by great differences of temperament. But anything I tried to do for you now would be a sham. It would only end in disaster. I do love you, but not as I did once, and we can't put back the clock. I think it would be best if we gave each other up, absolutely and for ever. You must go back to your work and try to remember that if you had married me you might never have gone to Yeshenku."

"Yes I should," said Ford obstinately. "I'd have married you. And I'd have gone there somehow or other. You'd have backed me up. Then you would. We'd have done it all."

"Oh Ford . . . Ford . . ."

"If you hadn't married him."

"If you hadn't turned back, that time you came for me. Oh Ford . . . why did you? You weren't brave enough."

It was just like her, he reflected, to fix the ultimate blame on to him. And then he was overwhelmed by the knowledge that he was losing her.

"I can't, Laura. I can't go. I was wrong to be so angry. I love you. I can't live without you. If you won't come with me, can't you, couldn't you . . ."

"No, Ford, no!"

"But if you love me . . ."

"It wouldn't be right," said Laura, through her tears. "We must do what we think is right. You'd better go away at once."

"I wonder you don't tell me I ought to stay and make friends with Bechstrader."

"You certainly ought. But that's asking rather much, I suppose."

"A very good stalking horse . . . your Mister Bechstrader . . ."

"Don't be so cruel."

He could not be just to her. He was suffering too much. And when they got close to the house he turned on his heel and went indoors.

Quite a lot of people had come down and were waiting about for some impulse to go into breakfast. Corny was in the garden, picking off dead heads, a thing he always assiduously did in the country. He knew exactly where Geraldine kept her scissors and gardening gloves, and he had appropriated both so that Hugo, also intent upon doing the right thing in the country, was obliged either to stand and watch him or tear his fingers upon the thorns. Laura lingered beside them to ask if anyone had heard

queer noises in the night. They had and Corny knew
what it was all about. He had been looking out of his
door when Geraldine brought Aggie upstairs again.
And he gave them an account which alarmed Hugo, who
was once more alertly on duty and braced by a night
spent in solitude if not in sleep. Aggie must never be
allowed to leave the house without having that play read
to her, and if she had departed in the middle of the
night he would only have had himself to blame. He must
exert himself and atone for yesterday's shortcomings.

Laura laughed and said that Aggie seldom stayed out a
full week-end nowadays. She went upstairs to take off
her hat, for she was not one of those who can fling down
their headgear in the hall without looking in the glass.
That Titian hair of hers took a good deal of time and she
had begun to grow it again.

Before going downstairs to breakfast she looked into
Alec's room with some idea of beginning immediately to
be a better wife. She found him still dozing, for he had
brought down a lot of work and had sat up half the night
over it. His early tea was already cold. Laura perched on
the bottom of his bed and told him to wake up, whereat
he thrust a yellow and wizened face over the sheets to
blink at her, and yawned tremendously, showing all the
beautiful gold fillings in his back teeth. In some surprise
he said that she was up very early.

"I've been to church," she said.

She looked down at her Prayer Book and at Ford's
rose, which she still held in her hand.

"Um, yes."

He poured himself out a cup of tea and sipped it.
Laura had been to church. That meant that his house
would very soon be rid of microgametes and macroga-

metes. Ford would vanish from their lives. He would be dismissed, after a certain amount of melancholy discussion. Laura always went to church at the penultimate stage of these affairs. She was a good woman. Alec was quite sure about that. A good woman but a silly one. Many of his friends had wives who were quite as silly and not good at all. It was silly of her to ask the fella to meet Bechstrader when the fella was in love with her. He stirred his tepid brew and nodded.

Laura suggested ringing for more and hotter tea. It was the sort of thing that a good wife should do.

"Oh it'll do," he said. "It's my own fault if it's cold. I did wake up when they brought it in, but I went to sleep again."

She put the rose and Prayer Book on the counterpane and felt the teapot.

"Shall we play a little golf to-day?" she suggested.

Very long ago Alec had told her that golf bored him unless she came too. And so it did, when first they were married. He looked surprised and mumbled something about a foursome that Gibbie had arranged.

"Oh. I see."

It was uphill work, being a better wife. She picked up her belongings and prepared to go.

"Is that a George Wode?" asked Alec, looking at the rose.

"No. I think it's a Mabel Jupp."

She did not quite know what to do with it, for it was still fresh and deserved cherishing, even though Ford had torn off some of its petals. But when she got back to her room she put it in the waste-paper basket. And then, sinking on her knees beside her bed, she buried her face in the quilt.

16. *A Quiet Sunday.*

Hugo, at breakfast, was very brisk and very determined
not to let the grass grow under his feet. He had made a
vow to read his play to Aggie before lunch time, and he
began at once to clear the ground. He must find out
where everybody was going to be that morning in order
to manœuvre Aggie into some other place. Laura, it
appeared, would be going to church again and so would
Lady Geraldine and Philomena. Corny was also to be
taken, because it was encouraging for Mr. Comstock to
see a man or two in the Syranwood pew. Gibbie, Alec
and Adrian were to play golf. At least there had been some
talk of it the night before.

"And Bechstrader?" asked Hugo, thinking that he did
not want an obbligato accompaniment on the gong.

"He'd better come to church," said Laura. "My
mother likes to have the pew quite full."

"But don't you want a foursome?"

Gibbie, to whom this was said, looked rather blue.
And Hugo, remembering with a shiver the menace which
hung over both their heads, hastened to reassure him.

"Oh, I can't come. I've got to read a play to Aggie.
But what about Usher? I was wondering if he'd like to
borrow my clubs. Where is he, by the way? Has he had
breakfast?"

"He's telephoning," said Laura.

"But he was telephoning ten minutes ago. He's
taking his time."

"He's ringing up the Guthrie Institute."

When they got out into the hall again Ford was still
telephoning in the butler's pantry. The door was open

and his voice rang harshly through the hall. It seemed that he had got hold of his assistant, for he was saying:

"No. I mean the carcasses we dissected yesterday. Yes, I know. I want you to look at the ovaries . . . All right. Ring me up when you have. It was just an idea. Somebody . . . it came into my head this morning. . . yes . . . well, ring me up."

Ford came out of the pantry and Hugo asked if he would like to play golf.

"With you?" asked Ford in surprise.

"No. I'm afraid I can't. But Alec wants to make up a foursome."

Ford explained that he must wait in the house all the morning in case a call came through from the Guthrie Institute. Meanwhile he proposed to go into the library and play for himself the records of five quartettes that he had found there. No power on earth should make him play golf with Alec.

"Then that's all right," thought Hugo. "I'll take Aggie into the drawing-room."

Having forgotten the girls he thought that he had accounted for everybody. So he sat in the hall, to make sure of catching Aggie when she came downstairs, and began to do the crossword puzzle in a Sunday paper. Everybody would be sure to pass through the hall sooner or later, and in this way he would be able to pass the time of day with each of them in turn and regain such good graces as he had lost the night before.

"A word in four letters, beginning with S, and meaning third thoughts," he said to Adrian, who was the first to appear.

"I don't degrade myself," replied Adrian sombrely. "I've always stood out against those horrible things.

What is everybody going to do?"

"You're going to play golf."

"Am I? You don't want the whole of that paper to yourself, do you? Give me some of it. I want to see what they say about Wrench."

As Adrian read the obituary comments he rustled the sheets and clicked his tongue.

"Nobody ever began to understand him," he complained. "As one of his few personal friends I can't but feel . . ."

"Could it be stet?" murmured Hugo.

"Of course, in the most vital period of his life, when he was living in that lighthouse, one didn't know him."

"I did," said Hugo.

"You did? Really! I never knew that. What sort of impression did he make on you? Was he writing then? Poetry?"

"I believe so," said Hugo. And added privily: "So was I."

He must have been writing poetry because his wash-hand-stand drawer was full of it. But he could not remember a word of it. Nor could he remember what sort of impression Wrench had made. But he recalled the lighthouse cottage, and the tamarisks blown flat by sea breezes, and the scratch of sand on the oilcloth of the floor. The rocks going up to the cottage had been covered with a queer low-growing fleshy plant that smelt sour when it was crushed. Perhaps he had written poetry about that. The Other Life flashed past him and was gone, as he thought of the tamarisks and the sand and the salt in the air. It was like being in a train that shot for a moment out of a tunnel into sunlight and then back into darkness. The glimpse was too short. He could not be sure of anything, only that there had been light and space and the sea tossing. *If you put your ear to the shell you'll hear the sea.* Once when he was a little boy he had a shell that he used to take to bed with him. He could shut his eyes and listen to it. Now his memory was like a shell. If he held it close, close to his ear, he could catch faint echoes. He was nothing now but a man listening to a shell . . .

Adrian's voice sounded pleasant and grieved in the resounding emptiness of the hall. He was taking the opportunity of saying all that he had been unable to say the evening before, at dinner. Indeed, he said it better, for he had had time to think it over and put it into shape. His full estimate of the loss to literature went booming gently out into the garden and up the curve of the stairs. So that Solange, running lightly down, caught echoes of it before she came into sight.

"One feels one must go," Adrian was saying.

"East Prussia is a long way off," Hugo pointed out. "Would you get there in time?"

"I doubt it," said Adrian quickly. "I doubt it. That's the difficulty. I doubt if it's possible."

Solange suddenly put her head over the banisters and said:

"Oh, I think it is. If you start to-night, or very early to morrow morning. There's a Continental Bradshaw in the library. I'll look out the trains for you if you like."

Adrian started and blenched. He had not meant to commit himself to more than a pious hope of being able to stand beside Paul Wrench's grave. The journey would be tiresome and expensive. If he had known that Solange was within hearing he would have been less definite. An expressed intention was quite enough for the world in general and would cost much less than a railway ticket. Many people would be sure to believe that he had, actually, gone. But not Solange. Not his family. They would know exactly whether he had been or not.

"The funeral is on Wednesday," she told them. "The paper says so. I'll go and look up your trains."

She skipped into the library and found the Continental Bradshaw. Ford helped her to find the place.

After a suspicious glance at Hugo, Adrian grew calmer. He doubted whether his discomfiture had been observed. The young man was in a brown study. His crossword puzzle had slipped to the floor and he looked as if he was listening to something.

"What are you going to do this morning?" asked Adrian, changing the subject.

Hugo ought to have spread the news that he was going to read his play to Aggie. But he had forgotten that. He was thinking that he had made enough money to live on for the rest of his life, and there was really no reason why he should not go and live in a coastguard's cottage and write poetry? Except that he would hate to live in a coastguard's cottage. The poetry, not the cottage, was the important part of it, and he could write that just as well in the Grosvenor Hotel, if he wrote it at all. What sort of poetry? he asked himself. And why did the memory of a tossed row of tamarisks make him want to write it? What magic lay in the scratch of sand on oil-cloth? Because they belonged to the Other Life. The significance was not to be sought in the subject, but in himself.

"It's gone," he thought gloomily. "It's gone."

Still, he could write poetry if he liked. It was not very difficult. He believed that he could be a successful poet as well as a successful playwright, if it were not for those moments when the train, flashing out of the tunnel, upset him. In the one career he had already gone as far as anyone could go, and perhaps it was time that he should try his powers in some other direction. He turned round and said to Adrian:

"There's something that I very much want you to do for me, if it isn't too much to ask. The fact is . . . I wish you'd read some things . . . some . . . some of my poems . . . and give me your candid opinion . . ."

Adrian was charmed. He liked encouraging young poets better than anything in the world.

Now I shall have to hurry up and write them, thought Hugo. He was for it now. It was strange how quickly these decisions were made. Now he was a poet, and his publicity was already prancing ahead of him.

"But my dear young friend, I didn't know that you . . . er . . ." Adrian made passes in the air, "perpetrated . . . these excesses . . ."

Hugo did not explain that he had perpetrated nothing yet. When the first idea for a new play occurred to him, it was always his habit to outline it to a sympathetic friend, before ever he set pen to paper. He fell into his new rôle delightfully. He blushed and was diffident and seemed to forget that he had three plays running at once in West-End theatres. Between them they had dug the foundation of his new career before Solange put her head out of the library.

"Is your passport visa'd for Germany?" she asked Adrian.

Adrian said hopefully that he did not think it was.

"Well then, you'll have to get it done to-morrow morning. You can catch the later boat train. I'll show you . . ."

She vanished into the library again and Adrian thought it best to escape before she could show him. Muttering something about the golf links he hurried upstairs. The church bells of Ullmer burst into a clamorous peal for matins, and a car for the golfers came purring up to the front door.

Presently Lady Geraldine came downstairs, putting on her gloves. Pausing in the hall, she slowly took them off and went up again. Alec came out of the drawing-room and went into the library. Adrian scuttled downstairs and got quickly into the car. Lady Geraldine reappeared unexpectedly from the baize service door carrying some string and brown paper. She went out on to the terrace and called for Marianne. Laura and Philomena came down the stairs and asked if there was to be a collection. Walter Bechstrader came out of the library and fell over one of the dogs. Corny rushed upstairs in a great hurry. Gibbie came and stood in the hall and tapped the barometer. The car in the drive turned off its engine. Adrian, tired of waiting, got out of it. The bells changed to another chime.

From the library came the strains of a gramophone. Ford and Solange were putting on quartettes. Lady Geraldine came in from the garden to remark, without much perturbation, that every one was going to be late for church. At last Alec, Adrian and Gibbie, all meeting by chance in the hall, were induced to go out and get into the car, but they waited for a little while before they realised that nobody else was playing golf. The engine started again, and the noise of it died away down the drive. The bells changed to a single note.

The telephone rang. Ford dashed out of the library. But it was a message for Bechstrader and he went back to

N

Solange. Somebody from the village appeared uncertainly at the front door with a note, and all the dogs began to bark at her, until Marianne, bounding across the hall, put a stop to it. Hugo could hear her courteously reassuring the flurried lady and promising to give the note to her grandmother. The competence and kindness of her manner puzzled him, for he had got it written down that she was shy. He must find out more about her, and some time, when everything was quieter, he would think with pleasure of her singing last night, and how it had made him feel like a ship at anchor. Instead of reading his play to Aggie, it would have been nice perhaps to go for a little walk with Marianne on the downs, and pick cowslips. 'Marianne,' he would say, 'do you still like me?' And she would be very much surprised. But in spite of her scarlet embarrassment he would succeed in learning that she did still like him very much.

The church bells had stopped. Three minutes later the party for matins had all assembled in the hall and were stepping casually out into the sunshine. The sound of their voices, their light laughter, Corny's chirp, and Bechstrader's gong, died away as the noise of the car had died away. Hugo was at last left to his crossword puzzle and the dawdling peace of a Sunday morning. On every side of him open doors and empty rooms gave promise of repose.

Flinging aside his paper, he went and stood at the garden door, looking out into a light that was already hot and blue. It was going to be another scorching day. The hills were hazy and far away, and the sun struck up from the stone terrace at his feet. But it was still morning. The noon siesta had not begun and though the world was tranquil it was wide awake. Bees swam heavily about among the flowers and from behind the brick wall, where the fruit would soon hang ripening, came cheerful farmyard cluckings. A sense of warmth, pleasure and well-being streamed up from the earth to Hugo, who was cold, sick and overtasked. He shut his eyes against the sunlight and felt the heat and dazzle beat against his eyelids. But it would not penetrate to the chilly core of his body. Something inside him remained frozen, even when he opened his eyes again, and saw Aggie coming downstairs.

17. *Beggar My Neighbour.*

After the first six pages all his doubts fell away from him. There was nothing the matter with his play. As he read he could see it staged down to the very pattern of those important divan cushions. He had achieved another winner. Aggie's face gaped at him, and he could see in it a whole dim theatreful of women, all Aggies in their own imagination, all of them dressed like Aggie, scented like Aggie and talking like Aggie. They craned up from the stalls, they leant down from the gallery, an entire audience responding as one woman to his infinitely skilful manipulations. Never had he managed his crescendo better, so nicely placed his climax or smashed the crockery at a more telling moment. He could do it every time. His light-hearted, tragic Irma was turning, before his eyes, into that Common Denominator which should identify her with every woman in the theatre. Aggie on the drawing-room sofa was all the audience he ever wanted, because she was thinking what he meant her to think, and feeling what he meant her to feel.

At the end of the first act she told him that it was terribly good, but that she feared it was going to be terribly tragic.

"Shall I go on?"

"Oh do."

The crockery-smashing in the second act was not quite as effective as it ought to be, because these things should be seen rather than described. But it held her. She had left off smoking and was leaning forward with her mouth slightly open. He went on without a pause to the third act.

Marianne came in just when Irma was telling her great sacrificial lie. For the sake of the man she loved, this magnificent adumbration of Aggie was tarnishing a reputation which had remained spotless, in spite of all appearances, for an hour and a half. Aggie was nearly weeping. She knew she would have done just the same thing herself. In two more minutes she would have wept, had it not been for the incursion of Marianne.

Hugo became aware, as he read, of a slight movement behind the screen which hid the door. Something was being done there, and he could see, reflected in one of the long glasses, a tawny head and sunburnt neck bent over a bowl of roses. She made so little noise that Aggie never knew she was there at all. But the fact of her presence remained. Hugo, ever acutely sensitive to Them, knew that he now had two listeners: that he was reading to a composite animal and not merely to Aggie. Instinctively he raised his voice a little. As he turned the page he had time to think what a pity it was that Marianne should have missed so much of the crescendo. But that could not be helped, so he must forget it. If she had heard the beginning she would not be fidgeting with those flowers.

She would be staring at him with her mouth open. He lifted up his voice and proclaimed:

"You've no right to ask me . . ."

What was she doing behind that screen? Was she standing enthralled, or was she still fussing about with those roses? He wished that she would either come in or go out.

"Is he your lover?"

Aggie's eyes were like blue saucers. She guessed that the Noble Lie was coming.

"Does it matter so terribly?"

Did it matter so terribly? Of course it did. It had to, or there would never have been any third act.

"Do you want me to say that he is, Gerry? Do you *want* me to? I believe you . . . do."

"I want the truth."

"Oh, no, darling. You've never wanted that."

"I've no proof . . . no evidence . . . if you tell me he isn't I suppose I must . . ."

"Must what, Gerry?"

"Put up with it!"

"Put up? Oh my God. Oh . . . wait a minute . . . I shall be all right . . . in a minute . . . have you . . . have you got a match?"

"Irma . . . for God's sake . . ."

"In a minute, darling. Just give me time."

"Time to invent something?"

"Yes. Yes. It wouldn't take a minute to tell the truth, would it? Only we don't want the truth, do we, Gerry? It's so ugly, isn't it? Have you got a match?"

"No."

"It doesn't matter. Your mother thinks I smoke too much."

"Irma!"

"All right. Don't look so terrified. You're not going to have to . . . to put up with it."

"Then you . . ."

"Oh yes, Gerry. I'm his mistress."

"I knew it!"

"Did you, darling?"

"Don't call me that."

"Sorry."

"You swear it's true?"

"Need I? When you knew it? But I'll say it again if you like. I'm his mistress."

But Marianne, behind the screen, would not know that this was a noble lie, because she had not heard the beginning. All the poignancy of it would be lost on her. In spite of himself he gave way to the temptation to drop her a hint. He broke off in order to explain:

"Each time she says it she looks at him in an awestruck way, like a person repeating a spell and not quite expecting it to work. They both know that it isn't true, and yet, it works. You see?"

Aggie blinked and came out of her coma. She said that she saw.

"Where was I? Oh yes. How-long-has-this-been-going-on?"

At all costs he must not allow himself to read it in that tone of voice, as if it was absolute muck, dead as carrion. Marianne did not matter.

"I'll—divorce—you . . ."

He shifted his chair a little so that he could see round the screen. But she was not there any more. She had finished her job with the roses and gone away. Perhaps she had even missed the little bit of explanation that had been aimed at her.

And Aggie's eyes were no longer like saucers. It had been a bad moment for an interruption. She was glancing furtively at the clock and then she sketched a barely stifled yawn. This sight was the last straw. Yawns are catching and Hugo had repressed his for just twenty-four hours too long. Like a tidal wave his fate overtook him. The words that he would have uttered were strangled in his throat. He had to give up, put down his manuscript, and keep Aggie waiting until the paroxysm was over. He yawned and yawned and yawned and yawned.

"I'm terribly sorry," he said at last.

"Go on," said Aggie coldly.

He asked where he had got to, though he knew quite well. But he had to cover his embarrassment at beginning again.

"I don't know," said Aggie. "Somebody was telephoning."

That had not happened since the beginning of the act. He found the place and was ill advised enough to apologise.

"I hope this doesn't bore you frightfully."

"Oh no," said Aggie, with straying eyes.

"I'll divorce you . . ."

"You'd got past there, I think," said Aggie.

He finished the play, but she never went into a coma again. Towards the end he felt that she only listened to one word in three. She fidgeted, she yawned, she lighted cigarettes, she looked out of the window to grimace at Corny who had just come back from church. When it was over she said that it was too marvellous and that she couldn't tell him what she felt about it. But he knew that her report to the others would be damning. And the news would spread like wildfire through the house.

"My dear, Hugo's play is dull."

"It's not true."

"The first two acts just possible, but it goes to pieces completely after that."

"Darling, I can't tell you how bad it is."

"Corny says it won't run a week."

"Well, that kind of success doesn't last for ever, does it?"

"I always did think he was dreadfully over-rated . . ."

". . . and conceited . . ."

". . . and after all, rather, rather . . ."

Nor was Syranwood gossip the end of it. On the contrary it was only the beginning. On Monday they would all go back to London and spread the tale. Hugo's play is dull. Hugo himself is getting to be a bit of a bore. He was asked down to Syranwood to meet Aggie and she wasn't amused. He won't be asked again.

It was all Marianne's fault. He could almost believe that she had done it on purpose.

The golfers had not returned, but voices in the garden and on the stairs told him that the church people were back. It was so nearly time for another meal that every one was waiting about. Through the window he could see Aggie strolling on the terrace with Corny. It had begun.

Not daring to join them he crossed the hall and slipped out of the front door. A blast of chilly air came up at him from the unwarmed turf. All that side of the house was still in shadow though the noonday sun was creeping up the drive. He shivered and strode on across the lawn, past the swimming pool, to the edge of the Syranwood shrubberies where trees and bushes could hide him and his humiliation in their sombre thickets.

After all, he was trying to remind himself, a failure here and there, an occasional rebuff, might do him a great deal of good in the long run. Unbroken success becomes monotonous, and he had to remember that cheerfulness in adversity was part of his public character. In the past it had indeed been so. He had enjoyed surmounting difficulties and his bouts of ill luck had been periods of great activity and stimulation. And he thought of his second play which ran for half a week. It had been so absolute a disaster that his agent had asked him if he really meant to write any more. And he had had great difficulty in getting anyone to look at the new one which came to him as he stood in the wings, that night, hearing a third act go to pieces and an audience get out of hand. His gallant cast, white-lipped and sweating, stood beside him, waiting for their entrances and avoiding his eye. Stoically they braced themselves to see it through, and he could do nothing to help them. He wanted to rush out himself upon the stage, to ring down the curtain, to do anything rather than see his helpless friends upon the rack. Their courage in the face of this common misfortune exalted him far beyond any petty sense of personal failure. He found himself excited, dominant, with all his powers awake and urgent. He had lived that moment intensely and in the weeks after, while he was writing his third, and best, play, he had been extraordinarily happy.

But he was not happy now. He felt no thrill, no renewed call to action, only a stifling melancholy. He had conquered Them and he was more afraid of Them than ever.

There was only one thing to be done. He must take

them by surprise. He must do something quite, quite new. For he had got to the top of the ladder too soon, and to stay there, perching nervously for the rest of his life, would look absurd.

He would become a poet. He would write those poems of which he had already spoken to Adrian. He would listen to the music in the shell. He would hold up the train as it flashed out of the tunnel. He would dive down into the Other Life. In that existence, experienced momentarily inside his soul, all things hung together: they had some collective relationship. That was why horses against the skyline, or a memory of a tossed tamarisk hedge, would start an echo. They threw shadows which were not their own.

"Hugo's poetry is marvellous."

"It's much better than his plays."

"Extraordinary career that fellow has had."

But poets were generally such dank people. They hid in the country or in basements and at luncheon parties they always looked a little unkempt. Or else they were very old and distinguished and got buried in Westminster Abbey. He did not want to be buried just yet. He wanted Aggie to think well of him. And he wanted to get out of the tunnel. Either one or the other, and, if possible, both.

For surely once, *once*, he had lived in the light: among the tamarisks, beside the chicken run, before he was born, perhaps. There had been a time when everything seen and heard, a dog barking in the street, the pattern of his aunt's tea cups, the whole texture of life, had been full of mystery and excitement. Nothing had escaped him; every experience, however small, had fed his flame, had become part and parcel of his dream. He knew that it had

been so once, just as he knew that the illumination had
failed him. It had happened. To make it happen again
might be, simply, a question of effort. Perhaps he had not
tried quite hard enough. But he needed help. He wanted
a call from somewhere, outside himself. He would have
prayed for it, had he known of any God disposed to
listen. And he was very nearly praying, for, as he walked
this way and that among the trees and bushes, a prayer,
long forgotten, came back into his mind.

"Renew . . ." he muttered. " . . . renew," (because
it had been there once) . . . "Renew Thy spirit within
me."

18. *Mrs. Dulcibel Usher.*

At the end of the shrubbery path there was a stile. It
led into the churchyard where a few villagers were paying
their Sunday morning visit to the graves and filling the
jam crocks with fresh bunches of stock and sweet-
william. Also a party of tourists were straying about
among the tombstones. He could see their car waiting for
them at the corner by the church. One of them had
climbed up on to the stile and was peering inquisitively
through the trees. She seemed to be in half a mind to
climb over and when Hugo drew near she asked him if
this path was private. Immediately afterwards she
exclaimed:

"Hugo Pott?"

He looked up at her and realised that it was Mrs.
Usher. The sight of her galvanised him at once. He felt
his geniality tap turn on with the explosive gush which so

often succeeds a slight air lock. For she was an old friend. He seized her hand and wrung it warmly, crying:

"Why! Look who's here!"

At least she did not know what a mess he was making of things. To her he must still be a miracle. He saw her frog-like mouth expand into a broad and happy smile. This was a wonderful piece of luck for her. She had only meant to trespass a very little way into the Syranwood grounds and pick up enough to make a short paragraph. Before ever she climbed up on the stile the opening lines were written in her head:

. . . I've been spending the week-end on the Downs near Syranwood, which is, of course, the famous Rivaz place. And oh, my dears, the beauty of it! The old church . . .

But here was something much more valuable than any old church—Hugo Pott, whom she claimed to have discovered, whose ghost still hovered benignly over her Sunday evening salons, was good for a couple of paragraphs any day.

. . . I ran over to Syranwood which is of course . . . and had a chat with Hugo Pott who tells me . . .

With his notorious good nature she could get quite a lot out of him. Casting an eye at her friends in the churchyard, who were rival journalists, she nipped lightly over the stile into the sacred ground.

"Be an angel and tell me who else is staying here?" she began eagerly. "And what are they all doing? Is there anybody . . .?"

Hugo understood and shook his head. As far as he knew there were no blacklegs in the party, and no gossip would be sold on Monday. But before giving her any information he hesitated a little. It was rather a return to the chicken run, this alliance with a breadwinner. If he was really going to make a habit of these week-ends he ought to rid himself of people like Mrs. Usher. But then Syranwood had not been so very kind to him, and he was not so sure of ever coming back. And a few crumbs of news, the outline of a 'story' might make all the difference to her, poor old thing. Even if the seven orphans were all grown up there were probably grandchildren. Here she was, still tapping away on her typewriter, sending her grandchildren to St. Paul's, or possibly Westminster, while peeresses with sons at Eton and bridge debts to pay snatched more bread out of her mouth every year. It was a shame.

"Well. There's Aggie."

"Lady Aggie? Ooh! Wait a minute while I get my stylo. Yes?"

"I've just been reading my new play to her," he added carelessly.

"Oh, have you? I'd just love to hear anything you can tell me about that."

It was curious how she licked her lips, a trait he had forgotten. And he had never seen her in country clothes before, only in an amber satin tea gown with an imitation jade string. Now she wore tweeds of a pepper and salt colour. She looked like some immense amphibian which might have come out of the pool to hop about secretively among the trees, something as unlike the inhabitants of Syranwood as a toad is unlike a man. As he told her about his new play and she took it all down with her stylo, his thoughts plunged down through the successive levels of his rise to glory, past Caroline Chappell and Antibes, the Acorn, club dinners, Joey and Squirrel, till it fetched up among the rancid cakes in Mrs. Usher's studio. They had discussed Aggie a good deal then, he remembered.

"And Cornelius Cooke . . ."

" 'Corny' Cooke . . . yes?"

"And Adrian Upward . . ."

She was not interested. Adrian was not news.

"And Lady Geraldine's daughter, Lady Le Fanu . . ."

"Dear little Laura!"

"What?"

"How is she? I've not seen her for ages."

"She's very well," said Hugo in surprise.

He thought that Laura must have grown a good deal since Mrs. Usher last saw her.

"Though I'm sure I don't know why I call her little. But then I always think of her as so, so young. And my goodness! What a handful! She lived with me for some time, you know."

"Lived with you?" cried Hugo, trying to conceal his astonishment. "No, I didn't know."

"I daresay you wouldn't. It was a madcap scheme she had. She wanted me to teach her how to run a house. Very sensible really. But I oughtn't to have taken it on with all my work. I couldn't look after her properly and felt she was running wild."

"I see. And that's how Ford got to know her."

"Oh, no," said Mrs. Usher quickly. "I don't think so. She never saw much of Ford. He . . . he wasn't at home at the time. In fact I don't think they ever met."

"Oh?"

Hugo opened his mouth to mention Ford's presence at Syranwood. But he shut it again, paused for reflection, and asked:

"Have you seen much of her since?"

"No," said Mrs. Usher. "As a matter of fact, I think she was very hurt that I wouldn't keep her. But do tell me, Hugo, who else is here? You see, to be quite frank, I'm very keen to get a good paragraph. You see, Mélisande, who does our Gossip Page, Lady Symes she is, has got phlebitis and I'm carrying on for her, and I believe I've got just the ghost of a chance of pinching her job. Of course, you know, Hugo, times aren't what they were, when I began. I mean you have to be in the know so much. With these society women wanting to earn money, the likes of me are getting crowded out, because of course they get all the chances, and all the plums go to them. But if only I could put it over that I can do as well as she can! Of course your play and how you've been reading it to Lady Agneta, that's the goods. But is there nothing else?"

Goodnaturedly he told her that Aggie was rehearsing *'Tis Pity*, that Adrian was going to Paul Wrench's funeral in East Prussia, and that Walter Bechstrader had been to church.

"Walter Bechstrader? Not really! Well, the luck some people have! I'd give anything, anything in the world for an introduction to that man. You wouldn't guess how often I've tried to wangle it. I know he could help Ford."

"And then there's Marianne," said Hugo hastily. "A granddaughter. Oh well. She's nobody much. Just a girl."

"Marianne Rivaz?"

"No. I don't think so. I . . . I've forgotten . . ."

He had never known. And it came to him with quite a shock that he should have lived so long without knowing Marianne's surname.

"She doesn't count," he insisted.

"Girls make quite good news nowadays," said Mrs. Usher. "I mean débutantes and the younger set and all that. Is there anything about her you could give me?"

"No, nothing . . . nothing . . ."

"Does she belong to this Monkey Club? Is she likely to be engaged or anything like that?"

"No. Oh, no. Certainly not. She does the flowers."

He would tell her anything she wanted to know about Aggie, but he was not going to betray Marianne.

"I see. What sort of flowers do they have? Do they have them on the dinner table, I mean? Do they have coloured glass? And a cloth? Or is the table polished? You see, *entre camarades*, it would be such a score if I could make it sound as if I'd lunched there. Where does this path go?"

"This goes to the swimming pool."

"The swimming pool. Oh, I must peep at that. I've heard of it. I could suggest that I'd bathed in it, couldn't I?"

"You could," agreed Hugo, with a faint quiver of mirth. "But be careful, for I think there's somebody there already."

They paused and heard a loud splash behind the bushes.

"Oh. Then I'll be very careful."

She peered over the top of an arbutus and asked in a raucous whisper which of them it was.

"Bechstrader," said Hugo, also peering.

"O . . . O . . . Oh!"

She craned up eagerly to look at the man who could do so much for Ford. But all they could see of Bechstrader was a brisk grey head travelling up and down the pool at a great rate.

"You couldn't . . . you couldn't possibly introduce me, Hugo?"

Hugo shook his head.

"It wouldn't do," he told her.

"Oh, Hugo. You're so kind. You're too kind to say no. To an old friend. You're always so good to your old friends. It would mean so much to me. I can't tell you how grateful I should be. It isn't for myself. It's for Ford. I know he might do something for Ford if he was approached in the right way."

"But it's lunch time. Really I ought to . . ."

"Just let us stroll along that path till we come out by the pool. We can stand and watch him for a little while and then you can do it quite naturally. I'll do the rest. You needn't say who I am. You can go in to your lunch when you've done it. Hugo! You won't refuse me."

"Mrs. Usher . . . it won't do."

"Since when have I become Mrs. Usher to you, Hugo?"

"My dear Dulcie . . . I can't. I ought to have told you before. I think he and Ford have met already."

"You think?" She stared at him. "Oh no. Impossible. I'm sure he hasn't. Ford would have told me. Why do you think that? Has he ever said anything about Ford?"

Hugo looked up at the trees and down at the path and wondered why such things should be fated to happen to him.

"Oh dear," he said dolefully. "I am in a mess! You see, as a matter of fact, he's staying here . . ."

"Yes. I know. You told me . . ."

"I don't mean Bechstrader. I mean . . . Ford . . ."

"Ford? Ford? What? Not here?"

"Yes. At Syranwood for the week-end. But I didn't like to mention it because evidently you didn't know. I was so taken aback that I thought . . . oh well, it doesn't matter what I thought . . . I behaved like an idiot . . ."

"Not here? Not in the house?"

"I thought perhaps he didn't want to tell you until he'd got something fixed up with Bechstrader, with *Bech-strader*, you know, in case you might be disappointed . . ."

Hugo looked at her hopefully, rather pleased at having hit upon so plausible a story. But she hardly seemed to be listening. Her greenish face was slowly turning purple and she was gasping for breath. And in her eyes there was such an expression of despair that he felt ashamed and lowered his own while he repeated:

"He came, I believe, expressly to meet Bechstrader."

There was a long pause, during which they heard a succession of splashes from the pool. Bechstrader was doing high dives. But she made no movement in that direction.

Hugo stood miserably, first on one foot and then on the other, fearing that anything he said might make matters worse, and a little afraid, also, lest she might be going to have some sort of seizure. But after a few seconds she pulled herself together. Sitting down heavily on a small rustic bench by the path she got breath enough to mutter hoarsely:

"No. He didn't."

"Didn't?"

"Didn't come to meet Bechstrader. You know he didn't."

"I don't know what else . . ."

"Yes, you do. He came for her . . . that woman . ."

"Oh dear, oh dear," thought Hugo.

But aloud he said, in assumed bewilderment:

"What woman? What do you mean?"

"Oh yes, you know whom I mean. Don't pretend you don't."

"Really and truly, Dulcie, I don't know a thing. I hardly know Ford. I knew he was brought here to meet Bechstrader."

She began to rock herself backwards and forwards on the seat.

"Oh, I knew there was something. I guessed there was some woman. He's been upset for months. I knew he wasn't always at the Guthrie when he said he was. I thought it was some little slut of a student working in his laboratories. I was ready for that. But this . . . this . ."

"Don't you think you're letting your imagination run away with you?"

"Oh no. No, I don't. Why should he lie to me? He said he was going to Sussex this week-end. He never lied to me before."

This was not true. Ford had lied to her for years, and she to him. They both knew it. He resented her domination and outwitted her when she tried to spy on him. She was his mother, but he did not love her any more. A remorseful gratitude was all that bound him to her now. But they both pretended this was not so.

"After all I've done for him!"

She had not been able to make him happy. She had never won his love. She was driven back into a recital of everything else that she had done.

"You couldn't know, Hugo. Nobody could ever

know. The years of overwork. It was such a cruel
struggle to get him educated. I gave him a better
education than the others. He was the youngest. I
adored him. He was born after my husband died. I had
nobody to turn to. I had to do it all myself. I've worked
all night, often. I've tramped round London . . .
people say I drink, and it's no wonder if I do. I've been so
tired. I kept him for years when he wasn't earning
anything. The others all began earning as soon as they'd
left school. But he was so brilliant. Everybody said so. I
was so proud of him. I believed in him. I always knew he
would make his way in the end. I backed him up through
everything. I sent him to Yeshenku. And now . . . just
when he's begun to make his way . . . now, to have this
awful business start again now. To see him ruined!
Yes . . . ruined . . ."

She began to cry, and Hugo's fatigued voice interrupted her, as he tried to think of consoling things to say.

"Oh, how can you say such things? Dulcie, how can
you? Why, he's marvellous! Everybody is talking about
him. He's been asked down here especially to meet
Walter Bechstrader . . ."

"She may give out that, I daresay. But if that's all there
is to it he'd have told me. It isn't that, and their being so
sly about it only makes it worse. It shows she's ashamed
of herself. You know as well as I do that he's come here
because of her. Oh God! I wish I'd died when he was
born. I nearly did. I wish I had."

Her tears, her obvious misery, upset Hugo. He could
not bear to see anyone so unhappy, and he sat down on
the bench beside her, patting her hands and murmuring
consolations. His head ached and he wanted his lunch,
but he put the thought of it out of his head.

"After all, you know, even if your suspicions are true, there's no harm done, is there? Nobody gets through life without affairs of some sort or another. She may attract him. I daresay she does. She's a very attractive person. But that won't hurt him. It'll probably do him good. Buck him up . . ."

"Oh no, it won't. He's got no time for that sort of thing. An affair with one of the girls at the Institute, yes! That's to be expected. But he hasn't the time or the money to take up with a woman like her. She'll waste his time. She'll exhaust him. She'll keep him dangling after her till he's fit for nothing but a lunatic asylum. She'll keep him from marrying some nice girl, who'd make a good home for him. I know. I've seen it before. She could always turn him round her little finger. She was always making eyes at him, from the moment she came into my house . . ."

"But . . ."

She had forgotten her easy lie of five minutes ago, and that Ford and Laura were not supposed to have met. But he did not remind her. He listened in silence.

"I might have known it. I might have known we should have trouble the minute I saw what type she was. I ought to have turned her out of the house right away without waiting. But I was working so hard. I was finishing a serial against time, and I did need help in the house. I couldn't afford a good servant . . . or of course I'd never . . . and after the last help I'd had, a French slut who stole my stockings, she seemed quite surprisingly capable and keen. So I trusted to luck in spite of Ford being in the house and her being so attractive. I hoped she'd think herself a cut above him. I hoped he'd be put off by her airs. She gave herself plenty, God knows. Not answering back, or anything like that, you know, and doing what she was told, but going about like a duchess in disguise. It was all I could do to keep my hands off her sometimes. I may be a vulgar old woman, but I was paying her twenty good pounds a year after all, and she seemed glad to get it."

"Paying? But did you know who . . ."

"No. Of course I didn't know who she was. What d'you suppose? She came to me, I tell you, with a false name and a lying tale about living in Ireland. Rivers she called herself. And why she did it, God only knows. I suppose they kept too strict an eye on her at home. I expect there was something behind it that we never found out. Of course I meant to send her packing the moment I could hear of anyone better. But when I did it was too late. I turned her out of the house. I parted them. But he's never forgiven me. I lost him. She took him away from me. He's never trusted me since."

"And if you'd known who she was?" asked Hugo curiously.

"I'd have acted very differently."

"Yes. But how?"

She could not tell him how, though she had been debating the point in her own mind ever since the day when she and Gertie had recognised Laura's photograph in a weekly paper. A great opportunity had been missed. That was clear. If she had acted differently she might have been spending this week-end at Syranwood herself instead of in a bungalow where all the cooking was done on an oil stove.

"But her people would never have allowed it," she pointed out.

"Allowed what?"

"Allowed them to marry. They were too young."

"But did they want to be married?"

"Why yes. Haven't I told you? He's never forgiven . . ."

"I mean, did Laura want to marry him, really?"

"I should hope so, considering the lengths she went with him."

"She really took him seriously?"

"And why not?" cried the mother bridling. "Oh yes. It was the real thing all right. I could see that in her face. I watched them coming in late one night, and I had her out of the house next morning before you could say knife. I asked no questions. But . . ."

But if she had known she would have asked a great many questions. And the Rivaz parents might have come to heel. They might even have insisted on the marriage, and in that case they would have been obliged to pay the piper. They and not she would have sent Ford to Yeshenku.

"The mistakes one makes," she sighed.

Hugo had left off patting her hands and looking sympathetic. He was frowning.

"She must have been very young," he said slowly.

"Eighteen or nineteen. And Ford not much older."

The age of Marianne, he thought.

"And you turned her out because you thought . . ."

"Oh! Now you're shocked, are you?"

He looked as though he was about to apologise for being shocked.

"It wasn't exactly a . . . a nice thing to do . . ." he mumbled.

"I had Ford to think of," began Mrs. Usher. "A mother . . ."

"I know. I know," agreed Hugo hurriedly. "I've never been a mother. I've no business to . . ."

He got up and went to look over the bushes at the pool. It was empty. Bechstrader had gone in to lunch.

"I really must go," he said.

But Mrs. Usher had risen too and was confronting him.

"Being a mother doesn't excuse everything," she said firmly. "I did wrong. I know that."

"I'm sure it was a horribly difficult position."

"I turned her out. I thought she was poor and had no friends. I left her to shift for herself. I'd have killed any woman who treated my own daughter like that. And I've often thought, since, when he turned against me: this is my punishment for doing wrong. I must bear it. People say I'm hard. But you've got to be hard when you're up against it as I've been all my life. I tell them that I could be damn soft-hearted on five thousand a year. But I was worse than hard to her. I was cruel. It's my cruelty I'm being punished for. And I thought I could bear it. I could have borne it. I could have stood losing him. But not this. Not seeing him making a fool of himself now, when it's too late. That's much too much. I must stop it. I must do something."

She began to walk hurriedly along the path towards the house, and Hugo pursued her, urging her to stop and think.

"You can't do anything now. This isn't the moment."

"Oh, don't worry me. I must see him. I must see her."

It was impossible to convince her that, this time, she could do nothing, and that the passions which she had thwarted once might now have passed beyond her control. Hugo argued and reasoned, but she merely continued her way along the path, buttoning and unbuttoning one of her gloves and muttering:

"Perhaps if I talked to her. She may still care for him. I'd humble myself, if that's what she wants."

"But not now. You can't just now. They're all having lunch."

"Are they? What time is it?"

"Nearly half past two. What about your friends? Aren't they still waiting for you in the churchyard?"

"I expect they've gone on to the Inn at Ullmer. We were going to have lunch there."

"Then hadn't you better . . ."

"No, I hadn't better. I've a right, I suppose, to call at a house where my own son is staying? Lady Geraldine may be an earl's daughter, but she can hardly show me the door."

"It's lunch time," persisted Hugo.

"Then she'd better give me some lunch. No. It's no use arguing. Where Ford is concerned you can't argue with me. If you don't want to be mixed up in it, you'd better go in first. I'll give you ten minutes and then I shall walk up to the front door and ask for him."

"Oh well . . ."

They were in sight of the house already, having emerged from the bushes on the far side of the lawn. But there were so many people standing about on the drive that even Mrs. Usher was daunted. Clearly they had all finished lunch and were waiting to see somebody off. A car was purring at the front door. Lady Geraldine and Aggie appeared in the portico. They were kissing one another on both cheeks. Hugo's heart sank with a thud.

"Is that somebody arriving?" asked Mrs. Usher.

"No. It's Aggie. Going away."

"What? Where is she? Oh, I see. In the fawn two-piece."

Aggie was going. There would be no more opportunities of pleasing her. Aggie was bored. All through lunch she had been telling them how dull his play was. She climbed petulantly into the car and was whirled off down the drive. He felt that everybody knew why she was going so soon, and now he would have to face them, hungry and out of spirits. If only he could snatch a meal first he would probably do it better.

"I don't see Ford anywhere," he commented. "What do you want me to do about it?"

"Aren't you going in?"

"They seem to have finished lunch."

He was edging away back into the bushes. And Mrs. Usher also felt that her courage was deserting her. She meant to get into the house, but would sooner have done it when fewer people were looking on. Later in the afternoon perhaps, when they had all gone away and she had reinforced herself with a large whisky and soda she might come back.

"I think," she said, "that I'd better join my friends at the inn after all. They'll be wondering what's happened to me and they might wait lunch. It's too late to ask for anything here. And I do feel that a little refreshment is indicated."

"Much better," agreed Hugo. "And, do you know, I think I'll come too. It's really too late to ask for lunch here. Do you mind if I come with you?"

She did not mind at all. She was pleased at the chance of showing him off to her friends.

"They're nice girls," she said as they set off again through the trees. "And they'll adore meeting you. It'll be the great thrill of their lives. As long as you don't mind lunching with a monstrous regiment of women."

"Not at all," said Hugo. "I do that everywhere."

And he tried to remember what it was that he had heard Adrian say about this quotation. He had an idea that there was a catch in it somewhere and had made a note never to use it until he had looked it up. Probably it came in Shakespeare.

The labour of living up to Syranwood did not grow lighter and it would be quite a rest to lunch at the Ullmer Arms with a few Joeys and Squirrels. Aggie might come and go, but they would be none the wiser. He could be sure of never boring them.

19. *Paradise Lost*

He hoped that nobody had caught sight of him, skirmishing about among the bushes. But, as usual, he had forgotten Marianne. She saw him and came to the conclusion that he was past praying for. He picked up women as a serge skirt picks up burrs. No sooner was Aggie out of the way than he must needs collect a new one. And when Solange, meaning to be kind, spoke in praise of him, she said nothing and looked glum.

"I shall go to see this play of his," said Solange.

She was in high spirits and inclined to think well of everybody. For she had discovered that it was quite possible to reach East Prussia before noon on Wednesday and Adrian's journey had been the main topic at lunch.

"It's just a sample of what I can do," she said. "I can

be very inconvenient unless I'm placated. Now he's got to get up at five and catch the six-thirty at Basingstoke."

"He won't. He'll manage to miss it."

"But wasn't your grandmother an angel, Marianne? She might almost have been one of us. She talked of nothing else at lunch and she's ordered a special breakfast for him. Do you think she guesses?"

"She may. She guesses most things."

They had gone up to Miss Wilson's room, but they were not practising their music. It was too hot. Ever since lunch the heat had been increasing in sudden jerks, like a car changing gear. Marianne sprawled on the battered sofa while Solange sat on the floor by the window sewing a button on to her shoe.

"I wouldn't mind being old, if I could be sure of being like your grandmother. She has such fun."

"Yes," said Marianne. "I've often thought that. Don't you think it would be a good plan if we could skip the next bit and jump straight into old age? I do."

"The next bit? What next bit?"

"The bit that comes after this. After we've left off being what we are now. We're all right now. We haven't made any frightful mistakes yet. But sooner or later we shall get into some muddle or other."

"I don't see why."

"Nor do I. But everybody I know has."

Solange did not agree. She thought that the next bit was going to be fun.

"I haven't done anything yet," she pointed out. "I've got to go to Freiburg, and be a toxicologist, and fall in love, and see the Grand Canyon, and have some babies (when I'm married I mean, not yet) and learn to play the recorder."

"You'll be busy," said Marianne. "I wonder if you'll do any of it."

"Why not? I'll do some of it, anyhow. What do you want to do?"

Marianne sighed and said:

"I don't know. It's too hot to think."

Solange looked round at her disapprovingly.

"What's the matter with you to-day, Marianne? Do you know, you remind me of an awful picture I once saw in a farm-house. One of those printed annual supplements, done, I should think, in the 'nineties. A pop-eyed girl in a fringe and a blue sash. And it said: ' *Standing with reluctant feet where the brook and river meet.*' "

"That's poetry," said Marianne suspiciously.

Solange laughed, and when she had finished laughing there was silence in the room. Both were aware that a slight chill had invaded their relationship. Those confidences yesterday had been a mistake. If Hugo had been a dancing partner Solange would have known what to say. She could have teased her friend about a May Week romance or shared with her the excitements of a first Commemoration Ball. But she winced and shied away from something inexplicable, some hint of profound gravity, which lay behind Marianne's ridiculous preoccupation. For her own part she had no intention of being bothered by such weighty problems until she had had her fling. They were a mistake and they spoiled enjoyment. She meant to have a lot of fun before she sat sighing and dreaming over anybody.

"You're getting sentimental," she said crisply.

Marianne did not deny it, because she did not want to argue.

"But what's the difference between emotion and

sentiment?" she asked after a pause.

"Well, a sentiment is a feeling that doesn't get you anywhere. I mean, it's sentimental to go to church and get very worked up and ecstatic and then come home and behave like a pig to your family."

"Um . . . yes . . ."

"And it's sentimental to . . . think too much about a man . . . unless you're going to marry him . . . or something."

By something Solange meant consummated passion and Marianne understood her perfectly well.

"But how can you help . . .?"

"Anybody can control their feelings if they try."

"Have you ever tried?"

"Well, once I had a rave on our elocution mistress at school. And she married and went to India. I thought my heart was broken. So I distempered our staircase and repainted the banisters bright red. It was a filthy job, but it cured me."

"I see."

Marianne lay for a moment on her back, staring at the ceiling. Then she leapt to her feet.

"I'm going to wash Tango," she said.

"I thought you hated washing dogs."

"I do."

"What nonsense! On a Sunday. Come and play tennis if you must do something energetic."

"No. I'm going to wash Tango."

The stable-yard was deserted, for all the men had gone off in their Sunday clothes to walk with their girls upon the downs. And Marianne rediscovered her equanimity in that tidy world of corn-bins, sluiced brick pavements, and polished leather. She even relished the tarry smell of the soap which she used for Tango. All the old-time noises of her childhood were around her; the jerk and squeal of the pump-handle, the clatter of her buckets on the stone floor, and the pigeons lazily coo-rooing on the roof. She was safe in the yard. She was shielded against the encroaching tide of the larger world, the future, which had begun to undermine the present. This place was complete and enclosed, a rectangle of plain stone buildings containing just what it needed for itself and nothing unnecessary. The pigeons never flew far away from their roof and the pale sky above it had no vagrant clouds. Only a little turret with a weather-cock stood up, breaking the long line of slates and pointing its four arms to wider horizons.

She put on a white overall and dragged Tango into an empty loose box. As she scrubbed him, and went clanking in and out with her buckets, she whistled the old tune that Bates, the coachman, used to whistle when he cleaned the harness:

> Have ye heard John James O'Hara
> Playing on his old trombone?
> Have ye heard John James O'Hara?
> Ain't he got a lovely tone?
> Old Sousa's band's all right . . .

"Oh dear!"
She sat back on her heels and pushed the tawny hair out of her hot face. She had a pain somewhere. But if Solange was right, then washing Tango ought to banish it.

> Have ye heard John James O'Hara
> With his tiddle-iddle-um-tum-tara . . .

Washing Tango was hard work and the buckets were heavy. But she wanted to work very hard and tire herself out so that to-night, when she went to bed on the roof, she would go to sleep at once. She did not want to lie awake as she had lain last night. Because in the daytime she could rule her thoughts, but at night she could not. Lying in bed, under the balmy canopy of the sky, she had let them stray down a forbidden road. And as her limbs grew relaxed and drowsy she had begun to dream of the impossible as if it could happen. For it was impossible that she should ever gather him into her arms and soothe him to sleep there, holding him safe, away from all these people. It could never happen. And very immodest too, she supposed, to think of such a thing. At least, anybody else would think it immodest. And she blushed deeply as she bent over her buckets and tried to think of herself telling Solange.

"I want to sleep with him."

Well, that was an awful thing to say. And not a bit true either. Because when people talked of sleeping with a person they meant something quite different, something that Marianne knew all about but never quite believed in. It happened to people, and some day it would happen to her, but not for ages, and when it did her grandmother had assured her that she would like it. Also she had been obliged, in the schoolroom, to read a great deal of poetry which hinted the same thing. But the hens and ducks and cows of the Ullmer Farmyards did not seem to like it much, and her earliest ideas on the subject had been gathered from them. Perhaps this was because they could not read. Anyhow the whole business was incredible. It had nothing to do with this pain that she could not banish, this longing to take him to her heart and, somehow, make him happy.

"To-morrow he will go away," she thought.

She took her bucket to the door and flung water out on to the bright stones. It glittered in the sunlight and rushed in a shining torrent towards the grating in the middle of the yard. Soon it was gone and the damp stones were drying. The little commotion, the splash and the clatter died down and she could hear the pigeons on the roof again. Leaning against the door-post she stood still for a moment in the sunlight, resting her tired back. And she felt a swift pang of envy for the stable men who could stay for ever at Syranwood, safe in this small solid world, listening to the pigeons, working all day amid the friendly companionship of the animals, keeping their domain so bare and clean, and standing sometimes like this, to rest, in the sunlight against a door-post. Very soon she would have to go away. She had only been sent there to be kept quiet, for Mathilde had thought the life of foreign legations too unsettling. At Syranwood she had grown up, under the care of her grandmother and a governess, had kept a Nature note-book, was confirmed in Ullmer church, and rode ponies which got larger as her legs grew longer. Now she was supposed to be all ready for the next bit. In the autumn they spoke of sending her to her mother in Rome.

Tango, smelling of soap, shot off to find a nice midden where he could roll, and Marianne went upstairs to change her overall. There was an empty Sunday feeling about the house, as if even time was giving itself a rest. Still whistling she pulled off her white shroud and sat down beside the window in her petticoat, while she got some of Tango's mud from behind her nails with an orange stick and a piece of cotton wool. When that was done she

P

whipped herself on to attack her Sunday reading. For a year, ever since Miss Fosdyke left, she had kept it up. She had promised. On Sunday she would sit down and read a Great Book for an hour and in this way she might hope to become, in a few years, really well-read. She did not enjoy it, but as she had promised she persisted. Miss Fosdyke had cried so much at leaving her that she felt bound to humour the poor thing. Last week she had finished *The Excursion* and now she thought that she would try *Paradise Lost*. She went over to the bookshelf and thought as she surveyed the smug façade of bindings:

"Oh dear! How I do hate poetry!"

Taking down Wordsworth she extracted the bus ticket which she used as a marker and transferred it to Milton. To lie down on her bed, as she would have liked to do, would be fatal. She had fallen asleep too often over *Sordello* to risk it. So she chose the hardest chair in the room, sat down upon it, and went to work with scrupulous and earnest attention. But the long strips of blank verse stood up like walls against her. They would yield no meaning. Her eye kept slipping off the page, although Miss Fosdyke had prophesied that in a year's time she would have conceived a passionate love of literature. She wished the miracle would hurry up.

In a small shelf at the head of her bed there were half a dozen books which had given her real pleasure. She had read them so often that she knew them by heart and wherever she opened them it was not like reading at all, but simply slipping off into another world where the very air was different. But not one of them would have passed Miss Fosdyke's censorship. They were not Great Books. They were not poetry.

After twenty minutes' hard labour she gave it up and

reached over to her own shelf. Without looking she pulled out the first volume that she touched, opened it, and read:

' . . . And how far a body can hear on the water such nights! I heard people talking at the ferry landing. I heard what they said, too, every word of it. One man said it was getting towards the long days and the short nights, now. T'other one said *this* warn't one of the short ones, he reckoned—and then they laughed, and he said it over again, and they laughed again: then they waked up another fellow and told him, and laughed, but he didn't laugh: he ripped out something brisk and said let him alone. The first fellow said he 'lowed to tell it to his old woman—she would think it was pretty good; but he said that warn't nothing to some things he had said in his time. I heard one man say it was nearly three o'clock, and he hoped daylight wouldn't wait more than about a week longer. After that, the talk got further and further away, and I couldn't make out the words any more, but I could hear the mumble; and now and then a laugh, too, but it seemed a long ways off . . .'

The green and white of her bedroom melted away. She was floating down an enormous river in a country which she had never seen but which she knew as well as she knew the Ullmer Downs. She was doing what she had always longed to do: floating on, and on, with the current, close down to the water on a raft, not high up on a noisy boat, floating all day and all night with no goal in front of her and no place where she ought to stop. She heard the lap of the water against her raft and saw the lights of a little town blink out from the shore a mile away. For it

was growing dark, and the river banks were long black lines under a dim sky. Only the water still had gleams of light in it somewhere, as if it had stored up lucence from the day. Between her and the shore it lay like a pale gleaming desert as the town swung past and was lost round a bend. She was happy. If only poetry could make her feel like that!

20. *The Invader.*

A knock on her door came from very far off and she took some seconds to answer it.

"If you please, Miss Marianne, Fletcher says there's a lady downstairs asking for Mr. Usher. She's in the drawing-room and we can't find anybody. Her ladyship's gone over to Brassing."

"Can't they find Mr. Usher?"

"No, Miss. Fletcher saw him in the garden with Miss Upward, about an hour ago, but he doesn't seem to be anywhere about. And Lady Le Fanu has gone over to Brassing too. The lady said she'd wait."

Marianne groaned and shut her book.

"Thank you. I'll come. Tell them to go on looking for Mr. Usher."

She knew that it was part of her business to entertain callers if Laura or her grandmother were out of the way. So she changed her shoes and stockings, pulled on a white pleated skirt, tucked her blouse in neatly, and pummelled her head severely with a brush. Remembering her nose, she rushed back to the glass to powder it, got to the door again, ran back to remove nearly all the powder, swung downstairs. Good drilling had cured her of some of her shyness. She knew what she had to do. She would walk this woman round and round and round the garden until somebody came.

But the drawing-room, with its open doors and windows, seemed, at the first glance, to be empty. She could not see anybody, though she was aware of a curious pause, a stillness in the long, shadowy room. Amid the airy spaces and motionless bowls of flowers some eye was watching her intently. She advanced a little way among the chairs and sofas and then came to a standstill, startled and confused, the smile of civility frozen on her face. A slight movement made her jump. In the darkest corner of the room, by the little table where the visitors' book was kept, somebody had turned a page. The book was quickly shut and a short, brown woman came into the light, saying in a voice that was odd and friendly:

"How do you do? Do you recognise me?"

Marianne did recognise her. It was the woman she had seen with Hugo before lunch.

"I . . ." she began confusedly. "I . . ."

But the woman had come closer to her and interrupted:

"Oh, I beg your pardon. I didn't see. I thought it was Laura."

"I'm so sorry they're out," said Marianne. "My grandmother will be very sorry. She . . ."

"I didn't come to see her," said the lady. "Or Laura either for that matter. So it doesn't matter. I want to see my son. Ford Usher. My name is Mrs. Usher."

"I think he's in the garden," said Marianne.

"So they tell me. But they don't seem to be able to find him."

"Perhaps he's gone for a walk."

"Perhaps."

"Could I . . . can we give him a message . . . or . . ."

"No. You can't give him a message."

The lady sat down with a very determined air and added:

"I'll wait. I suppose I may wait?"

"Oh yes," said Marianne. "I'm sure he'll be back quite soon. Wouldn't you . . . would you care to walk round the garden?"

"No thanks. I've walked quite enough to-day."

Marianne sat down too because that seemed to be the only thing to do. The lady looked so angry that it hardly seemed safe to talk to her. And it was very strange that she should speak of Laura by her Christian name. It looked like impertinence, and Marianne knew how to deal with that in a general way. But it might not be. It might be a form of shyness.

A long silence ensued during which the stranger examined her young hostess from head to heels most attentively, and then stared about the room. Presently she said:

"You're not out yet, are you?"

Marianne stared at her. What did the woman mean? Out?

"You haven't been presented?"

"No. Oh no," said Marianne, beginning to understand.

"When shall you come out?"

"Next spring, I believe."

"Really? You'll be presented then, I suppose?"

"I suppose so."

"How old are you?"

Marianne wanted to say thirty, but contented herself

with twenty-one. Mrs. Usher looked surprised and then suspicious.

"That's very old to come out."

"Is it?"

"Older than most girls. Are you looking forward to it?"

Marianne drew herself up and began to reply very coldly. But Mrs. Usher went on. She asked if Marianne had been to school, and if she meant to take up a career and if she did not think it splendid the way girls took up careers nowadays, and if most of her girl friends had taken up careers, and if she thought modern freedom was a good thing, and if she despised post-war young men, and if she was going to grow her hair, and whether her grandmother would give a dance in London for her next year.

At last Marianne could stand it no longer. Murmuring something about telling them to bring tea, she made her escape into the hall where she found Hugo loitering among the dogs.

"There's a most extraordinary person in the drawing-room," she told him. "I think she must be a reporter or something. But she says she is Ford Usher's mother."

"She's both," said Hugo. "And I'm afraid I brought her here. I had to. I met her in the village and she wants to see Ford. Did she ask you a lot of questions?"

"Yes. She was very rude. But Hugo . . ."

"I know . . . I know . . ."

He looked at her to see how much she also knew. But she was merely puzzled.

"I don't know what to do," she said.

"I'm afraid she won't go until she has seen Ford. So the thing to do is to get hold of him as soon as we can. I've been all over everywhere, and nobody has seen him apparently."

"I think he's gone for a walk with Solange. Must I go on talking to her till he comes?"

"I'm terribly sorry. I didn't tumble to it, till we were actually on the doorstep, that she was . . ."

He paused and looked nervously at the drawing-room door.

"But is she always so very queer?"

He shook his head.

"The fact is, I'm terribly afraid . . . you see I lunched with her . . ."

"I know."

"Did you? How did you know?"

"I saw you with her in the garden and you didn't come in to lunch, so I concluded you were lunching with her."

"Holmes, you're . . . wonderful!"

So at least one person had noticed his absence. They had not all taken it for granted that he should fade away as soon as Aggie has ceased to find him amusing. He could not keep himself from asking anxiously:

"I suppose it was all right?"

"What?"

"Your grandmother didn't mind my lunching with them? She didn't think it rude?"

"Oh no," Marianne assured him. "I don't think she knew. Lunch went on a long time because the golfers came in late. I think I was the only one who . . ."

She stopped and flushed. Hugo was relieved but a trifle resentful. Remembering his triumphant exit from the Acorn yesterday he felt that Marianne ought not to have been the only one. But there was something that he wanted to ask her.

"I say," he said impetuously, "I'm quite mad, but do

you know I don't know your surname. I suddenly realised it this morning."

"Fleming," said Marianne. "But about Mrs. Usher?"

"Oh yes. Mrs. Usher. I'm afraid she's rather . . . upset."

"Has she got bad news for Ford?"

"Something of the sort."

"I see. Well, I'll ply her with tea and keep her soothed till he's found."

"No," said Hugo. "I'll give her tea. And you look for Ford. I expect I'll manage her better."

He pulled himself together and went into the drawing-room. Mrs. Usher was still sitting as though she defied anyone to remove her. She glared up at him and said truculently:

"You think I'm drunk, I suppose?"

"Yes," said Hugo. And then: "No. Not really. But you aren't quite yourself, you know. I think you braced yourself up a bit too much at lunch. If I were you I shouldn't see Ford just now. You won't do any good. Go away and have it all out with him when you've thought it over."

"Go away? What a hope! Go away? Now that I've got here? I suppose you're ashamed to be seen with me. Oh yes. I daresay they would like to get me out of the house. I know too much, don't I?"

Her voice was rising to a pitch of uncontrolled fury. It rang and jarred through the spacious quiet of the room, until three rose petals fell from the bowl behind her as if the shaken air had disturbed them. They floated slowly to the carpet and Hugo picked them up. He made no further protest, but the silence, when she had finished speaking, was like a rebuke. She seemed to feel it and she drew herself in with a suspicious glance behind her. The disadvantages of her position were dawning on her clouded mind and her next remark showed a vacillation of purpose.

"You'd do the same if you were me, wouldn't you?"

"I don't quite know what it is that you want to do."

"I want to save him . . . from her."

"Yes. But how? You won't do it simply by making a scene. And are you quite sure what it is that you're afraid of? You say she'll waste his time and make a fool of him. But at the bottom of your heart you're wondering . . ."

"What?"

"If she doesn't still care for him."

"Oh no!" said Mrs. Usher quickly. "That's impossible."

"Are you sure?"

She was not sure, and that was why she had forced her way into Syranwood.

"You mean I've come here to see her, not him?"

"I think you'd better make up your mind which you've come to see, and what it is you want to find out."

She shook her head, and said that she could not make up her mind about anything. She was too much upset.

"When that girl came in I thought she was Laura."

"Did you? Marianne? How strange!"

"She's very like Laura."

"Not a bit," said Hugo crossly.

"Very like Laura ten years ago. She's her niece, I suppose. Not so pretty, but she has the look. Only Laura was always more . . . what's the word? . . . voluptuous or something. Came dashing into the room like a cavalry charge and then pulled up and wondered where she was. I thought: 'Here's our Laura.' That sounds funny, but it's quite true. 'Our Laura,' I thought. As if there was nothing to worry about. And there wouldn't be if she was . . ."

Fletcher came in with tea for two and set it on a little table in front of the sofa where they were sitting. Hugo poured out and induced her to eat a cress sandwich. And when Fletcher was gone he distracted her mind by describing all that he could remember of the domestic arrangements of Syranwood. He felt that time was everything and still hoped to get her away without a scene. Her truculence had quite disappeared. She drank three cups, listened to his gossip with a sombre attention, and at length accepted a cigarette.

"But you're being nice to me," she said suddenly, as he lighted it. "I think you're being very kind. You're so sympathetic."

"Am I?"

"I mean you understand."

"Not the same thing," said Hugo grimly.

She looked at him quickly. Her mind was growing clearer.

"No," she agreed. "You understand with your head and sympathise with your heart. But you can do both, Hugo. That's why everybody likes you."

"Does everybody like me?"

"Oh now! Don't fish! You're the most popular . . .'

She was shaking a playful finger at him, but he gave her a look so grave that she left off laughing and said soberly:

"Well, anyhow, you've been an angel to me. Because you really think I'm quite in the wrong, don't you ? You think I oughtn't to interfere."

"I think it's too late. You can't live his life for him, you know."

"I want him to be happy," she cried.

Hugo leant back in his chair and shut his eyes. They ached and his head rang with all the jokes and giggles that had gone on at the Ullmer Arms. Also he could listen sympathetically if he was not looking at her. That voice, speaking in the darkness, had accents of grief which convinced him that she suffered. But sitting before him he could only see Mrs. Dulcibel Usher, whom he had so often mimicked, and who wanted to pinch Mélisande's job. Those pepper and salt tweeds, that greedy mouth, were too impenetrable a disguise.

"He might have been happy," toiled on the sorrowing voice. "He was happy before she came. I had a premonition . . . yes, a premonition. That first night. I knew. I was working very late with my serial. And when I went to bed I saw a light under his door. I suppose, at the back of my mind, I was afraid of her. I don't know. I didn't think anything specially, but I felt frightened."

There was a pause and Hugo murmured:

"Umhum?"

"I looked in. He was asleep. He'd fallen asleep reading a score. He used to read scores in bed. I . . . I looked at him . . . and I was so unhappy. I felt as if I could never do anything for him really. As if all that I was doing was no good. I don't know. It . . . was . . ."

Her voice trailed off as though she had found no words adequate to the emotion which she was attempting to describe. She could never lay bare to another mind that picture of her son, lying asleep among his scores, so lost, mutinous and young, his clumsy boy's hands flung out empty across the counterpane. His bare little room rose up before her, and the deal table where he worked, with a shelf of scores above it and a picture of the Himalayas which he had torn out of the *Illustrated London News* and pinned up on the wall. And once more she saw his life as she had seen it then, not as a thing which she had made but as having travelled already far beyond her keeping. She knew, even then, that he was looking forward to a time when he should get away from her. And she would let him go.

"I was determined to give him the life he wanted. Not to let him set up as a G.P. when he was through with his exams., but to pay for him to specialise if I could. But we had such heart-breaking disappointments. You see, when he'd got his diploma he got quite a good post at Goddard and Cabells' research laboratories at Dorking. But he threw it up because he wanted to get on to tropical diseases. So he went as medical officer to a plantation in Siam, thinking he'd have more opportunities for experience. But it wasn't what we'd expected, nothing but poulticing coolies and dosing them with castor oil. So after a few months he came back, and then of course his job at Goddard and Cabells' wasn't open any longer. But we thought he might have a chance for one of the Sandemann travelling scholarships, and that would just have suited him, because then he could have got to Yeshenku. But as luck would have it, the scholarship was given to the man who'd taken his job at Goddard and Cabells': so if he'd stuck on there and not gone to Siam he'd have had a better chance. So then he got into the Guthrie Institute as a sort of bottle-washer, and I slaved and scraped for three years, and we got the money together to send him to Yeshenku ourselves. You say I can't live his life for him, but I say that I have."

Still Hugo said nothing. He was floating away on the tides of sleep and the word Yeshenku boomed emptily about in his head. But he knew that this was rude, and struggled back to consciousness with an effort. She was saying:

"They've gone back in the car. But I can take the bus from Ullmer Cross into Basingstoke."

He opened eyes that were glazed with sleep and stared at her. For she was getting up. She was going. He jumped to his feet.

"But how very noble of you," he exclaimed.

She laughed and brushed the crumbs off her skirt.

"Let's hope it's all chalked up somewhere. We don't get our rewards in this world, that's certain. But perhaps it'll all turn out better than I fear. Where's my gloves? Oh, there! Well, good-bye, Hugo. And thank you for that excellent lunch. I don't think we ought to have let you pay."

"Oh, not at all. I enjoyed it."

"No, you didn't. You're looking very seedy. If you'll take my advice, as an old friend, you'll take a long sea voyage or something. You're overdoing it. Good-bye."

She moved towards the door and then drew back, for there was a sound of talking and bustle in the hall.

"Can't I get out by those French windows?" she asked. "I'd rather get away without seeing any of them."

Hugo looked out on to the terrace and saw that the garden was empty. He knew that a path went from a small gate just below the yew parlour and that she could get to Ullmer Cross that way by crossing a couple of hay-fields. So he conveyed her out on to the terrace and hustled her through the garden into the pleached alley.

"They'll never know how much they owe me," he thought. "They'll never guess what a scene I've spared them."

The alley was delightfully cool, and as they were by now out of sight of the house they both began to walk more slowly. The green arch at the far end of it framed a picture of fields and downs too vivid, in the strong light, to be quite real. But when they had got halfway towards it the picture was blotted out. Somebody had come in from the yew parlour. She walked quickly towards them, bending a burnished golden head under the roof of leaves. Hugo pulled up with a jerk of dismay and looked behind him. But there was no escape.

"Here is Laura," he said in a low voice.

"No," said Mrs. Usher, clutching his arm. "No . . ."

Laura came on towards them. They met in the middle of the leafy tunnel.

21   *Our Laura.*

It was Waterloo. He saw that at once, in the long silence while the two women surveyed one another. That pause was an admission of crisis. There were to be no preliminary skirmishes either, no explanations or feigned misunderstandings. And it was Laura who bore the appearance of an attacking force. Her very tread, as she came towards them, had been quick and vengeful, and in her face there was a white and flaming anger. She spoke first, in a high, rapid voice:

"I've been expecting you, Mrs. Usher. I've been thinking about you so much this afternoon. I felt sure you must be near. What do you want?"

She had to stoop a little in the green gloom to look into the eyes of her enemy. She bent downwards with such a

gesture of fierce pouncing that Hugo was not surprised to
see Mrs. Usher draw back quickly. And, though it would
have been discreeter to leave them, he lingered, feeling
that it would be almost inhuman to leave the poor
battered woman in the claws of this angry white
seagull.

"I'm going," said Mrs. Usher hurriedly. "I've got a
bus to catch. You needn't worry. I shan't trouble you
any more, Laura. You've won."

"What d'you mean? I've won? *I've* won?"

"I shan't try to interfere. I'm going. No harm's
done . . ."

"No harm? But don't you know . . . haven't you
seen Ford?"

"No," said Hugo. "We couldn't find Ford."

Laura looked suspiciously from one to the other, as if
trying to gauge the truth of what they said.

"But what have you come for then?" she asked.

"I came to see him, but he couldn't be found."

"Then it's not your doing after all?"

"What?"

"Ford's gone."

"Gone?"

"You mean to say you didn't know? I thought it
was you who . . . when I saw you there, I thought:
now I understand it all. But you tell me you didn't
know?"

"I swear we didn't know," said Hugo. "We've been
sitting in the drawing-room ever since we came, waiting
for somebody to find him. When did he go?"

"I don't know. After lunch some time. I went over to
Brassing with my mother. And when I got back I found
they'd gone."

"They?" queried Hugo.

"Ford and . . . and . . ." Laura grew even whiter than before, "and Walter Bechstrader. He left a note for me." She swooped down at Mrs. Usher again. "You can read it if you like. Hugo can read it if he likes."

Straightening herself she turned away from them and stared fiercely back along the path at the vivid picture under the green arch. Hugo and Mrs. Usher read the note. It was a formal apology for going without bidding Laura and Lady Geraldine farewell. Macdonald had rung up to say that he had found traces of zygotes in the eggs of one of the mosquitoes, and so Ford was obliged to return to the Guthrie Institute at once and he had availed himself of the kind offer of a lift from Walter Bechstrader. They had departed in a hurry by road more than an hour ago.

"Solange was there, it seems," Laura told them.

Her face was averted and her voice was quivering, but she went on:

"You ought to be delighted, Mrs. Usher. Mr. Bechstrader was rather sceptical about Ford's work last night; but it appears that they had a friendly conversation after lunch, and Ford seems to have taken the trouble to explain things rather more. Solange said that they went off on the best of terms, and Mr. Bechstrader is going up to the Guthrie to look at Ford's specimens this evening."

"Bechstrader?" repeated Mrs. Usher. "Bechstrader?"

"I asked him down here to meet Ford," explained Laura drearily.

"Yes. I know. Hugo told me. But . . ."

"But you didn't believe it? Nobody did. Did they, Hugo? Oh! He's left us to fight it out. What tact! Well, there's nothing to fight about, is there, Mrs. Usher?

Q

You've no need to get worried about Ford. Not the slightest."

"I had thought . . ." stammered Mrs. Usher. "I was afraid . . ."

"So was I. But we were mistaken apparently. He has as good an eye for the main chance as even you could wish. Oh, my dear woman! Don't cry! I can assure you there's nothing for you to cry about."

"I've been through so much to-day," gulped Mrs. Usher. "I c-can't help it."

Laura eyed her coldly.

"Can't you understand that you've won," she repeated. "Without even having to fight for him? Surely, knowing Ford, you couldn't have thought he was in any real danger? Surely not? What were you afraid of?"

"I thought he'd come for you."

"And what were you proposing to do about it?"

Mrs. Usher dried her eyes and blew her nose.

"I'm sorry," she said. "I've been so upset all day. When I heard he was here I was so wild, I hardly knew what I was doing. I couldn't bear to feel that he might have to go through it all again, a second time. After getting over it once . . ."

"Was there really ever anything to get over?" demanded Laura sharply.

"Of course there was. How can you ask? You must know. He was heartbroken. And I thought, now he's going to break his heart a second time. I hardly knew what I was doing. I felt I must do something, I didn't know what. But while I was waiting here, I thought it over . . . and I felt that I didn't know . . . how much you still cared for him . . . oh my dear! My dear girl! Don't look like that!"

She put out a timid hand and touched Laura's arm almost caressingly. But Laura drew back and said:

"You can afford to console me."

Mrs. Usher dropped her hand.

"I don't know, my dear. I don't understand."

She was groping about for the relief that this news ought to have given her. For of course it was a relief. Ford was not going to break his heart a second time. He had been faithful to his zygotes and all her terrors had been for nothing. Walter Bechstrader had taken him up. This queer sense of disappointment was merely the result of having been so much upset. It seemed that she had screwed herself up to a pitch of generosity which was, after all, excessive. The reward which she had never expected to reap in this world had arrived before she was ready for it.

"I can't understand Ford," she said with a sigh. "I've never understood him."

She began to walk down the path towards the yew parlour and Laura pursued her to say hastily, almost as if defending Ford:

"But he did ask me. He did come down here for that. He asked me this morning to go off with him."

"Oh? He did?"

"Yes, indeed, and I told him that I couldn't. To him it must have been quite definite. He was under no obligation . . ."

They had reached the end of the alley and turned, as if by common consent, to pace the length of it again.

"Definite to him," said Mrs. Usher, when they had walked some yards. "But you're angry with him. You feel he's treated you badly?"

"Yes," said Laura, in a low voice. "But he hasn't."

"You feel he oughtn't to have gone away suddenly, like this, without saying good-bye?"

"It was cruel. It was meant to be cruel."

"Oh no, dear. I don't think it was meant to be cruel. He thought, probably, that it was the most sensible thing to do."

"Oh yes, terribly sensible. If he'd gone immediately after breakfast, that would have been quite sensible enough. I'd have understood that. But I forgot about Walter Bechstrader."

Her voice tightened on the last word.

"But didn't you ask them down here to meet one another?"

"I did. And I scolded Ford last night for not taking more pains. He only did what I told him. He couldn't know . . ."

But he ought to have known. That was her quarrel with him. He ought to have known that she found it hard to send him away, that her struggles all day had been severe. He ought not to have stayed till after lunch unless he meant to make another appeal to her. All through that long hot drive to Brassing she had wrestled with her conscience knowing in her heart that she could not resist him for ever. The thought of their ultimate happiness kept breaking through, until she found herself regarding it as a certain event. But he had not stayed for her, only for Bechstrader. He couldn't know. But he ought to have known. Just as he ought to have known ten years ago. It was the second time that he had failed her.

"He couldn't know, could he?" she said, turning to Mrs. Usher.

"That you care for him? I should have thought it was as plain as the nose on my face, and always had been."

"Oh, Mrs. Usher? You do believe it?"

"I do."

"Then he ought to have believed it."

"He's stupid," said Mrs. Usher crossly. "He always was. Can't think of more than one thing at once. But he didn't mean to be cruel. He hasn't enough imagination. And, mind you, I'm not saying that it isn't all for the best, now. Of course I think more of his happiness than I do of yours, and I do think he'd be better to go off now and forget all about you. It's too late. Things might have been different . . . what I mean to say is . . . I'm sorry. I've never been comfortable in my mind about the way I came between you that time, and now I've seen you I feel worse than ever about it. I . . I . . could have loved you so much, Laura. You and he . . . I might have seen him happy . . . his life might have been different."

She was not thinking of the man who had hurried off with Bechstrader, but of a rebellious boy asleep in an attic. She sighed.

"Well, there's no use crying over spilt milk, is there?"

"None at all."

They came out into the garden where Hugo was sitting on a derelict roller. Everybody else was drinking tea in the dining room but he still felt glad of an excuse to hide himself. He had not faced them collectively since the fiasco of the morning, and though he had Marianne's word for it that nobody had noticed this long disappearance he could not help feeling that he ought to stage his come-back very carefully. He would wait until Laura had put Mrs. Usher to flight and then he would go into tea with her, which would look so much better than strolling in alone.

But he had not expected to see them come out of the

pleached alley arm in arm. The spectacle surprised him so much that for a moment his own dilemma went out of his head. He got up from his roller and stood at attention, but they did not come his way. Turning out into the garden they took a slow promenade round the paths, sometimes hidden behind the box hedges and sometimes passing into view. As far as he could see and hear they said very little, but they seemed strangely loath to part, as if some common emotion held them in a wordless bond.

Solange came bounding from the house, a tennis racket in her hand, and stopped to ask him if he would make up a four.

"No," said Hugo. "I haven't had tea yet. I'm waiting for Laura."

He nodded at the two women standing beside the fountain in the middle of the garden.

"Who's that with her?" asked Solange.

"Mrs. Usher. Ford Usher's mother."

"Ford's mother?"

Her eyes sparkled with excitement and interest. She sat down on the roller beside Hugo.

"Does she know about Ford?" she asked. "Isn't she excited?"

"What?" asked Hugo cautiously.

"I was there when the telephone message came through. It was one of the most thrilling things that have ever happened to me. I mean, next to actually discovering *Pseudopictus*, I suppose it's the most important thing he's done. I mean, they never thought it could be transmitted to another generation, though of course he says it's only a possibility even now and you mustn't rush to conclusions. But it does break entirely new ground. And he's going to let me come up to the Guthrie and see for myself, one day. Does his mother know?"

"Yes. Laura told us."

"Isn't she very excited?"

Laura and Mrs. Usher seemed to have finished their silent contemplation of the goldfish in the fountain. They came towards Hugo's roller discussing the time table of buses from Ullmer Cross to Basingstoke.

"You must be sure to go through the gate and not over the stile," Laura was saying. "The other path takes you out on to the downs. It's a little difficult to find. Hugo! Perhaps you . . ."

"Let me go," put in Solange eagerly. "I know the way. I could take Mrs. Usher right to Ullmer Cross."

She jumped off the roller with a pretty, smiling readiness to oblige, and waited impatiently while Mrs. Usher made her farewells. She was longing to talk about the elusive zygotes. To her eyes there was nothing strange in the kiss which Ford's mother gave to Laura, for she was sure that they must all be very pleased. Ford was wonderful. One day he would win the Nobel Prize and found an Institute of his own and become a perfectly happy man, so that it was no wonder if his mother did want to go about kissing people.

22. *Waning Star*.

From the dining-room came sounds of laughter, and Hugo stood outside the door, listening nervously. He wondered if a sudden silence would fall on them if he went into the room. He could not, as he had hoped, slip in behind Laura, for she had gone straight upstairs. And after a little while he reminded himself that he had had tea. He would put it off a little longer. He would go into the library and be very busy writing something.

But before he had time to escape the dining-room door opened and Alec came out, peering short-sightedly and almost bumping into Hugo as he hovered on the mat. The two of them set to partners, for Alec thought that Hugo was trying to go through the door. At last he realised that it was not so, and something of the uncertain misery in Hugo's soul must have reached him, for he closed the door and suggested that they should go for a walk.

Hugo accepted eagerly, though he hated going for walks. It was another respite, nor did it occur to him, until they were well away from the house, that even Alec might regard him as an unsuccessful guest. Taunting memories came back to him. Alec had a reputation for kindness to people in misfortune. Laura had said that she always put the bores next to him at dinner.

"Who sat next to him last night?" wondered Hugo. "Philomena! Hell! At least I won't start thinking about Philomena."

For he was growing very angry with Philomena. He was angry with all of them. They had all conspired to make a fool of him. But Philomena had done worse. She had led him on to make a fool of himself. She had got him into a false position, taking advantage of a moment's folly, and now he had a suspicion that he was going to be set free in a way that was even more humiliating. To get out of it adroitly was one thing: to be dropped was another.

Perhaps Alec had been expressly told off to entertain a failure. But a country walk was poor entertainment. Over a great many stiles they went and conversation languished. Courting couples, embracing in the lanes, made way for them respectfully. Courting couples lay prone upon the downs. In some cases they lay right across the path so that Alec and Hugo had to walk round them. Hugo, accustomed only to the more urban forms of licence, was embarrassed. He could not achieve the imperturbable serenity of his companion, who strode on and looked the other way. Occasionally they stopped to peer at small, uninteresting flowers and wonder what they were called, and at one time Alec grew very angry over a new red bungalow which had been built just on the edge of the Syranwood property. Geraldine, he said, had tried to prevent it, but a speculating builder from Basingstoke had been too many for her.

"It's positively indecent," he complained. "It ought never to have been allowed."

"I should think so," agreed Hugo, trying not to look at two people on the grass ten yards ahead of them.

"It's the thin edge of the wedge," said Alec. "We've kept the place from being vulgarised up till now, but in another ten years it'll be quite spoilt."

When they got to the top of Chawton Beacon he pointed out the walk which they were going to take, a pleasant circuit of seven miles or so, which they could easily do before dinner. Hugo, who had thought the walk already too long, broke into a cold sweat. He murmured something about having some writing to do, whereat Alec relented so far as to point out a shorter route whereby they could save three miles. To its modified horrors they committed themselves. As might have been expected, a blister had already begun to form on Hugo's heel. And a deadly fatigue settled upon all his limbs, the frozen impotence of a nightmare, so that he had absolutely to force one foot in front of the other while he listened to Alec's dry savourless voice.

They spoke of the drama, because Alec was always careful to talk to people upon their own subjects. He used, he said, to like going to the theatre, but now he could never hear what they were saying. It was not that he was deaf, but that modern enunciation was so bad. But he still made an effort, in spite of his work, to keep up with all that was going on. He could make a few dim little comments about each of the well-known dramatists. Concerning the elder generation he had already made up his mind. Palemon White was very clever, oh, very clever indeed, but not an Englishman of course. Alan Chrome was clever too, but there was something ill-natured about the fella, Alec thought; he left a nasty taste in your mouth. And as for Edgerton, well, Alec knew Edgerton. They had a place nearby, over at Brassing, and he liked the fella. They had been contemporaries at Cambridge and nobody would then have suspected such a thing. But he did not like Edgerton's plays. He thought them subversive. They were too serious, that was the point. Clever Mr. Palemon White could be dismissed with indulgent laughter because he was not, after all, an Englishman. Not so Edgerton. The fella was always raising points which he did not himself seem able to answer. Those were not the sort of points which ought to be raised in a play. A serious play might possibly teach a lesson, but it ought not to make the public feel uncomfortable. There was no such thing as ideal justice in this world and Edgerton was an educated man who ought to know it. But he seemed to be always demanding it, and that was the sort of thing that might make ignorant people

discontented. Not that Edgerton was biased exactly.
That was another thing. You could never tell which side
he was on, so that you could not even be sure if you dis-
agreed with him. Still, he liked the man. Had always liked
him.

But it was the younger generation that he wanted to
discuss with Hugo. Which of them would live? Which
had a message?

Hugo, as they forged up the next hill, panted out the
names of his three most prominent rivals, adding that
formula of praise which he could, by now, have repeated
in his sleep. But Alec wanted to hear more than that. He
wanted to get the young dramatist's point of view, and he
asked tactlessly whether any of them were really any good.
Would they live? Hugo wanted to say that they were all
quite healthy as far as he knew, but he restrained himself.
His head was empty of ideas and his heel hurt him
abominably. He said that one of the three would live, he
thought. Well, which? asked Alec. Cecil Hopkins, said
Hugo, believing that he spoke at random, but guided unconsciously by a determination not to be jealous. But
why Cecil Hopkins? Because he was so very clever. But
they were all clever. And vitality was apt to be overrated,
nowadays. After all it was merely raw material. And had
Hopkins anything in particular to say? That was what he
wanted to know. They limped up hill and down dale, and
Hugo felt that the conversation was becoming more and
more imbecile.

Before the end of the walk they had both given it up.
Hugo could think of nothing but his heel, and Alec had
gone back to the problem of a cargo of china teapots,
shipped from Bristol to Honolulu. They had arrived in
pieces and it was his own opinion that this was due to a

monsoon, but it was his business to convince a judge that
there might be reasonable grounds for saying that it was
not so. Since Hugo did not want to talk he might as well
go on thinking about that. But it was a pity, because he
really did desire to keep up his interest in the arts and
nobody would help him. Hugo was not the first person
who had fallen into a kind of blank stupor when out on a
walk with Alec.

The afternoon was sultry and they had to go out of
their way in order to avoid a field with a bull in it. When
they got home it was after seven o'clock, and they found
the hall full of people who all seemed to have come to the
end of their resources. They were just sitting about, too
much exhausted to go up and dress for dinner. Aggie's
departure had left them all at a loose end, and their several
preoccupations were far from pleasant. Laura had lost
her lover, Adrian had got to go to East Prussia, Philomena had decided that she would never be able to
"manage," and Gibbie was making up his mind that the
Good Man takes a firm line. But Hugo thought that they
were all displeased with him. He had grown so nervous
that he could not consider them as individuals any longer.
They were just a public which had turned against him.

Sitting down beside Corny he rallied sufficient spirit to
make a very small joke. Corny laughed abruptly. In that
quarter abruptness was a well-known danger signal, for
Corny had never been known to desert a friend in
trouble. His friendships generally dissolved urbanely before
trouble of any sort set in. After the laugh there was a long
silence as though everyone was waiting for a lead. Now,
if ever, might Hugo have seized the opportunity to re-
instate himself. He should have rushed in and held them
all spellbound. He said nothing.

Failure, as he now saw, is like success in that it is cumulative. It generates its own fuel. Because a man is out of humour he has to go for a walk with a first-class devitaliser like Alec, is reduced to a mass of thirst and blisters, and automatically becomes incapable of recovery. Failure is a quicksand, an octopus, anything that drags you down if you struggle. All these people, so ready yesterday to applaud his good fortune, were quite indifferent to-day at the sight of his collapse. They would sit round and coolly watch him sink. Not one of them cared to give him a helping hand, not even Philomena, who ought, at least, to have laughed when he made jokes. He looked across at her, almost appealingly, but she stared back as solemn as an owl. And this final proof of his falling credit left him quite hopeless.

When, at last, he went upstairs to dress he could think of nothing save Philomena's inconstancy. He promised himself a rich scene with her later on. She should be forced to explain herself. He would have it in plain English. If she had dropped him because he was not being a success, then it must have been the purest snobbery which had flung her into his arms twenty-four hours ago, and he would make her say so. The whole business had been ugly and insincere. He did not want her. He had only made love to her because he was bored and she seemed to expect it. She ought to be ashamed of herself, and he would tell her so.

Seething with indignation he tied his tie and saw in the glass that romantic young face which had been his fortune and his undoing. Ill temper could change but not spoil it. He snarled:

"At least you can still make Joey giggle."

And flung out of the room.

23. *Hugo's Heavenly Crown.*

At dinner he found himself placed between Marianne and Mrs. Comstock, the rector's wife. Of course this was not accidental. It was another milestone on the road to ruin. He had only to compare it with his position last night, between Aggie and his hostess, to know how far he had sunk. And his anger stiffened into a black sulkiness which kept him as silent as either of his neighbours. Nothing should make him speak until they did, and if they began he would give them a bad time. He ate up his soup and his fish and looked straight in front of him.

After twenty minutes his silence had become conspicuous. Lady Geraldine threw him one or two disturbed glances, and he was aware that Laura had said something about him to Adrian. He was being inexcusable and they all knew it. He was dramatising his own failure. As, in prosperity, he had been swift to impersonate a darling of the gods, so now, in adversity, he gave them a very good imitation of a pariah. But never again would it be said that he put on no airs. His dissatisfaction with his neighbours was far too obvious. Yet, a fortnight ago, when he was still in his glory, this accident would have fallen to his greater credit. He would have been quite as charming to Mrs. Comstock as he had been to Aggie. And in the midst of his spontaneous good fellowship he would have been thinking:

"This isn't insincere. I'm not doing this to make an impression. I'm nice to them because I like them."

Now he did not like anybody, so it would be insincere to hide it. Marianne wanted to speak to him. He felt that she was trying to catch his eye. But he was not going to help. He was a celebrity and celebrities are sometimes difficult to entertain. They are fools if they do not, occasionally, claim some licence. All this pose of being simple and unspoilt—he had overdone it. He had cheapened himself by being too pleasant. If he had been rude, now and then, perhaps they might think more of him. Common sense told him that a waning star cannot afford a sudden change of policy, but he was past listening to common sense. He kept his eyes on his plate until he heard her voice, speaking low and clear under cover of a burst of laughter all round them.

"The lady on your right is very deaf. She never talks to people because she's afraid of being a nuisance. But she loves it if they talk to her."

"Oh?" said Hugo.

He had not expected this and he was taken aback. As soon as he could do so naturally he looked at Mrs. Comstock and saw what he ought to have seen long ago. It was a plain, elderly face, but the look of endurance upon it gave it a kind of grim beauty. She had just leant forward in the hopes of catching some joke that was passing at the other side of the table. Such as it was, she missed it. And he saw her sit back again, disappointed, into the solitude of her deafness. There was a terrible patience about the gesture. Every day, every hour of her life, she must resign herself to missing things. A twinge of sick compassion shook him. Perhaps she liked people.

"I see," he said, turning to Marianne. "Thank you. I didn't know. Er . . . what shall I talk to her about?"

"Flowers."

"Flowers? Just my luck!"

Flowers were not his strong point. He knew a rose from a delphinium of course. But Mrs. Comstock looked

as though she might be the sort of person who knows
wild carrot from cow parsley. And after so long a silence
he could think of no opening remark about flowers which
would not sound silly, especially if he had to shout it.
Already he was paying for his bad manners. A nervous
lull seemed to have fallen upon the table. Everybody
began to converse in undertones. He waited for two
minutes and then braced himself. Valiantly crashing into
the unpropitious quiet he asked Mrs. Comstock if the
soil of Ullmer was good for roses—the soil, the *soil* of
Ullmer was good for roses, *Roses*, ROSES. She said that
it was on the whole, and waited, in pleased surprise, for
more.

"I suppose you're a great gardener?" bellowed Hugo.

He must forget that he was making himself ridiculous.
Of course this sudden interest in horticulture after half
an hour's huff would do nothing to restore his lost credit.
He was not trying to restore his lost credit. If Corny had
really tittered at the other end of the table, so much the
worse for Corny. He would concentrate upon his
heavenly crown, and permit his own good nature to put
him, for the first time in his life, at a disadvantage. Mrs.
Comstock should be persuaded that her conversation was
a pleasure: she should go away feeling, not that he had
been kind, but that she had been interesting. So he persisted until dessert was put upon the table. And by that
time he had made so complete an exhibition of himself
that nothing worse could ever happen to him. There
was almost a touch of æsthetic beauty in this rounding off
of his disasters. It was so complete. The very complete-
ness of it, together with the champagne he had drunk,
made him feel rather better. He turned to Marianne
almost cheerfully and perceived for the first time, that she

had very beautiful eyes. They were fitting the heavenly crown on to his head as neatly as if it had been made to measure. She had the air of being in his debt. Perhaps the moment for coping with her had come. For he had been wanting to cope with her ever since his arrival and had never secured the opportunity. He took a sip of port and said jovially:

"Well, Mary . . . Ann . . . ?"

"Have a gooseberry?"

"Thank you. I wanted to ask after that girl who used to live here. A mere child. But she used to be so nice."

"Nice?"

"Oh, a darling. A pearl. What's happened to her?"

Marianne opened her eyes very wide and frowned a little.

"You know," she said, "I'm not very good at . . . at *badinage*. Is that a word?"

"Yes. I believe it's a word. Though I never dare use it myself because my accent's so good. Tell me about the other Marianne."

"Have another gooseberry."

"Thanks. I'm only trying to say that I feel we're strangers, but I'm pleased to meet you."

"Why?"

"Oh, you are bad at it!"

"I told you I was."

"What are you good at?"

"Swimming."

"So was the other Marianne."

"And so was the other Hugo."

"Ah! That's just what I was coming to. There isn't another Hugo. You've been misled."

R

Marianne said nothing, and he was obliged to continue.

"Why do you disapprove of me, Marianne? You do, don't you? Except when I'm talking about the ivy-leafed campanula at the top of my voice. Oh, I know you're plying me with gooseberries now, but that's merely a reward for elocution. You don't really approve of me. Do you?"

"That is a thing," said Marianne gravely, "which we have to guess for ourselves. Whether other people approve of us or not, I mean. It isn't fair to ask, though one would often like to."

"I am answered, Mademoiselle."

He was deeply offended. The other slights which he had suffered were as nothing to this rebuff. Because he had really come to hope that Marianne's good opinion was independent of the general judgment. After all, she had liked him when her mother mistook him for a Rhodes Scholar. It was a bitter blow to discover that Aggie's writ ran here as everywhere else. Flushing resentfully he turned away from her and bit into a gooseberry, but even there he was betrayed, for the ripe fruit exploded and sprayed the table with little pips. In spite of himself he could not help glancing at her to see if she was laughing, and found that her face was as crimson as his own. She was not laughing. She was nearly crying.

"Marianne," he exclaimed desperately. "What has happened to us? I think you might try to explain it. We used to be such friends."

"I was very young then," said Marianne.

"And now that you're so frightfully mature you've crossed my name off. But why?"

She murmured something lamely about people in different generations never quite understanding one another. But this could not placate him.

"Different generations? What are you talking about? I'm not so awfully, awfully much older than you are, you know."

"Not in years. But your mind is a lot older, Hugo. And all your friends are older."

"My friends?" He paused and said quickly: "I doubt if I have any."

Marianne did not contradict this, but she amended:

"Well, the people you go about with. And the people you write plays for. I mean, you go in for rather old-fashioned kinds of plays, don't you?"

Hugo, the White Hope of the Moderns, nearly spilt his port.

"You're the first person who's ever suggested that," he said.

"Oh, I know they're frightfully good," cried Marianne. "And they don't sound old-fashioned. I meant more the point of view . . . the ideas . . . the sentiment . . . I should have thought it was the sort of thing that appeals to middle-aged people."

"Would you? How? Give me an instance. Are you repeating something you've heard Aggie say?"

"Aggie? No, of course not. She likes that sort of thing."

"Did she like that play I was reading to her this morning?"

"I don't know. She didn't say. I should think so. It sounded exactly the sort of thing she would like. Of course I didn't hear much of it . . ."

"You only heard about three words. Not enough to judge."

"I know. But it sounded . . ."

"How did it sound, Marianne? Tell me! How did it sound?"

"Oh, I can't talk. I don't know enough."

"Yes, you do. Tell me. I'm interested. I shan't be annoyed. Really I shan't. I want to get your point of view."

"Well, I only mean that Aggie, and people of that age, what they really like is a great fuss about nothing. I mean that when a woman has a . . . a lover . . . they still call it 'granting him everything.' At least they mayn't call it that, but they think it's that. But it isn't, is it, Hugo? It's only granting him one thing. But so often it's the only thing they've got, so they like to feel it's frightfully important. And they like plays and books that make a fuss about it."

"But it is important," said Hugo gravely.

"Always?"

"You don't understand. When you're older . . ."

"There! You see!"

"What?"

"You've said it yourself. I told you. We belong to different generations."

"If you could see the letters I get from girls no older than you!"

"And you think they're silly?"

"Well, yes, I do. Most of them. But for all that, it isn't, as you seem to think, a great fuss about nothing. And some day you'll know that it isn't."

"But isn't it very often a great fuss about nothing, Hugo? I know that it can be tremendously important. It can mean a great deal in two people's lives. But not always. And there's a kind of insincerity in pretending that it has meant more than it has. When you're my age, you take it for granted that some time or other there is going to be this great thing in your life. But perhaps you're unlucky and it never comes to you. So you pretend that it has, and the less important that you really in your heart know it's been, the more fuss you make. But if you're lucky . . ."

"How do you know all this?"

"But if you're lucky you don't need to make a fuss. I don't know it. But I suspect it. You think that's all wrong?"

"No, I don't. But you know, Marianne, very few people are . . . lucky as you call it."

"Oh. Lots are. They must be."

"Really? I'd like to see them. Tell me where to find them."

"Oh . . . in the Underground, and . . . and shopping at the Stores and places."

"And where are the unlucky ones, then?"

"Listening to your plays."

"At least I console them, poor things. By the time you're forty-five, my dear, you may be very grateful to me."

"Probably," said Marianne.

"You don't really think it's in the least probable. You mean to be lucky, don't you?"

"There's my grandmother getting up."

"Don't you?"

"I wasn't talking about myself," said Marianne, getting up.

"No. But I was. And I'm obliged to you for telling me so much."

She gave him a startled look. But she was out in the hall before she had really begun to blush and Solange was the only person who noticed her agitation.

"How red your face is, Marianne."

"It was so hot in the dining-room."

"You're blushing at something."

"Well. I can't help that."

"I know. We shall have outgrown it by the time we're twenty-one. It's something to do with our circulations. I read that in a book called the *Psychology of Adolescence.*"

The night was hotter than ever and they all went straight into the garden. Geraldine wanted to cut some roses for Philomena to take to London in the morning. She called to the girls to bring her basket, gloves and scissors.

"Only the buds," she said. "They can be in water all night and then they'll travel better."

"I can't see which are buds," said Marianne, peering into the dusky bushes. "We ought to wait till the moon rises."

"No, but you can feel them," said Solange. "All hard and firm."

She pulled at one, scattering the dew over her hands, and she laughed. Her spirits were so high that she hardly knew what she was doing. But she tugged at the rose again, humming:

Rosen brach ich nachts mir am dunklen Hage . . .

"That's a silly song," grumbled Marianne. "I think it's the silliest song anybody ever wrote. I'm sure it can't be good poetry, even in German. 'Also of the kisses the perfume me as never before drive mad which I by night from the stalk of your lips plucked.' "

"Come a little further down the path, Marianne. I want to tell you something. Listen. My father has climbed down."

"What? When?"

"At dinner. Oh I had a lovely time at dinner. Did you see?"

"No. I didn't notice."

"Well, to begin with, he simply wouldn't speak to me. He just sat there wisihng that modern parents could give their children *lettres de cachet*. You see, I'd offered to see him on to the boat train and meet him on the way home. And he's realised that he can't go on leading a double life. After this he'll never know what I mayn't say or do unless he buys me off."

"You're sure he doesn't want to go?"

"Of course he doesn't. He hates travelling at his own expense, and he can't afford it, anyhow. So at last I opened negotiations, I said how I envied him and how I wished that I could go instead. And I said that if anything should stop him at the last moment perhaps I might use his ticket. So he said: 'Well, that wouldn't be much use.' And I said: 'No, I should want some money as well.' 'Which I haven't got,' he said. So I told him that it wouldn't mean very much, and all that Ford told me about the cost of living for a student at Freiburg. So then he said he'd think about it. And he said, very cautiously, that he wasn't sure if he could go to East Prussia after all, because he'd just remembered an important appointment on Tuesday. So I said: 'Well, then you'll be able to think about me going all the sooner.' I saw that he was debating it all in his mind, and wondering whether it would seem ridiculous or not, to say he was going and then not go. If he hadn't been so terribly solemn and impressive about it to begin with, he wouldn't be in such a hole. So he said: 'Well.' And after a bit, 'Well' again. And I really think it's all right,

Marianne darling. I can't thank you enough for helping me to manage it. I've had a perfectly wonderful week-end, getting to know Ford and everything. I'm wildly happy. What did you talk to Hugo about at dinner? You seemed to be having a sticky time at first."

"Nothing in particular. I cheeked him rather."

"Good. He needs taking down a bit, as I told you before. Did you ever hear anything like the way he showed off to Mrs. Comstock? Pretending to be so keen on gardening. All at the very top of his voice."

"He had to. She's deaf."

"Well, it sounded very silly. I'm sure everybody thought so. Corny said: 'Hugo's always so kind-hearted,' in a very nasty voice. What happened? Did you catch a thorn?"

"No."

Marianne straightened herself with a jerk and flung down her basket. She wanted to cry out. Solange was intolerable and so was everyone else who laughed at Hugo for being nice to Mrs. Comstock. She could not bear it for one moment longer nor could she ever look him in the face again, in case he had guessed. What had she said to him? Had she given herself away?

"I'm going," she said in a choked voice. "I've got a headache."

"Are you going to bed?"

"No."

To shut herself up in a stuffy room would do her no good. She wanted to find some spacious and quiet place where she and her troubles would seem small. She would change her frock and shoes and slip up to the downs. Up on Chawton Beacon, where the wind whistled through the harebells, she would be able to cry as much as she liked. She would stay there all night and never see him again.

Solange was offering eau-de-Cologne, and insisting that it all came from washing Tango on a hot afternoon. But they both knew that the headache was a myth. The image of Hugo hovered between them, beloved by the one and contemptible to the other. Solange thought, as Marianne left her:

"It isn't as if he'd really ever done anything to make up for being so affected. Only a few rubbishy plays. It isn't as if he'd made a great discovery or anything like that."

She went on cutting roses and feeling for buds and singing so loudly that the three elder women beside the fountain said to one another:

"How happy that child sounds!"

24. *A Great Fuss About Nothing.*

The moon, wheeling up over the trees, turned the topmost drops of the fountain to silver, and gilded the head of the marble cupid with his dolphin. When Solange left off singing there was no sound in the night save the soft continuous whisper of the water. But Philomena's thoughts were so restless and noisy that she could hardly believe they had not been spoken aloud. She stood on the path and watched Geraldine's thoughtful clipping and wondered why nobody should have asked what was the matter with her. Rebellion flowed from her, but it was lost in the quiet and the darkness. She was sacrificing her youth and her happiness. But

Geraldine went on cutting roses. Nobody would ever know. Hugo would never know, Gibbie would never know, the children would never know, what a martyrdom she was going through. It was unfair, and some time, some day, she would make somebody pay for it.

Solange, that happy, happy girl, sang on and the fountain played and a sound of music drifted out of the drawing-room windows. Corny was playing his pieces. He did this so seldom that many people were unaware that he could do it at all. He liked taking them by surprise. Towards the end of a visit he would sit down nonchalantly on the piano stool and strum a little, picking out tunes with one finger. And then, suddenly, he would break into quite an impressively difficult piece. Nobody had ever heard him practising and there was no piano in his flat in Whitehall Court. But his agility and dash suggested a high level of accomplishment and an astonished group would always gather round him.

Now he was executing a Liszt Rhapsodie and his hard, firm notes rang out into the night, breaking up its quiet like a shower of stones thrown into a pool. The rose-gatherers flocked into the house again and the Comstocks took their leave. Geraldine took Alec, Adrian and Laura into the library to play bridge, commanding the rest to play a round game in the drawing-room. But Solange had gone to put the roses in water, and Corny was determined to show how well he could play the *Noveletten* so that only Hugo and the Greys were left. It was the first time that the three of them had met at close quarters since Philomena talked to Gibbie. They none of them realised what was happening until too late. They were still standing and looking blankly at one another when Geraldine came back for her cigarette case. She said nothing but, as she went out again, her glance accused Philomena of managing very, very badly.

Gibbie was the first to recover countenance. He muttered something about having manuscripts to read and disappeared into the hall. And Philomena said rather petulantly, under cover of Corny's music:

"I don't think you're very tactful, Hugo, I must say."

"I didn't know I had to be tactful," growled Hugo. "It's you who've got to be tactful."

"Hush."

"Corny won't hear us. Come over here and sit down on this sofa and let's get it over."

"What do you mean?"

His eyes were bright and angry. While Corny's music filled the room he took her over to a sofa by the fireplace and forced her to explain herself.

"You're going to leave me cold, aren't you?"

"Oh, Hugo, I'm so sorry."

She explained to him that she was in a cage, and that she could never get out of it without hurting other people. One should not hurt other people. It was wrong. She reproached herself bitterly for having led him on, but maintained that being a wife and mother had turned out to be more of a whole-time job than she had thought. Not that she actually mentioned Ada or the children's summer holiday, or even several other complications which had occurred to her during the day—a party for which she had already sent out invitations and the re-decoration of the drawing-room which would certainly be muddled if she were not there to supervise. But she went on saying vaguely that she was in a cage until Hugo said:

"You weren't in one yesterday."

"I hadn't thought it out then."

"Is it Gibbie? Has he put his foot down or what?"

Oh no, it was not fair to put the blame on poor Gibbie. As far as Gibbie was concerned it seemed that she might go off to-morrow.

"But the world isn't properly organised yet," she said. "One can't do these things."

"My dear Philomena! One can do these things perfectly well if one wants to. You talk as if no woman had ever done it before. Be reasonable!"

Philomena gave him a surly look. She was being reasonable and he ought to have been trying to argue her out of it. He must have experience enough to know that he ought not to appeal to her reason in order to make her change her mind. But he did not, as she now began to understand, really want her to change her mind. He was making no great efforts to move her, though his vanity was clearly wounded by her defection. She had been sorry for him, but now she began to be offended. Each resented the other's want of urgency.

"The fact is you've weakened," he told her. "If you wanted to come you'd come. But you're glad of an excuse, because you mean to drop me and I know why."

"You know why, Hugo?"

"Yes. I do know why."

"Not so loud. Corny'll hear you."

He was trying to light a cigarette but his hand shook so much that he could not manage it. Suddenly his brain seemed to go molten with anger. He felt all power of self-control sliding and slipping away from him. The blood in his ears began to hum and his voice, high and shaking, rose above the noise of Corny's piano.

"I don't care if he does hear. I don't care if anybody

hears. I'm not saying anything that they don't all know already. Oh yes, I know why. Oh yes, I know why. I know why. I know . . ."

"Hugo!"

"I'm not such a feather in your cap as you thought I was. This week-end's been a flop and so you find you're in a cage. You needn't think I don't know. You needn't think I don't know. If Aggie hadn't gone we shouldn't hear so much about cages . . ."

"Hugo! Be quiet! Don't make such an exhibition . . ."

"I suppose you all think she knows a good play from a bad one. I didn't want to read the thing to her. But as it was written to amuse a lot of frustrated old women I thought I might as well try it out on her. I don't know what she's been saying about it. I only know you've all dropped me as if I had the plague."

"You must be mad. Nobody's been saying anything about you that I know of. You're so eaten up with vanity, your head's so turned, you'll soon be quite impossible."

"You didn't think so yesterday."

"Going off to lunch with a lot of reporters! I didn't believe it, at first, when I heard about it."

"Who told you?"

"Corny. And let me tell you, Hugo, that you can't do that sort of thing here. You may as well know that we had some difficulty to persuade Geraldine to invite you. She was afraid you'd bring your publicity manager with you. 'Isn't he rather a shallow little *arriviste?*' she said. We told her you were very amusing. But the only time you've been amusing was when you were shouting at Mrs. Comstock and that was in very bad taste."

"So you 'find you're in a cage!' Thank you."

"Thank heaven I did. I don't like hysterics."

"Yes, you ought to be thankful, oughtn't you? My God, yes. I'm no catch now . . ."

"How dare you talk like that! I thought I loved you!"

"You certainly behaved as if you did. But how far did you mean to go? And when did you change your mind?"

"I'd have given you all you wanted . . . everything . . . if . . ."

"Everything! Don't make me laugh."

"Don't be more of a cad than you can help."

"When women like you talk of giving everything . ."

"Hush!"

Corny, at last aware that something exciting was going forward at the other end of the room, had left off playing. Hugo's voice rang through an attentive silence as, ignoring her gesture, he shouted on:

"It means you've only got one thing to offer. And if I want that I can get it elsewhere without having to ask Gibbie's leave."

Philomena did not reply. She was looking at Corny on the piano stool and to him she said:

"Please go on playing. Hugo is having a nerve storm."

Corny played middle C very softly and shook his head.

"I've played all my pieces," he said.

He was smiling to himself and Philomena had a suspicion that he might have heard a very great deal. She looked at Hugo in despair, wondering what else he might be going to say. But he was beginning to recover. Her gesture of appeal was not lost on him.

"All right," he said. "I've finished."

"Shall I go?" asked Corny, getting up.

"Wait a minute," said Hugo.

Something must be done to keep Corny's mouth shut,

and his brain cleared rapidly as he came to this conclusion. He left off shaking. He made up his mind.

"Tell them this," he said.

Crossing the room he pulled Corny's nose very hard
indeed. Then he nodded reassuringly at Philomena and
walked slowly out through the French windows on to the
terrace. For a few minutes he stood waiting just beyond
the circle of light thrown out on to the stones. He
wondered whether Corny would choose swords or pistols,
or if a simple apology would suffice. He would be quite
ready to apologise, for he was certain that his end was
gained and that there would be no talk.

But no sound came from the astonished room behind
him. They might both have fainted, they were so quiet.
And, just when he was wondering what he ought to do
next, a fresh torrent of music flowed on to the terrace.
He crept back on tiptoe to look. Philomena had disappeared and Corny, still with a very red nose, was
executing a Bach Prelude. There would be no duel this
time.

He went into the hall to get a drink and found Solange
putting away the basket and the scissors. She said:

"Where have you been?"

And he said:

"Listening to Corny."

"Isn't he clever?" said Solange admiringly. "I didn't
know he could play Augustus Harris."

"Play what?"

"That fugue. At school we used to call it Augustus
Harris. Because of the rhythm. It says:

     'AuGUStus Har-ris
     Caught a FLEA in his COFF-ee.'"

"Where's Marianne?"

"Gone to bed. Thanks. I'll have some lemonade."

They sipped and listened to Corny playing Augustus Harris. Solange looked thoughtful. Presently she asked if he had had a row with Marianne at dinner.

"I don't know," said Hugo. "It isn't finished yet. I'm sorry she's gone to bed."

Solange pondered again. She made up her mind.

"I don't think she has gone to bed, as a matter of fact. She's gone up on to the downs."

"Oh."

He finished his drink and wandered out into the garden again. Solange tip-toed to the door to watch him. As soon as he had got off the terrace and believed himself to be unobserved he set off down the garden at a great rate. She smiled to herself, looked doubtful, and then smiled again as she went up to bed.

25. *Michal.*

"But Gibbie . . . Gibbie . . ."

"It's no use, Philomena."

"Can't you understand that it's all over. I've given it up. Nothing's happened. Don't look at me so angrily. I've done you no wrong."

"Yes, you have. You've made a fool of me."

"I've always been quite frank with you."

"That has nothing to do with it. You've made a fool of me."

"How?"

"To him. And you can't undo that. First you'll go.

And then you won't go. What does he think I am?"

"Gibbie! Don't be childish. I've done nothing."

"Nothing? You've only told him and God knows whom else that I can't keep you in order . . ."

"Keep me in order. I'm not a child."

"You behave like one."

Philomena sat down in front of her dressing-table and buried her face in her hands. She felt that it ought to be quite easy to dispose of Gibbie, but she was shaken by that awful, outrageous scene downstairs. She must have a little time for recovery before she could deal with this new mood of Gibbie's.

"Let's talk about it when we go home," she said faintly. "I'm too tired. I can't go into it to-night."

"But I'm not going home. I've told you. I'm not going to live with you again."

"You're mad. I've done nothing. I've been absolutely faithful."

"That has nothing to do with it. Plenty of men can manage to be happy with unfaithful wives. But nobody can live with a woman who makes a laughing stock of him. At least you might have kept up the decent fiction that I'd kick him if I found out."

"Oh well. Forget it. You've not been the only person to suffer, I can assure you."

Gibbie shook his head stubbornly.

"You don't understand, Philomena. I've been thinking it out all day. I've been trying to get it clear."

"That you weren't going to let me go, you mean? Well, I'm not going and that's that."

"No. Your going has nothing to do with it really. You can go or not as you please. I'm not going to live with you any more."

"But what have I done?"

"You've wrecked our marriage. That's what you've done. You've made it impossible for me to respect myself. You don't seem to understand in the least what a man expects from his wife. He doesn't merely want a sort of permanent concubine. He wants a woman who'll share whatever prestige, standing, honour . . . you can call it what you like . . . that he's been able to win for himself out of the pack. That's why she takes his name.

"He has to trust her. She gets to know things about him. She knows his weaknesses. But as long as she helps him to keep his own end up she's a good wife . . ."

"You talk as if I'd given you nothing. I've had your children. I've taken risks for you. I've loved you."

"A mistress might do that much. That's a matter of our private life. It's our public life I'm talking about. Marriage is a public contract. You've let me down."

Even yet she could not take him seriously. His manner was too didactic. He was off again on his eternal theorising. A man who is about to break up his home does not trouble to distinguish between the private and the public life. She shrugged her shoulders.

"You've argued yourself into thinking that you ought to leave me. A nice point in moral philosophy. For once you've decided what the Good Man does."

"Yes," agreed Gibbie. "For once I have decided that."

"But you've forgotten one thing."

"What?"

"That you love me."

"No. I haven't forgotten that. I do love you, un- fortunately. But I'm going to leave you for all that. Too much can be sacrificed for love."

"Oh Gibbie!"

It was nonsense, but his air of resolution began to frighten her. That solid structure of home, marriage and security, which she herself had always put first, must not be attacked, even in theory.

"Please don't say such things. I can't bear it."

"I want you to understand why it is that I can't forgive you. You thought you knew how to get round me, and you very nearly did. But you oughtn't to have told him. If you'd simply deceived me I shouldn't feel that you had brought me so low."

"Please, Gibbie . . ."

She got up and would have gone to him, but he held her off.

"It's no use, Philomena. I know my own mind now. I ought to have known it yesterday, I admit. But you did try to rush me, didn't you?"

"But Gibbie . . . Gibbie . . ."

He turned away from her and went into his dressing-room. The manuscript which he had been trying to read lay strewn about on the writing-table. He switched on the reading lamp and picked up the next chapter.

"Poor thing," he thought. "She didn't understand a single word that I said."

To-morrow he would go to sleep at his club until their separation could be arranged. And after that he did not know what he would do. But a kind of triumph upheld him. He had for once made his decision by the light of reason, as all decisions ought to be made. He had argued out his case with himself as though it belonged to another man. And now he had only to act upon it. Having once acted he believed that his whole life would become quite different. He would himself be the Good Man.

26. *Springs in Deserts Found.*

The night grew warmer and brighter. Each rounded cock in the hayfields had its own blot of shadow. There was no sleep indoors or out. Small things rustled and twittered in the black thickets and a million grasshoppers were sawing away in the fields. Yet every sound was slight and clear, etched distinctly against the large quietness of the sky and the hills. Noises from far away, a dog barking from an upland farm, a car changing gear in the valley, fell into the cup of fields like single notes from a bell.

Hugo's moon shadow dogged him through the fields and at first he hurried and stumbled as though he was trying to escape from it. But when he came to the gate on to the downs he went more slowly. The hill grew steeper. Gradually, as each step took him out of the human world of the valley, all sound slipped away from him. His breath returned and his heart left off hammering. He fell into a steady plod up the chalk path to the crest of the ridge. Soon he could hear nothing save the ghost of a whisper as a small wind blew among the dried hare-bells. The air was cooler up there, but a lingering warmth stole from the earth which had lain baking in the sun all day.

He got to the top and saw more, and yet more sky. Half the world was sky, and when he looked back he could not see the Ullmer valley, only a smudge of blackness below the silvery slopes. He stood still and his shadow stood still beside him. He had got to a place of absolute silence.

It was too silent.

A strange thing had happened to him, but he did not immediately know what it was. His private orchestra had stopped. For the first time in years he was able to listen to his own thoughts, to that secret voice which he shared with no one else. He had given his tyrant the slip and was walking alone with his shadow as anybody else might walk. He need no longer think of himself as the most successful young man who ever wandered in the moonlight.

But he was not ready, yet, to be alone. His success might be a tyrant but at least it was company and he had come to depend on it. He had not stumbled up this hill for the sake of solitude but because he wanted to find Marianne. For he must sleep soon, and he never could until he found her. When Solange said that she was on the downs he had gone in immediate pursuit. Not to argue, or to explain, did he go, but simply to be with her. For he knew that he had come very near the edge, down there in the drawing-room with Corny and Philomena. He was very near the edge still. He would go over if he did not find her.

There was no sign of her anywhere. The night was empty and the downs were bare. He went on a little way, scanning the faint, grey levels for her moving figure. But it seemed that she was not there. And then his loneliness grew to panic size. He began to hurry. He tried to get off the downs and lost himself. The Ullmer valley had disappeared, but he slipped and stumbled a little way down into another one, looking for the path that he had missed. A sea of gorse bushes cut him off and he tried to crawl through them, gashing his hands and arms. At last he got to the top of the ridge again, where his moon shadow dodged and bobbed beside him. It looked like a shadow cast by some other man and he grew afraid of it. At last, blindly terrified, he began to run, round in circles, and up and down over the grass, trying to find some shelter from the cold eye of the moon. But there was no refuge, even from that, only endless miles of turf full of rabbit holes that tripped him up. His shouts and calls were muffled in his throat and choked him. He went round and round like a squirrel in a cage.

When he had run for a long time he was walking again with Marianne beside him. She seemed to have come suddenly out of nowhere, to have taken shape out of the void sky. The moon glistened on the white frieze coat that she wore, and her lanky shadow stalked along the ground beside his. She had taken his arm, as they swung along, and tucked it under her own, thus preventing him from falling into rabbit holes as they took the path along the top of the ridge.

"Where were you?" he asked when they had gone a little way.

"Up there."

She nodded at the great mound of Chawton Beacon, looming above them.

"Did you see me?"

"No. But I heard you calling."

"Oh. Did I call?"

"Yes."

"More than once?"

"Yes."

"Was I calling you?"

"Yes."

"You must have thought I was getting queer in the head."

She did not answer that. Instead she pointed across the valley and said:

"Look!"

On the slope opposite a flame had spread out like a fan. The whole hillside was burning.

"They've lighted the grass," she said. "Look, there's another on Chawbury. And a little one on Callow Down. And do you see the one on Ullmer Ridge? They light it there in a ring and if it burns all the way round at the same time, then it's going to be a lucky year. But it's better when there's no moon."

They went along the ridge counting the fires, of which there were about a dozen. Hidden in the hills there must have been scores of men setting the grass alight and a faint shout floated now and then across the valley. Marianne kept spinning round and naming the more distant flickers. For the most part they looked wan and ephemeral under the steady light of the moon. But Ullmer Ring burnt bravely long after the others had gone out.

"We might go across and help them to keep it up," she suggested. "Why are you limping?"

"I've got a blister on my heel. I don't want to walk any more. Let's sit down."

"It'll be cold here by and by. We'll go along to the haystacks and then we'll have something to lean against."

"Where?"

"Just below here. Where the fields run up to the Down. There are two stacks. We can sit against them and see Ullmer Ring as long as it burns. Mind the rabbit holes."

They went down, slipping a little on the cropped turf, and Hugo asked where Syranwood was. She pointed to an enormous mass of shadow like a dark lake, just below them.

"You know," said Hugo, as he slithered along, "I did an extraordinary thing to-night. I pulled Corny's nose."

"Did you? Oh, look out! Have you sprained your ankle?"

He had stepped into a rabbit burrow and fell sprawling.

"Why didn't you put on thick shoes if you wanted to come up here?" asked Marianne unsympathetically.

"I didn't want to come up here. Did you hear what I said? I pulled . . ."

"Yes, you can tell me when we're safe at the bottom."

"Should I try rolling down?"

"You could if you liked. But if I were you I'd take my shoes off. The grass is quite dry."

Hugo sat down and removed his shoes and socks. The grass was not only dry but warm, and his feet gripped it comfortably. But he encountered a good many thistles.

"I believe you take me over them on purpose," he grumbled.

"It's better than gorse. Here we are."

The haystacks leant together like two little houses. But one of them had been cut on the side facing Ullmer Ridge and Marianne scooped out a nice warm hollow in the loose hay. It was soft to sit in but it tickled Hugo's feet until he had to put his shoes on again.

"Now are you settled?" demanded Marianne.

"More or less. How long are we going to stay here?"

"I'm going to stay till the Ring is burnt out. But you needn't unless you like."

He did like. As far as he was concerned they could sit there all night. For it was still quite early. As they came down the hill he had heard the stable clock striking twelve among the trees below.

"Do you mind if I go to sleep?" he asked.

"Do."

He stretched himself at full length in the hay and stared up at the sky.

"Why aren't there any stars?" he asked presently.

"Because it's a full moon. There never are."

"Why?"

"I don't know. Go to sleep."

"I can't. The hay scratches my neck."

He shuffled and fidgeted about for a few minutes and then sat up. Marianne, who had been watching him, said gravely:

"You can put your head on my lap if you like."

"Can I?"

He did, and sighed with contentment.

"I'm so comfortable."

Marianne said nothing. She looked straight in front of her at the uncertain ring of fire across the valley. And after a little while Hugo went on, in a placid, drowsy voice:

"You know, Marianne, I can't bear it any longer."

"I know."

"You don't know. You couldn't. Nobody could unless it had happened to them. I'm like a man driving some terrible, high-powered car and losing control of it. He tries to think, poor devil, that he's driving it. But all the time he knows it's driving him."

He spoke slowly, pausing for words, as if at any moment he might drop off to sleep. But he went on:

"Something outside of me has got hold of me. I'm a slave. Even my thoughts aren't my own any more. I haven't got a private life any more. I always seem to be leading a public life, even when I'm alone. Do you understand?"

"Yes."

"My mind is simply an enormous reverberator for other people's thoughts. I'm hardly a real person any more. The nearest to reality I get is to give a marvellous imitation of myself."

Marianne moved, as though she was going to speak. But he stopped her.

"I know what you're going to say. Why not go away? I'll tell you why. There's nowhere to go to. People can't get away nowadays. Wherever I went, they'd come too. Nothing will make any difference. I'd thought of trying something new: writing poetry instead of plays. But I hadn't considered the idea for more than ten minutes before I found myself telling Adrian all about it. Doing a little advance publicity. When a man gets into the state I'm in he can only produce abortions. When things grow you have to hide the roots of them. But I've got nowhere to hide them in."

"I know," said Marianne. "So if I were you I shouldn't write any more."

"What?"

He turned his head round on her knee and peered up into her face to see if she was laughing. But she looked quite serious.

"How do you mean . . . not write?"

"Do something else," suggested Marianne.

"But, my dear, I'm a writer. What else could I do?"

"Anything else. Anything you like. Why not? If anybody could do what they liked I should think it was you. You must have made an awful lot of money."

"Not as much as people think," said Hugo instantly.

"But still, quite a lot. Have you spent it all?"

"No. I've saved enough to live on, if it comes to that."

"Then, my goodness, why go on doing things you don't like. Plenty of people that don't have any money at all have a nicer time than you. Why should you go on writing?"

"I've got into a habit."

"It's a bad habit."

"And then, you can't get away from it. I'm so successful. To leave off writing altogether, to give up, that would be failure, wouldn't it?"

"Well?"

She seemed to scrutinise the word as if trying to discover the secret of its menace. And Hugo lay there wondering idly what he would like to do besides writing. He might sail a small boat perhaps. He liked sailing.

"Well," pronounced Marianne at last, "you've tried success and you don't like it. Now try failure and see."

It was absurd. He left off toying with his little boat.

"But darling . . . what am I to do with my life?"

"Oh I don't know. Just live it. Do nothing at all for a good long time, till you find there's something you really and truly want to do. Don't you realise how lucky you are? You're free. You don't have your living to earn. And you quite like doing nothing, don't you?"

"Do I? I don't know. I've done nothing this weekend, but I can't say I've liked it."

"Done nothing? You've been at it the whole time, I should say."

Hugo considered this but found no answer. So he went back to the impossibility of getting away.

"Darling, you don't know what you're talking about.

My agent would never allow it. I'm afraid of my agent."

Marianne made a movement of impatience. It was a hard task to disentangle his mind from its mesh of publicity.

"Nobody need know," she insisted. "Give an address to your bankers or your solicitor or somebody like that, so they won't think you've fallen off a cliff. And then disappear."

"Where to?"

"Oh, I don't know. I should go to a cheap hotel at Torquay or somewhere for a bit till you've thought of a place you'd like. Nobody would think of looking for you at Torquay."

"You've got it all very pat. Have you been thinking it over?"

"Yes, I have. Ever since dinner."

"Nice of you. But you know there'll be an awful hullabaloo. Disappearance of Hugo Pott."

"Oh no, not if you say you've gone a pleasure cruise. You've no idea how quickly they'll forget you. They'll say: 'Oh, by the way, where's Hugo? Still cruising?' And then they'll leave off even saying that. They'll find another King Toad to . . ."

She broke off with a gasp.

"Go on," murmured Hugo contentedly. "I don't mind. A King Toad, did you say? So that's what you really . . ."

And then, thinking of his arrival, and those two faces looking down at him from the old schoolroom window, he laughed.

"I didn't really . . ." stammered Marianne.

"Oh yes, you did. And you wouldn't tell me at dinner. You think I'm a King Toad, Marianne, but you're terribly nice to me all the same, and in three minutes I shall go to sleep on your lap. Do you mind?"

"No."

And in three minutes he did, slipping off suddenly into that dreamless void which he had so desperately desired. He lay absolutely still, breathing slowly.

Marianne settled herself more comfortably into the hay and leant back. She watched the fires die out, one after another, and heard the stable clock chime out beneath her. The night was a little cooler now and as the moon slipped down the sky it grew darker.

She was so completely happy that she had almost left off being herself. The barrier between herself and everything round her, the dark cooling air, the huddled stacks, crumbled away, so that her peace was one with the peace of the sleeping world. This was her whole life, since an entire existence is no longer than its moment of highest fulfilment. She knew that when she was old she would not think: I have lived long. She would think: 'He slept one night with me in the hay.' She held his sleeping spirit in her hands and she was content.

To-morrow he would go away. And perhaps she might never have him near to her like this again. To-morrow night, and for many, many nights after she must lie alone with her grief. He would be lost to her arms but never to her love. For her love would send him out, away from her, just as, to-night, it had brought him close. To-morrow and its loss would be born of this happiness just as surely as light follows darkness and sweet flowers bear bitter fruit. But in this hour, when all time seemed one, she could think of it without sorrow.

The moon had slipped out of sight. Its milky beams grew dim and the outline of the hills disappeared as it set.

All the fires were out now. Hugo lay still as death, but when she moved a little, to ease her cramped limbs, he sighed and said something about ringing up in the morning.

His head rolled off her lap but he did not wake. Very softly she lay down in the hay beside him, took him in her arms and pulled his poor head into that hollow of her breast where it ought to lie. In a few minutes she was fast asleep herself.

27. *Open the Door.*

The silent pageant of night and day streamed past them unseen. For a time there was nothing, no colour and no shape, while the unlit world swung over in the void. And then a faint ray, distilled from the east, turned nothingness into a dark pearl. Marianne dozed fitfully, floating on the tide of her happiness in and out of sleep. But Hugo lay all night long in a profound repose. Once she woke to see the morning star hanging over Ullmer Ridge and then she slept again while the light grew and the grey fields found their shapes. She was still asleep when the first banners of colour were flung up into the sky and Hugo started, broad awake, as if he had been summoned.

He sat up and took a deep slow breath, smelling the early morning air. An extraordinary feeling of newness infused his body, as if he had been taken to pieces and put together again during the night. He looked about him in a puzzled way, at the colourless fields and the pearly sky and Marianne's grave, sleeping face. Fragments of their conversation came back to him, confused with many things that he might possibly have dreamt. He had been in great distress, but it was over now, and on the other side of the night.

He looked again at Marianne and realised that he had been lying in her arms. How that had come to pass he did not know: he was deeply moved, almost frightened, when he thought of it and yet it seemed quite natural. Very gently he touched the rough frieze of her coat sleeve. Although she did not move he knew that she was going to wake. Her face was losing its sculptured calm and for a few seconds he watched as the truant soul flowed back into her body. Then she opened her eyes and smiled at him.

"You've got hay in your hair," she said.

"So have you."

They sat up and pulled bits out thoughtfully while he tried not to think of what might happen next, or how the sun was whirling up behind the downs, and how it would soon be breakfast, and then lunch, and tea, and dinner, and night again. He was a little cold and cramped, but so conscious of refreshment, slaked fatigue and nerves relaxed that he wanted to make the moment last. Suddenly he flung an arm round Marianne and drew her down into the hay again.

"Let's go on sleeping."

He had not nearly finished sleeping. He wanted to sleep all day and wake up at this hour to-morrow morning. But Marianne pulled herself away, saying that she had slept enough and was going to pick mushrooms. A great many of them had appeared in the night, small, firm and white, in the short grass of the next field. She took Hugo's handkerchief and began to search for them, swearing mildly at an occasional puff ball. The collector's glare came into her eye. She ranged far over the field while Hugo limped after her.

Below them, like a scene reflected in a sheet of grey glass, lay the motionless trees, the church tower, and the chimneys and roofs of Syranwood. Hugo turned his eyes away from it and scanned the turf for mushrooms. For beneath those chimneys there were rooms, and in those rooms They were all asleep in their several beds. Asleep, but not for ever. They would wake up and with them there was still a young man called Hugo Pott, created by them for their pleasure. This monster had not vanished in the night. He might at any time rise like a phœnix in the morning sun. By lunch time he would be wide awake and very much the better for the nice sleep he had had. Power had come back to him and he could use it in any way he liked. It would be quite easy to make up for the ground he had lost in the last two days. If he wanted to go back there was nothing to stop him. The battle was not over. It was beginning.

He called to Marianne, up the slope, with a subdued but urgent summons, pitched to the dreaming quiet of the air. And she called back to him in the same low key. Stooping occasionally to pick another mushroom they drew together by the haystacks again. He said:

"Marianne, what are we going to do?"

"We?"

"What am I going to do? When I go back there it'll all start over again. Do you realise that?"

He looked at the little hollow in the hay where they had spent the night, and then he looked into her eyes. The light was quite strong now so that he could see himself there, dishevelled and alert. It was the first time that he had ever been reassured by the sight of his own face.

"Marianne," he said hurriedly, "will you marry me?"

"Some time."

"Why not now?"

"Because you've got to go away now."

" Then you come with me."

"No."

"Why not?"

"Because going away is your affair, not mine. I've got nothing to do with it. All those things that you told me last night have nothing to do with me. You'd be in the same hole whether I was here or not. Getting out of it is your kettle of fish and you've got to boil it. Nobody else can."

"But you will marry me some time?"

Marianne hesitated and then said seriously:

"I hope so. But we won't talk about that now, please. We'll talk about you going away."

Hugo looked at his patent leather shoes, at the hay on his clothes and his crumpled dinner shirt. His collar and tie were gone.

"I expect they're on the top of Chawton Beacon," said Marianne, seeing his hand go up to his neck. "They were gone when I first saw you, anyway."

"Extraordinary thing," said Hugo thoughtfully. "But you see my point. I'm not dressed for going away."

"You want some clothes and some money. That's all you want. Come down to the house now, before they wake up, and change. I'll see that the rest of your things are packed and sent back to London. I'll say that you had to leave by an early train."

"And then what do I do? The open road, the knapsack, the wayside fire and all those horrors?"

"Not if you don't like it. I should go away in a train."

"Which train?"

"Well, there are plenty of trains at Ullmer Halt. You can walk that far, I should think."

"I see. I take a train. Where to?"

"That's as you please. But as I said before I should pick Torquay. It's not nice enough for you to want to stay there long."

"And my tooth brush? Do I put it in my pocket or carry a small suitcase, or wrap it in a red handkerchief and hang it on the end of a stick?"

"Oh, toothbrush my elbow! Can't you buy one in Torquay?"

In this unreal pearl of a morning he found it difficult to believe that she was talking nonsense. And whenever they were not speaking there was always that repose, that quietness in his mind which had so alarmed him the night before. Now it was heavenly. It gave an effect of soberness to her fantastic proposition. And it heightened the horrors of the alternative—a lifetime of meals at the Acorn.

"But I must have something to eat," he pointed out. "I'm hungry. I can't do all this on an empty stomach."

"Come down now and I'll find you something to eat."

In the valley fields there had been a heavy dew. Their feet made silvery tracks in it as they crossed the grass, and the rose bushes sprayed them from the high garden hedges. Everything looked strange and spellbound. The house with its blank eyes floated before them like some flat old engraving.

Marianne had the key of the garden door. The hinges creaked and a fusty indoor air blew out at them. On tip-toe, with cautious looks they shut out the cool morning world and felt their way along a stone passage. It was in the oldest part of the house, amid flagged kitchens and corridors which still smelt of the eighteenth century, of new bread and beer. A clock ticked loudly and hastily in the baking house and there was a faint scurry of mice over the floor. Somewhere behind a shut door there was a seismic snoring.

"Be frightfully quiet," whispered Marianne. "Fletcher sleeps down here next the pantry."

"I can hear him doing it."

They got past Fletcher's door and into a small larder where Marianne found bread and cheese.

"Start and eat some now," she told Hugo, "while I go and make coffee. Then I'll show you the backstairs to your room."

Hugo hacked off a bit of bread and stood leaning against the larder shelves, biting off large mouthfuls. There were some stone jars beside him full of almonds and raisins, and when he had finished his bread and cheese he ate some of then. Everything tasted very nice. He nosed into a canister which said TEE and found some lumps of sugar. He ate them.

Somewhere among the rooms and passages he could hear faint footsteps which might be Marianne brewing the coffee. The rhythmic power-house throb of Fletcher's snore continued and he felt fairly safe, though he knew that people snore loudest just before they wake up. But he thought that she might have come a little more quietly down the passage. Her heels clicked against the stones right past Fletcher's door. He could hear them stop from time to time as if she was pausing to look into all the rooms along the corridor. They approached. His door was pushed a little way open and an old wary face

T*

looked in. It was Lady Geraldine, all muffled up in white shawls, a silk handkerchief tied over her head.

"Is that Mr. Usher?" she asked, peering uncertainly.

"No. It's Hugo Pott."

"What are you doing?"

"Eating sugar," said Hugo truthfully.

"Where is my granddaughter?"

"Making coffee."

She nodded and shut the door behind her.

"I saw you come across the garden," she told him. "I was looking out of the window."

Hugo, realising that the house might not have been quite so fast asleep as it looked, made a noise of dismay.

"Quite so," agreed Lady Geraldine. "That is why I came down to talk to you." She looked him over severely. "It seems to me that you are a most inconsiderate young man. If it had been poor Aggie, or Philomena, or even Laura, I shouldn't quarrel with you. But can't you understand that Marianne is quite different."

"Oh, absolutely. If she hadn't been, I shouldn't have been so inconsiderate. Please don't think . . ."

He stopped, embarrassed.

'Well?" said his hostess sharply. "What am I not to think?"

"It's . . . it's not necessary for me to point out, to you, what you must, or mustn't think about Marianne. Crude of me even to begin."

"Oh, I know that. But what am I to think about you?"

"Only that I worship her," said Hugo.

"I don't want her to be worshipped," said Geraldine, with some heat. "I only want her to be left alone."

"I quite understand that."

"Then what happened? What have you been doing all night?"

"We went for a walk on the downs, and then we sat down in some hay, and then we fell asleep," said Hugo lamely. "It was quite early. We didn't mean to stay there all night. But I haven't been sleeping properly for a long time, and I suppose I was overtired. I dropped off and Marianne was too kind to wake me. So I slept till the morning. We woke about an hour ago, I should think, and then we picked some mushrooms. Marianne has them. And then I asked her to marry me."

"You can't. It's quite impossible."

"And she said she would . . . some time . . ."

"Absolutely impossible. She's a great deal too young. I won't have it. You must go away at once."

"That's what she says."

"What?"

"That I must go away at once."

"Oh? She does, does she? And are you going?"

"Yes, I'm going. But I don't promise not to come back some time or other."

A tray jingled outside the door and Marianne appeared with the coffee cups. She had heard their voices in the passage, so she was not surprised to see her grandmother, and merely said:

"Don't talk so loud unless you want Fletcher to hear."

"Fletcher hears nothing that he shouldn't," said Lady Geraldine. "Mr. Usher tells me that he has to go away at once."

"Pott," said Marianne.

"Give me that cup, child, and fetch another for yourself."

When Marianne had gone again, Hugo remembered

that he ought to return thanks for the Syranwood hospitality.

"Thank you very much for asking me," he began. "I've enjoyed myself tremendously."

"Hmph!" said Geraldine. "You looked very ill when you came, but you seem brisker now. I daresay a good sleep was what you wanted. But I'm sorry it wasn't a more amusing week-end. It's a pity Mr. Usher had to go away so soon. He talks so well, doesn't he?"

Hugo made a strange noise as he sipped his coffee.

"Wasn't it Mr. Usher who was so amusing at dinner on Saturday night?"

"I don't remember," confessed Hugo.

"Nor do I. But I remember thinking the party was going to be a success. And then somehow it wasn't. I suppose you're going back now to that place . . . that place . . ."

She was about to say the Guthrie Institute when a doubt assailed her. So she finished:

"That place where you came from? I think you're so right."

Her mind toiled through the thickets of imperfectly remembered things. For the life of her she would never be able to remember Mr. Pott from Mr. Usher. One wrote novels and the other hunted butterflies, and she had asked them because she had been told to ask them, and when next Laura or poor Aggie came to stay with her she would be instructed to invite a couple more. But they were so right, these young men, to go back to the places they came from because, poor things, they were not always a success. They talked well at dinner on Saturday night, but it was hard work for them, and they often looked unhappy, and one of them had upset Laura so much ten years ago that she was not going to allow the other to upset Marianne. She would send the child to Rome immediately.

"Mathilde must look after her," she thought. "I can't stop her from meeting these queer people here, with Laura coming so often. This is no place for her till she's married."

And she nodded sagely at Hugo who was going back to the place where he came from.

"I think," said Marianne reappearing, "that Hugo ought to go up and change his clothes. He has to walk to Ullmer Halt."

"Walk?" echoed Lady Geraldine. "But surely, didn't I order a car for him yesterday? You want to go to that funeral, don't you? Surely we arranged . . ."

"Oh no," cried Hugo and Marianne together, "that was Adrian."

"Oh yes, I remember. But can't you go with him?"

Hugo looked at Marianne. He did not much fancy the idea of walking to Ullmer Halt and he waited for her to say that he might drive with Adrian. But she buried her face in her coffee cup and said nothing.

"What about it?" he ventured at last.

"It depends where you're going," she said.

Which meant that she did not trust him alone with Adrian. But she was quite wrong. He made a face at her, behind Lady Geraldine's back, as he said:

"All right. I'll walk. If you'll see that my things are sent back to the flat."

"Yes," said Marianne. "I'll see that's done."

"Then I think we'll say good-bye," said Lady Geraldine, putting down her cup. "You must want to be going. We've been very glad to see you here. Marianne, come with me. I want you."

"What?" exclaimed Hugo, blankly. "What?"

He had not thought that she would be whisked away from him like this. He had supposed somehow that she would at least come with him to Ullmer Halt. They had settled nothing beyond Marianne's vague promise about marrying him some time. There was something which he ought to have asked her. But perhaps he needn't as she had promised to marry him. Still he wanted to ask her and it was impossible in front of her grandmother.

"I say!" he cried, pursuing them into the passage. "I say . . . Marianne! I haven't said good-bye!"

He seized her hand and tried to pull her back into the larder, but Lady Geraldine kept a firm hold upon her other arm so that he could not pull one without pulling both.

"No, no," said Lady Geraldine. "You've had plenty of time to say good-bye in, and Fletcher will be coming."

Marianne laughed at both of them and told them not to quarrel.

"And don't pull me in half between you. It's not necessary. I'm not going to be bullied by either of you. I'm going upstairs now. If Hugo has anything more he wants to say, I think it will keep. And if there's anything more that grandmamma doesn't want me to say I think that'll keep too."

She spoke so firmly that they both released her. And as Fletcher poked a tortoise-like head out of his door she ran off down the passage. Hugo looked after her and said to Lady Geraldine:

"I think we must call it a draw."

"No, you don't," said Lady Geraldine. "You don't think anything of the sort. You think it's mate in one move. Well . . ." she gathered her shawls about her. "You may be right. If you are, you'll be an exceedingly fortunate young man. Good-bye, and mind you catch that train."

She pattered off upstairs to her own room and immediately sat down to write to Mathilde. *I am worried about Marianne*, she wrote, and then she wondered if she really was worried about Marianne. She had been worried yesterday, foreseeing all the pains and perils of a first love, knowing, fearing, yet powerless to defend. She might send the child away to Rome, but she could never teach her to ride her own fate. Ride, or be ridden, that issue could only be determined by Marianne herself. It had been the same with each of her daughters in turn and not one of them had ever taken her so completely by surprise. Experienced old horsewoman that she was, she had never seen such a magnificent leap into the saddle as Marianne had taken that morning. Her darling Marianne, her last, and best beloved: The child of her age, and the soul of her youth. No, she was not, ever again, going to be worried about Marianne. She crossed out the sentence and wrote:

Marianne has fallen in love. Nobody much. One of those young men who come down here to meet Laura and Aggie. But if you don't want her to marry him you must set to work at once. She ought to see people, and as I can't take her about I think she had better come to you. Put him out of her head if you can: she's perfectly reasonable. It's nobody's fault but yours, Mathilde, for leaving her here so long. So if you have anyone up your sleeve you'd better waste no time. Will you come home to fetch her, or shall I send her out?

She chuckled, as she blotted the page, for she knew quite well whom Mathilde had got up her sleeve and she thought him very undeserving. Hugo Pott might be nobody much, but at least he would serve as a spoke in Mathilde's wheel.

Twenty minutes later, spying from her window, she saw him go down the garden. The grey light was gone and the heavens were rosy and warm. Chawton Beacon, caught by the unrisen sun, turned yellow above the violet shadows of the valley. A light wind ruffled the leaves and the small birds, waking all together, sang from every bush. Hugo went quickly across the terrace and disappeared into the pleached alley.

"Gone back to his mosquitoes," she thought, with extreme satisfaction.

Long might he stay there!

28. *I Have No Name.*

Hugo had no intention of walking to Ullmer Halt. He did not know the way for one thing, and his heel hurt him. Nor did he believe that Marianne would require anything so unnecessarily dramatic: it would be almost as bad as the knapsack, the open road and all those horrors. The fact that he was going should be enough for both of them, and the means of transport might safely be left to the suggestions of common sense. So he went to the village and hired the Ullmer taxi as soon as its sleepy owner could be dragged out of bed.

It was nearly seven o'clock before he finally went rattling up the hills over the downs in the very oldest

Ford that he had ever seen, and he might just as well have gone to Basingstoke and enjoyed the larger choice of trains to be had there. But he did not think of that, and was in no hurry, anyhow. It would be possible to get from Ullmer Halt to Torquay in the course of time and that was all he cared about. The taxi took him over the downs and over the edge beyond where the grassy hillsides fell away to the plain again.

"You want the Up train?" asked his driver, as they began to rattle downhill again.

"No," said Hugo. "No. The Down train."

"Then you won't catch it. Not the Down train you won't. That's the Down train."

And he pointed to a little snake of smoke which crept along amid the chequered fields and woods below them. It seemed to be crawling across country at the rate of one inch an hour.

"It's gone," he said. "And you'll have to wait an hour for the next. There aren't many trains stop at Ullmer Halt. You'd better have gone to Basingstoke, if it was a Down train you wanted."

"It doesn't matter," said Hugo.

They went on rattling down the hill. In the fields the haymakers were already creaking out with their carts. Hugo was beginning to feel quite hungry again already, in spite of the bread and cheese and almonds and raisins and sugar that he had eaten. He had that slight dizziness and headache which is the lot of people who take unaccustomed exercise in the early morning. His mind worked slowly. He was in no hurry to make plans for the future, unless they were forced upon him. His freedom was too large for him. He refrained from thinking about it, but sat dozing in the warm sunlight on the tiny platform of Ullmer Halt more conscious of his heel than anything else.

A solitary porter pottered in and out of a signal box or rolled a milk can from one part of the station to another. Presently he went off to breakfast. Hugo wondered what he would have to eat. An egg perhaps; for there were hens clucking and scratching about in a paddock behind the station and a woman who might have been the porter's wife came out of a cottage with a tin pan of food for them. She might sell eggs, but he could not eat them raw. He had better wait for his breakfast till he got to the junction. A train of some sort would come in time, though at present the bright line of metal running away through the fields looked as if it might be deserted for the rest of the day.

He put all his pennies into a slot machine and got some slabs of mouldy chocolate which he was not hungry enough to eat, and when a gong clanged loudly in the signal box he stared hopefully along the line. But nobody else took any notice of it at all. The hens clucked drowsily and a bumble bee buzzed up and down the hollyhocks. Hugo tried lying down upon the station seat, but it was too narrow and he rolled off it. The booking office had no seat in it at all, only a weighing machine and a notice about sheep scab. So he began to walk up and down the platform until he heard the hopeful sound of a car driving up. If other people were coming there must be some train soon.

There was a trample of boots in the booking office and a chauffeur appeared with several suitcases. The man looked familiar somehow. He stacked them up and returned without noticing Hugo. And then Gibbie, with a face of thunder, came striding out on to the platform.

He did not notice Hugo either, but went straight to the very end of the station as if he could summon the train by looking angrily down the line.

There was more luggage than could ever have belonged to Gibbie, and Hugo wondered how many more of the Syranwood party were about to join him. Not Corny, he hoped. For there was nowhere to hide but the signal box. How right he had been to say that he could never get away! He was so much afraid of meeting Corny that the face of Adrian, peeping timidly out of the booking office, was a positive relief. He hailed it with a friendly grin.

"Hullo?" said Adrian surprised.

"But I thought you were going to Basingstoke," said Hugo.

Adrian explained. They had missed the train at Basingstoke and Gibbie was very unreasonably annoyed about it. Apparently they had had a most unpleasant drive. For Adrian, not knowing that he was to have a companion, had come down with a politic lateness to find Gibbie champing on the doorstep. The chauffeur had said that they could not possibly reach Basingstoke in time and had insisted upon bringing them to Ullmer Halt to catch a slow Up train with two changes. It was not at all what Adrian had intended. For Gibbie had no right to be so put out since he had given no notice, the night before, of his intention of coming too. But he behaved as if Adrian had made them late on purpose, and, by the time they got to the station, they were scarcely upon speaking terms.

"It was entirely my fault," said Adrian, candidly, as he drew Hugo with him to the opposite end of the platform. "But I think he might have kept his temper."

He assumed that Hugo was also taking the Up train, and he was so much pre-occupied with his grievance against Gibbie that he asked no questions. To him this meeting was a godsend, for it put an end to an uncomfortable situation. They would travel together and Gibbie could take his ill temper to a separate carriage. He liked Hugo, especially since their conversation the day before. To encourage young men was always his darling passion and few of them had been more open to encouragement than this one.

"So you're going to Paul Wrench's funeral?" asked Hugo respectfully.

Adrian laughed. These young people, these strenuous young people, were very endearing. Solange, he explained, would never forgive him if he did not go. But for all that, he would confess to his dear Hugo that he very much doubted if he ultimately would. He had looked up trains, but only Solange could have expected that to result in the so different activity of catching them. Solange, as was natural, at her time of life, mistook the value of . . . of gesture. One had made the same mistake oneself twenty, thirty, forty years ago. The vigour of middle age fell away from Adrian as he talked and he took on a look of distinguished decrepitude as though a whole headful of grey hairs had sprouted in the course of the night. Alas! Alas! One did not, relish a stormy crossing . . .

"But you'll have a very calm crossing," Hugo pointed out. "It's marvellous weather."

Adrian continued as though he had not heard . . . or night journeys in a third-class carriage. And when his young friends had left their forties behind them they might find, dared one say it? that the relative . . . the

relative . . . Adrian sawed the air as the right word
eluded him . . . gravity of these considerations had
undergone a subtle alteration. To the hot blood of
youth it might appear that one did not, to put it quite
crudely in the idiom of Solange, care. But did one? He
admired Paul Wrench. He considered a great poet to
have been lost in Paul Wrench. But he was not going to
Paul Wrench's funeral and it was a relief to be able to say
so to somebody.

"And you, my dear Hugo, situated as you are, midway
between the two of us? How do you look at it?"

Hugo saw that he was expected either to be so extremely young that Adrian could laugh at him gently, or
else to exclaim languidly:

"I think you're so right."

Habit was so strong that he hesitated for a moment
before remembering that he need never again do the
expected thing. For this freedom he was paying the price
of sitting hungrily at Ullmer Halt with a blister on his
heel and no prospect beyond Torquay. He remembered
it with a gush of gratitude and relief which almost
banished his headache. If Marianne thought that he
could not be trusted in a car with Adrian she was making
a great mistake.

"I should be shocked if you went," he said. "There
was nothing Wrench loathed more, when he was alive,
than humbug of any sort. I don't think he's a proper
subject for it now he's dead."

"Humbug?" queried Adrian fastidiously.

He minded the sound of the word more than the
implication. It jarred. It was the kind of word that
Hugo, in his right mind, would never have used to a
critic. Because after all, one was a critic, and a critic of

some distinction, and if Hugo was going to take to writing poetry he had better not forget it. Malice one could forgive, but undistinguished abuse was quite another matter. Paul Wrench, who was often angry but never malicious, had made this mistake, but it was a pity that a promising young man should model himself on Paul Wrench.

"Humbug?" he said, eyeing Hugo. "Dear me!"

Hugo did not apologise. Having delivered himself of his declaration of independence he walked away and was leaning over the station railing among the hollyhocks, to watch the porter's hens in the field. A signal clanked down some way along the line, and Gibbie was plodding back towards the booking office.

"I do hope," said Adrian, joining Hugo at the fence and laying a friendly hand on his arm, "I do hope you won't forget to send me those verses we spoke of. It's possible that I might be able to help you."

"Thank you," said Hugo.

"Not that you'll have any difficulty in finding a publisher, of course. I don't mean that. Even in these hard times I imagine that your success in the theatre and, if I may say it, your personal success, would ensure that. They'll tell you that they don't make money on it but they'll take it. But you, I gather, in an adventure of this kind, aren't thinking of success in the er . . . vulgar sense of the word, so much as recognition."

Hugo, whose object was to avoid recognition for the rest of his life, swung round at last.

"Recognition?" he exclaimed. "But of what?"

"An artist," began Adrian . . .

But his reply was lost in an outburst of self-advertisement from a hen which had just laid an egg. And Hugo would in any case have lost the thread of the argument, for the word 'recognition' had set some curious machinery spinning in his brain. It was as if a door had been opened somewhere, as if he were looking down some immense vista, at a little figure advancing towards him out of the future, a nameless man too small to hail him yet; moving already down the avenues of time. The thing was coming to him, but nobody else in the world would ever know that face. He smiled with an indulgent but unseeing eye at Adrian, who shouted something about Keats.

"*Chork*-chuck-chuck-chuck-chuck-chuck-chuck-chuck-chuck-chuck: *Chork*-chuck-chuck-chuck-chuck-chuck-chuck-chuck . . ."

". . . thought the critics killed him," persisted Adrian, "and they probably did. He knew, all poets know, that an artist can't live without recognition. Without success . . . I grant you. But even Paul Wrench . . ."

"*Chork*-chuck-chuck-chuck-chuck-chuck-chuck-chuck-chuck."

". . . must keep in touch with the critical minds of his period. Wrench never saw that till too late in his life. And in consequence we all know how little recognition he ever got. Indeed I don't think he'd have had any if it hadn't been for . . ."

"Chuck-chuck-chuck-chuck . . ."

"You and Corny," suggested Hugo.

Adrian, mollified, made a little deprecatory gesture. It seemed that his point had gone home, though it had not been necessary to bring Corny into it. He had been able, possibly, to enlighten his young friend as to the difference, the immense difference between recognition and success, without being too much obliged to stress the purity of the former or the vulgarity of the latter. There was no reason why Hugo, under proper guidance, should not in time achieve a chaste marriage of both.

Far down the line a small dot appeared, framed under the foot-bridge and topped by a puff of smoke. It enlarged itself rapidly as the porter collected their suitcases. It filled up all the space under the bridge and the smoke, striking the archway, belched all round it. With a hiss and a rumble that drowned the clucking of the hens it drew into the station, while Adrian composed an illustrative epigram about names writ in water and names writ by aeroplanes across the sky.

"Or names on visiting cards," agreed Hugo, helping him into the carriage. "All of them means of identification. Good-bye, Adrian. Thank you for being so kind to me. Gibbie seems to be getting in further down.

"But aren't you . . ."

"No, I'm taking the Down train. Good-bye . . ."

He shut the door with a slam which was echoed from Gibbie's compartment at the other end of the train. For a moment, in the silence before they moved again, the voice of the chicken-field triumphed.

"Chuck—chuck—chuck—chuck—chuck—chuck—chuck—chuck . . ."

Hugo turned to listen with a grin of pleasure, as if an old friend had called to him. He did not see the departing train, or the startled face which Adrian thrust out of the window. He saw only those uncharted regions of his Other Life, lying all round him, open to the adventures of thought and sense. And to his ears the diminishing thunder of the wheels came faintly like the beat of muffled drums, a last reverberation from the land of his captivity.

THE HISTORY OF VINTAGE

The famous American publisher Alfred A. Knopf (1892–1984) founded Vintage Books in the United States in 1954 as a paperback home for the authors published by his company. Vintage was launched in the United Kingdom in 1990 and works independently from the American imprint although both are part of the international publishing group, Random House.

Vintage in the United Kingdom was initially created to publish paperback editions of books bought by the prestigious literary hardback imprints in the Random House Group such as Jonathan Cape, Chatto & Windus, Hutchinson and later William Heinemann, Secker & Warburg and The Harvill Press. There are many Booker and Nobel Prize-winning authors on the Vintage list and the imprint publishes a huge variety of fiction and non-fiction. Over the years Vintage has expanded and the list now includes great authors of the past – who are published under the Vintage Classics imprint – as well as many of the most influential authors of the present. In 2012 Vintage Children's Classics was launched to include the much-loved authors of our youth.

For a full list of the books Vintage publishes,
please visit our website
www.vintage-books.co.uk

For book details and other information about the classic
authors we publish, please visit the Vintage Classics website
www.vintage-classics.info

www.vintage-classics.info

Visit www.worldofstories.co.uk for all your
favourite children's classics